RETURN TO HOPE'S RIDGE

SILVER MCKENZIE

HOPE'S RIDGE BOOK #3

CONTENTS

*M*att cursed as his phone pinged with another text message. He glanced at the screen, his father—again. He stopped, the cool night air nipping at his collar as he quickly sent a reply. *Yes, I'll be on time.* He slipped the phone back into his pocket and carried on toward O'Reilly's. He would be early, not on time, but that was a detail his father didn't need to know. One thing he knew for sure, he'd be glad to return to Hope's Ridge the next day. Two days in the city were two too many as far as he was concerned.

Matt shivered as he stepped off the sidewalk and into the warmth of the Irish pub. He glanced at his watch. He had fifteen minutes before they were due to meet. Walter wanted to speak to Matt about a business opportunity and had organized for the two of them to meet with Susan Lewis, a venture capitalist. Matt had to admit to being slightly intrigued. Both he and his father had made their money in property development, both residential and commercial. If Walter was planning to diversify his investments, then that was something new.

He made his way to the bar, deciding he needed a shot of something warm. It was mid-May, it should be mild temperatures by now, but the recent cold snap had taken them all by surprise. He glanced at the live band as it started the opening notes for a song he recognized as the Cranberries and froze. Brad Campbell was across the room, seated next to a gorgeous redhead, one arm casually wrapped around her waist. Matt shook his head. What was Brad thinking?

Forgetting about the drink, he wove his way through the crowded bar toward them. Brad was now whispering something in the woman's ear. Even from a distance, the chemistry between them was undeniable. Matt shook his head. The wedding was only two weeks away. Was he insane?

Matt reached their table before Brad noticed him. When he did, he looked up and a guarded smile spread across his lips. "Matt, how are you, man?" He rose and stuck out a hand. "Let me introduce you. This is Nadia."

Matt ignored the outstretched hand, his gaze shifting to Nadia. "Nice to meet you."

She nodded politely and Matt looked back at Brad, whose smile faltered. He could only imagine how much Brad was sweating at this moment.

"Got a minute?" Matt asked. "I'd like to talk in private if you don't mind." He forced an apologetic smile for Nadia's benefit.

"Why don't I leave you two to chat," Nadia said. "I'll head to the restroom."

Matt waited until Nadia was out of hearing before

turning to Brad. "What are you doing? You're getting married in two weeks."

Brad forced a smile through clenched teeth. "Settle down. I'm well aware of that."

"Is Nadia?"

"What do you care? You're hardly the poster child for successful relationships."

"I care about Jenna."

Brad snorted. "Since when."

Since always. Matt silenced the thought. "How long have you been seeing Nadia?"

"I'm not seeing her. It's a fling. She knows that and she's happy with our arrangement."

"So she knows about Jenna?"

"It's really none of your business, Matt."

"You're unbelievable. Where does Jenna think you are? You guys live together, don't you?"

"She went home to her folks. Something about a catch-up with Asha and some others this weekend. Look, don't stress about it. In two weeks I'll be committing to Jenna, and that will be the end of any other relationships."

"There's more than Nadia?"

Brad shrugged. "Maybe. Casual stuff."

"And Jenna knows nothing about it?"

His eyes narrowed. "It's none of your business."

"I don't get why you want to marry someone if you're cheating now."

Brad sighed. "It's not cheating, okay? Jenna and I have an arrangement. She knows that once we're married, she can depend on me."

"Depend on you? As in, you won't cheat once you're married?"

"Something like that."

Matt sucked in a breath. It was almost impossible to believe that Jenna knew and condoned what Brad was doing. "You said that Jenna knew nothing about it and then said you had an arrangement. Which is it, Brad?"

"Both. We have an arrangement, but I haven't mentioned Nadia to her. And as you so clearly pointed out, as the wedding is in two weeks' time, I'd prefer not to." He glanced toward the restrooms. "She's coming. Say goodbye and disappear."

Matt stared at Brad. He was a dog. They'd known each other for a number of years and often laughed and joked about Brad's conquests. So why was it bothering him now? A vision of Jenna, dressed in white, head thrown back, laughing during her engagement party only a few months ago flashed into his mind. That was why. Jenna wasn't one of Brad's conquests. She was different. For a start, she was his friend Zane's sister. But also, Matt had known her since they were teenagers. They weren't exactly close, but he'd always liked her and felt protective of her.

Nadia reached the two men, looking from Brad to Matt. "Everything okay?"

Matt shifted his focus to Nadia, her wavy red hair cascading down her back. He could see why Brad would be interested in her, but Brad had no right to be. He forced a smile. "I'd better get going. Nice to meet you, Nadia." His eyes locked with Brad's. "See you in two weeks—at the wedding."

The smile on Brad's lips did nothing to hide the anger in his eyes. For Nadia's benefit, he clapped Matt on the back and laughed. "Wouldn't miss it for the world."

Nadia's face lit up. "I love weddings." She winked at

Matt. "I might have to twist Brad's arm to be invited as his plus one."

Matt hesitated for only a second as Brad laughed at Nadia's suggestion. Did she know it was Brad's wedding and was therefore joking? He honestly couldn't tell. He turned and walked toward the bar area to wait for his father.

———

Jenna pulled into a spot outside the Sandstone Cafe, debating who she'd go and see first. Asha was expecting her to drop in for coffee, but she also wanted to say a quick hello to Margie. Other than a couple of brief conversations, she hadn't had a chance to spend any time with her since she and Ryan had returned to Hope's Ridge earlier in the year to run the Sandstone Cafe. The last time she'd seen Margie was at the engagement party.

The sun glinted off Jenna's Tiffany diamond engagement ring as she glanced down at her left hand, a feeling of warmth enveloping her. Two weeks from tomorrow, she and Brad would be getting married. She could hardly believe it. It had all happened quickly—the proposal, the engagement party, and now the wedding—but it was how Jenna operated. When she was ready for something, she pushed all reservations aside and made it happen.

Pushed all reservations aside? Did she have that thought? She gave herself a mental shake. She didn't have reservations. She was head over heels with Brad, and she knew he felt the same way about her. They were perfectly matched. It was other people who'd tried to plant a seed of doubt in her mind: her brother, father, even Asha had been concerned about the speed of the relationship. But they lived in Hope's Ridge, and she and Brad lived in the city. They hardly knew him, so they weren't in a position to judge.

She pushed open the car door and stepped out onto the sidewalk, admiring the development next to the cafe. It was nearly complete, and she had to admit, it looked fantastic. While there had been many objectors to Matt Law's development, the look and feel of the Sandstone Cafe had been carried across the apartment blocks. The three levels housed twenty-four apartments, and it appeared from the outside that they were complete.

"I see you are admiring my project?"

Jenna turned to find ninety-six-year-old Charlie Li smiling at her. "Hello, Mr. Li. Your project? I thought it was Matt's."

"Ah, that Matthew, yes, I guess you could say it is his project, but I have brought it to life."

Jenna smiled. "I did hear you were doing a fantastic job." She, like most of the town, had been beyond surprised when Matt Law had offered Charlie the job of foreman on the construction of the buildings. Only a few months earlier, Matt had tried to have Charlie declared unfit to look after himself or make financial decisions. His plan to cheat Charlie out of his properties had luckily been stopped, and Matt had spent many months trying to win back the respect of the town. His genuine remorse toward Charlie and the offer of the job had certainly helped.

"And I hear you are soon to be wed," Charlie said.

Jenna smiled. "Hear? You RSVP'd yes to the invitation we sent you. You are coming, aren't you?"

"I did, and I am delighted to be attending." A frown crossed his features. "Although, this Brad, is he good enough for you? I've heard he has wandering eyes."

Jenna blushed. "I think you'll find that was before Brad met me, Mr. Li. He's grown up and knows what he wants, which is a future for us."

"Very good. But Jenna, call me Charlie. This Mr. Li nonsense is making me feel old. Now, I'd better get on with my day." He glanced at his watch. "Those landscapers will be here any minute."

Jenna smiled as the older man shuffled toward the apartments. She turned and walked the short distance to the entrance of the Sandstone Cafe and pushed open the front door.

"Jenna!"

Jenna grinned as Ryan walked up to her, his arms outstretched and dimples deepening as his smile widened. She had to admit, as much as she loved the city and couldn't imagine living in Hope's Ridge, she did love coming back to her hometown every now and then. She walked into Ryan's embrace and hugged him back.

"It's so good to see you," Ryan said, releasing her. "I didn't think we'd see you before the wedding."

"Brad's got a few commitments this weekend, so I decided it was a good chance to have a final visit as an unmarried woman."

Ryan raised an eyebrow. "That suggests you'll be up to no good. Are you having a bachelorette party?"

Jenna shook her head. "Not officially. I'll catch up with Asha tonight, and then a friend in the city has organized some pre-wedding drinks next week, but I didn't want to do anything big."

"But Brad is."

Jenna laughed. "Yes, the bachelor party sounds like it's going to be massive. That's the weekend before the wedding. He'll probably need a few days to recover."

"And you don't mind? I've heard Brad can be pretty wild."

"Why would I mind? It's a chance to celebrate with his friends that he's moving to a different stage of life. I'm sure you'll all have a great time."

Ryan nodded, his face reflecting that he perhaps didn't agree. "Now, coffee? Cake? Margie made the most incredible frosted carrot cake this morning. Come and have a look."

He directed her to the glass-front display case.

"Wow." Jenna's mouth watered at the sight of the masterpiece. "I'm supposed to be having coffee and cake with Asha over the road, but this looks too good to pass up."

"Hey, Jenna." Margie walked through from the cafe's kitchen area.

Jenna smiled, doing her best to hide her shock at Margie's appearance. She was dressed neatly but had dark rings under her eyes, deep lines etched on her face, and her dark hair was limp and lifeless. She was only a year or two older than Jenna, but the trauma of losing her husband to pancreatic cancer a few months before she and Ryan moved back to Hope's Ridge was clearly visible in her appearance. "Hey yourself. It was you I wanted to see."

"Oh? Anything wrong?"

"No, but I've hardly seen you since you and Ryan returned to the Ridge. I'm here for the weekend and wondered if you'd like to catch up?"

"She'd loved to," Ryan said.

"Ry!" Margie shot an annoyed look at her brother. "I can answer for myself."

"And you'll say no. We both know that. You need to start doing things again that don't revolve around work."

Jenna looked from Ryan to Margie, noting the anger that flashed in Margie's eyes.

"Look, there's no pressure. I'd love to spend some time with you, that's all. If there's an issue, then you can say no."

Margie sighed. "There's no issue, and I'd love to. Ryan's overprotective. He thinks since we've arrived back here that I've become a hermit."

"*Think*," Ryan muttered. He shook his head. "I'll go and clear some tables and leave you to it. Don't leave without a firm commitment from her, Jen."

Jenna turned to Margie after Ryan left. "Are you okay?"

Margie's eyes instantly filled with tears. "Sorry. Those three words usually undo me."

"It can't be easy," Jenna said. "I couldn't imagine how I'd feel if I lost Brad."

Margie nodded, wiping her eyes on her sleeve. "I'm okay. Some days are harder than others, that's all. The memories are a bit overwhelming." She did her best to smile. "Enough about me. I want to hear about you and the wedding plans. I'm finishing at one tomorrow if you want to catch up in the afternoon? A walk beside the lake, perhaps?"

"Sounds great. Now, in order to support both your and Asha's businesses, I'd like two slices of that amazing-looking carrot cake to take across the road. Ash can supply the coffee."

Margie grinned, opened the door to the display unit,

and took out the cake.

Matt replayed the conversation he'd had the previous night with his father and the venture capitalist, Susan Lewis, in his mind as he left the city behind and with each mile drew closer to Hope's Ridge. The discussion had unsettled him. Walter was talking about selling off numerous assets in Hope's Ridge and neighboring Drayson's Landing and using the funds to join Susan in a scheme she was investing in. It didn't make sense to Matt why his father would suddenly risk his assets by putting a large majority into one investment when he'd always talked about diversifying and the importance of spreading risk. But it was more than that.

There was something about Susan that didn't sit right. Matt had never heard of her before, yet the way she was talking to Walter, you'd assume they had known each other for years. If Susan wasn't half Walter's age, he'd wonder if there was something going on between them. But then again, Walter hadn't seemed particularly happy to have her meeting with them. He'd nodded and agreed with everything she'd said, but it felt like he was doing it with an underlying layer of resentment.

He maneuvered the Chevy Colorado down the winding hill leading into Hope's Ridge, deciding to push all thoughts of Walter and Susan from his mind. He smiled as he looked around the pick-up's cabin. He could already imagine the comments that were likely to be made when people saw he'd changed his vehicle. The BMW Roadster had been a pleasure to drive, but he knew it was also the cause of many head shakes and nasty suggestions about his work ethic. *He has to rip everyone off in order to cover his fancy lifestyle.* That was the comment that had made him wake up to what the townspeople thought about him. He'd done enough damage to his reputation through his own actions. The last thing he needed was something as simple as a car to be a constant reminder to the town that he was successful. As a result, he'd spent part of his visit to the city changing vehicles. While the Colorado didn't offer the same luxury as his Roadster, it was comfortable, had heaps of grunt, and most importantly was practical.

He'd almost laughed when his father had seen the vehicle. His mouth had literally dropped open. "What's that heap of junk, Matthew? It hardly sets you apart from the rest of the town. They'll think you're one of them."

There was no point explaining to Walter Law that that was what he wanted them to think. He'd tried for many years to emulate his father's approach to business but recently had seen that he could be successful in all areas of his life, and it didn't have to be at the expense of others. His ninety-six-year-old mentor had helped him realize this, and he hoped, as a result, he would be a better man. A man that someone might find attractive enough to consider a relationship with. If that dog, Brad Campbell, could get someone like Jenna, surely there was someone out there for him.

Matt gripped the steering wheel tight, his knuckles turning white as he thought of Brad and his smug smile. Thinking it was okay to cheat on Jenna. He said it was going to stop when he got married, but Matt didn't believe him. His anger rose as he thought about the situation. Back in high school Matt had had a crush on Jenna. He'd never told anyone, and if he was honest, she'd scared him with her confidence and sarcastic sense of humor. And anyway, she was way out of his league, so he hadn't acted on his feelings, and then she'd moved to go to college in the city.

The road leveled out as Matt reached the Welcome to Hope's Ridge sign on the outskirts of town. He slowed and turned onto Lake Drive. He would grab a coffee from Asha and then head over to Holly's. It was hard to believe how much work had already been achieved on the wellness retreat. Another aspect of his life his father had looked down upon. "A wellness retreat? That's prime land, Matt. You could develop that into something profitable. It's that girl, isn't it? That business partner of yours."

"Steph?"

Walter nodded. "You've got a thing for her, haven't you? This is your way of trying to make something happen. An incredibly stupid and expensive way."

"No, I don't have a thing for Steph. She's in a relationship, and she's definitely not my type." More accurately, he knew he wasn't her type, but that wasn't the point. He'd been so happy for Steph and Buster when they'd found love earlier in the year. He'd give anything to have what they had, but with someone suited to him.

"Then why?"

It made Matt angry that he had to spell it out to his father. Surely he could work it out himself as to why Matt might want to help people. "Because of Mom," was all he said.

"Your mother's been dead for fifteen years. Do you honestly think a wellness retreat is something she would have wanted to see in Hope's Ridge?"

"Definitely. It would have helped her, and it will be an

opportunity to help others like her."

The look of incredulity on Walter's face had Matt curling his hands into fists. If she hadn't died, Matt could only assume his mother would have divorced his father. Her illness had been an inconvenience for him and her death a relief. "You want to help others with MS?"

"Not only MS. All sorts of illnesses. But that's not all it's set up for. It's also a yoga retreat. It will attract a variety of clients."

"Total waste of money, and some of that is my money, don't forget."

Matt was unlikely to forget that his father had a vested interest in most of his businesses. On paper, he owned a larger share than Matthew with most of them, but in reality, he stood back as a silent partner and allowed Matt to handle the day-to-day running of the projects.

He did his best to change the subject. His father had suffered a heart attack four months earlier and still had to take it easy. A heated argument over how Matt conducted his business wasn't going to achieve anything.

He knew his father was getting healthier every day and was almost back to normal by how arrogant and controlling he was. It was a good reminder that this was not how he wanted to be seen. Charlie had been the one to say that to him. "Look at your father, Matthew, and decide which qualities you admire and which you don't. Write them down. Two lists. Check them regularly and make sure your behavior doesn't fit with the list of qualities you don't admire. He was your teacher and your role model. Unfortunately, while some of his teachings were educational, some of them were less than desirable. Use your knowledge to build a better you."

Matt pulled to a stop and parked in a parking area designated for customers of the lakeside coffee venue, Irresistibles. He pushed open the pick-up's door, relieved to have the opportunity to stretch his legs. Glancing across at the Sandstone Cafe, he was pleased to see the outdoor tables full and hoped inside would be the same. He hesitated. A white Jeep was parked outside with the license plate *Jenna*. He wasn't sure he could face Jenna right now. What would he say? He could hardly imagine she'd want to hear from him that her fiancé was a cheat.

He walked toward Irresistibles, stopping when he saw Jenna and Asha sitting at one of the tables. So much for not having to see her.

Asha waved him over, making it impossible not to talk to her. He plastered on a smile as he reached their table. "Taking a break?"

Asha nodded. "Orla's helping out today, so it gives me a chance to relax and see what it's like to be a customer. Although," her eyes twinkled, "the cake is one of Margie's. Jenna's spending money with the enemy."

Matt smiled. "The enemy is here to spend money with you, so I guess that helps even things out."

Asha laughed. "It does. But Matt, I don't expect you to buy your coffee here. You own the Sandstone Cafe. I'm pretty sure you don't have to pay over there."

Matt shrugged. "True, but I'm doing my best to show you I'm genuine about us all working together and being friends."

"And let me guess," Jenna said, "Charlie's forced you to spend a certain amount of money here each week."

"Forced is not the right word," Matt said. "Strongly suggested would be more along the lines." He switched into an impression of Charlie. "*It is good for relationships, Matthew. People see you are genuine. That you are part of the town. They like that, Matthew.*" He grinned. "I agree with Charlie, and I need the town behind me, so I should treat everyone how I want to be treated. Now, I should let you get on with your catch-up and order something from Orla." The two women looked at him, no doubt expecting him to leave them alone, but he found himself glued to the spot. He felt he should say something. If Jenna was his sister, he'd hate for her to be marrying such a pig. But was it his place? Should he talk to her brother, Zane, instead?

"Everything okay, Matt?" Asha asked, breaking into his thoughts.

He cleared his throat and locked eyes with Jenna. "I bumped into Brad last night at O'Reilly's."

Jenna frowned. "O'Reilly's? He must have had a change of plans. I'm sure he said he and the boys were going to the Manson bar."

"The boys?"

Jenna nodded. "Yes, some of the crew he works with can't make the bachelor party and were taking him out for pre-wedding drinks. He only invited a couple of the guys from work, but the rest of the office decided it was a good excuse for a night out."

"Can I ask you something?" Matt asked. "This will sound a little strange. But do you and Brad have an arrangement? One where you can see other people up until you're married?"

Jenna's face paled. "He wasn't with someone, was he?"

Matt took a deep breath. "He was, and I didn't see any of the guys from work. A woman—Nadia."

Relief flashed in Jenna's eyes. "Red hair? Gorgeous? Tall

with flawless skin?"

Matt nodded. Jenna had described her perfectly.

"She's one of the realtors at Bold Realty where he works. What time did you see them?"

"About six. I was meeting Dad at six-thirty and was early."

She nodded. "Their night out started at seven, so the other guys probably weren't there yet, that's all. No big deal. I'm sure it was completely innocent."

"Jen, I mentioned the wedding and Nadia laughed and suggested to Brad she'd like to come as his plus one."

Jenna smiled. "That sounds like Nadia. According to Brad she's very funny and at times deliberately inappropriate. She wasn't invited to the wedding since Brad only invited a couple of people from work, so it was probably her way of reminding him of that. She might have wanted to come."

Matt nodded. He'd been unsure at the time if she was joking. It was awful to think that she was having a relationship with a man she knew was about to get married. In his eyes, it made her as bad as Brad.

He forced a smile for Jenna. "Sorry. I saw them together, and it concerned me, that's all. I would have felt guilty if I didn't say something with Brad's reputation for being pretty wild."

Jenna's eyes hardened. "As you pointed out at our engagement party. I'm pretty sure you have a reputation you'd like people to move on from too, Matt. Why don't you allow Brad to do the same?" She turned her attention back to Asha.

Matt's cheeks burned with embarrassment. How he wished he'd never seen Brad the previous night. He turned, deciding to forgo the coffee, and walked in the direction of the Sandstone Cafe. He should have gone there first. So much for following Charlie's advice of keeping nice with Asha. It was good advice. He knew that. Asha served coffee to a large percentage of the town, and having her as a friend rather than the enemy was what he needed. He hoped she didn't think he was trying to interfere with Jenna's relationship. He wasn't. He was—what? He sighed. He didn't know what he was doing. He'd been around plenty of cheating guys before. But this one got his back up. A guy like Brad did not deserve a woman like Jenna.

Jenna shook her head as Matt walked away. "Sorry, it looks like I cost you a sale. What's Matt's problem anyway? He made some snide remark at the engagement party about how he was amazed Zane was letting me anywhere near Brad and now this. Can't he handle us all moving on while he remains single?"

Asha frowned. "Is he interested in you, do you think?"

Jenna threw her head back and laughed. "You've got to be kidding. I've hardly seen the guy since high school. I've seen him a couple of times in the last twelve months. Early on in our relationship he hung out with Brad occasionally. They got to know each other a few years ago on some development Matt's father was buying, and Brad was the realtor. But something happened recently, and they had a falling out. Brad didn't say what, but it was some kind of argument, and Brad decided he didn't want Matt hanging around. When you look at all of the terrible things he's done here, that's no real surprise."

"He's made a real effort to change, Jen, which is why I'm surprised he'd try to stir up trouble for no reason."

Jenna picked up her coffee and took a sip. She replaced the mug on the table. "Brad's done nothing wrong."

"I'm not saying he has."

"Well, it sounds like you are. I'm getting married in two weeks, and you, Zane, and my parents all give me this vibe that I'm doing the wrong thing."

Asha reached across the table and took her hand. "Sorry. That's not my intention. We all love you, that's all. We don't want to see you get hurt. None of us knows Brad well, and the fact he's had little interest in coming out to the Ridge hasn't been in his favor."

"He's a city boy, that's all. He's not keen on *the sticks,* as he calls it."

"But *the sticks* is where your home is. Your family, your friends."

"I've lived away from here for ten years, Ash. Home is the city and Brad. The problem is none of you seem to realize that. I moved on. As for friends, you're here. Everyone else is in the city. You've hardly come to the city since I've been with Brad, and Zane and my parents are the same. You had the chance to get to know him and still do if you make an effort."

Asha nodded. "You're right. I'm sorry. I guess I'm used to seeing you when you're here. Zane and I will definitely come and visit once you're back from the honeymoon."

"Good. And as for Brad's reputation. Sure, he dated a lot before we met. But he's chosen me." Her lips curled into a smile as the words left her mouth. "I can hardly believe it. He could have picked anyone, and he chose me."

Asha didn't respond, but Jenna could see from the look

on her friend's face that she was holding something back.

"What?"

"You make it sound like he's doing you a favor. It should be a case of him falling in love with you and having eyes for no one else."

Jenna's phone pinged with a text message before she had a chance to respond. She plucked it from her bag, her heart swelling. *Miss you babe. Can't wait for Sunday night. It's time our bedroom got a proper workout.* She held her phone up for Asha's benefit, a smile spreading across her face.

Asha put her hand to her mouth and laughed. "Ew, I don't want to read that. Way too much information."

Jenna dropped the phone back in her bag. "I'm making a point. He loves me. I've never been with a guy that's made me feel this way before. I'm not stupid either. I'd know if he was cheating." A flush of heat pricked her cheeks. "And as you can tell from that text, there's no reason for him to cheat. I'm pretty sure every fantasy he's ever had has been played out."

Asha pretended to put her hands over her ears. "Like I said, too much information. Now, what's the plan for today?"

"I'll drop in and see my parents, and then it's dinner with you and Zane tonight."

"And Steph and Buster," Asha said. "If that's okay? Steph wanted to come."

Jenna grinned. "Sounds great. I'm so happy for them. They're perfectly suited. I'm glad Buster's found love. He deserves it after everything he's been through."

Asha nodded. "They both do. The accident brought them together. It's so sad that he no longer has Holly, as I think Steph would have adored her too."

The two women lapsed into silence in memory of the little girl who'd lost her life the previous year.

"Do you think you'll have kids soon?"

Asha's mouth dropped open. "Where did that come from? Zane and I aren't even engaged, let alone married."

"Which surprises me," Jenna said. "I thought Zane would have proposed by now. Did you want me to give him a kick up the backside?"

Asha shook her head, her cheeks coloring. "No, I think he'd propose in a heartbeat if I let him."

"Let him? Isn't he the one who gets to decide when he's going down on one knee?"

"Yes, but he knows I'm not ready. I like to take it slowly, Jen. You know me."

Jenna frowned. "Do you have doubts about Zane?"

"None. He's the love of my life, and we'll get married and have kids at some point, but right now, I'm concentrating on building my business and following my plan."

"Your *plan*? That sounds ominous."

Asha laughed. "Let's get you married off first, and then you can worry about Zane and me."

Jenna finished the rest of her coffee and stood. "Traders at seven then?"

"Perfect."

Matt had Margie make his coffee to go, wishing again that he'd gone to the Sandstone Cafe first. He smiled as Margie placed his to-go cup on the counter.

"Thanks."

"Ryan said he saw you talking with Asha and Jenna over

at the food truck," Margie said, raising an eyebrow.

Matt sighed. "You can't do anything in this town without someone commenting."

"Sorry," Margie said. "I was being nosy. I said to Ryan, you were probably buying coffee there for a change, but he said no, that it looked like Jenna was getting mad. Flapping her hands as she does."

Matt stared at Margie. She was someone he could trust. "Can I ask you something?"

"Of course."

"If you'd found out that your husband was seeing someone else quite close to your wedding, would you have married him?"

Margie's mouth dropped open. "Brad?"

Matt nodded. "I saw him with a woman last night at a bar in the city. He was all over her, and when I asked him about it, he said he and Jenna had an arrangement where they could see other people, which would end once they got married. It sounded a bit odd to me, so I asked Jenna if this was the case."

"I take it it isn't?"

"No. I didn't say much, only that he was there with a woman, Nadia. Jenna knows her and said she works with Brad. She said Brad was going out with people from work, and the others would have arrived a bit later. It's definitely not what Brad told me. I'm not sure whether I should say anything else. What would you do?"

Margie considered her response. "I'm not sure. It's a tricky one. If you say more and they end up getting married, you'll always be the guy who tried to break them up."

"Not ideal when I'm trying to show people I've changed." Matt sighed. "I guess I'll stay out of it."

"You're sure that they were together?"

"Definitely. He mentioned other casual relationships too. If they have an arrangement, then that's fine, but I'm guessing the only one who knows of this arrangement is Brad." He picked up his coffee from the counter. "I'd better go. I've wasted enough time on Jenna today. I promised Steph I'd be at Holly's by now. We're breaking ground for the pool today."

"Tell her I said hi," Margie said. "And I promise I'll be at one of her weekend classes." She laughed. "I can even get through an entire hot yoga class now without having to lie down. She's a great instructor."

"She is." Matt raised his coffee. "Thanks for this."

Matt considered Margie's words, that Steph was a great instructor, as he drove the short distance from the cafe to Holly's. The yoga retreat and wellness center was situated at the far end of town, back from the lake, tucked at the base of Mount Hopeful. It had taken a few months to confirm plans and have approvals in place, but now Holly's was in the construction phase. Steph had taken Matt's vision to a whole other level. His gut feeling had been that she would be exceptional. The yoga studio was all Steph. Her energy coursed through it, motivating, caring, inspiring. And her touch was on everything, both the look and feel. Her own home, which was like a retreat you'd find in Thailand or Bali, was the same. But her design ideas and the touches she'd suggested for Holly's went beyond anything he'd imagined. She had a flair for design, and he was beginning to wonder if she was wasted in her role as a yoga teacher. Once Holly's was completed, they intended to employ staff to run the retreat side of the business. Steph had planned to step up her role to manage the staff while still running and teaching in the yoga studio, but Matt could see her being valuable on other projects.

He pulled into the long driveway that wound from the main road through a forested area up to the yoga studio and retreat development. He found himself smiling as the property came into view. He wished his mom could see this. See that he was doing something that would help so many people. She would be proud of him. He knew that. His smile slipped as a sense of longing and loss overcame him. A loneliness he hadn't experienced before had crept into his life in the last few months. It was strange as he was more settled than ever, calling Hope's Ridge home and doing his best to improve it. Maybe that was the problem. He finally felt like he had a place to call home yet had no family and no one special to share it with.

———

2

*J*enna was glad she'd only had one glass of wine at dinner the previous night and had woken clear-headed and ready to enjoy what looked like a beautiful sunny Saturday in Hope's Ridge. She stood in her childhood bedroom, looking out of the large bay windows. Being up on a hill, she had a clear view over the rooftops to the lake. It was a relief to see the sun shining again after the unseasonable cold snap during the week, and a couple of boats were already out taking advantage of the warm May day.

"Hon, you awake?" Her mother tapped gently on the bedroom door before opening it.

Jenna, already dressed, turned to face her mother.

"I can't believe my little girl's about to get married," Janet said. "Who knows, there might be grandchildren coming to visit soon."

Jenna laughed. "I'm not sure about that. I'm in no rush."

"You'll be thirty soon," Janet said. "I said the same to

Zane the other day. You don't want to leave it too late, especially if you plan to have more than one."

"Well, it's not on the radar yet. My job's too important to me to take time out."

"Speaking of that, Dad was hoping to have a chat with you. You know that he and Zane have been working on ideas for a new website and signage for the mill."

Jenna nodded.

"Well, between you and me, I think they're way off track. The look they're going for is modern corporate, and that's not what we are. We need to look professional but with a rustic feel to it. The mill's got a history, and that needs to be reflected in what we do."

"Definitely," Jenna said. "Some beautiful red cedar with the lettering burnt into it would look stunning for the signage. Like the sign behind the bar at Traders. And that should be carried through to the look and feel of the website."

Janet smiled. "I knew you'd have ideas. Would you be willing to speak to Dad about them?"

"If you think he'll listen."

"He'll listen. Will you be home for dinner tonight?"

"Yes, I'm meeting Margie this afternoon for a few hours, but that's it. Ash said she and Zane were coming for dinner tonight, so I'll be here."

"Great. Perhaps you can give some thought to ideas, and we can discuss them tonight. Now, I'll leave you to it. Coffee's made downstairs, and there's plenty of fresh fruit for breakfast. Or I can make you something more substantial?"

Jenna patted her flat stomach. "Fruit sounds good. Brad

won't be impressed if I put on weight between now and the wedding."

Janet turned to leave, hesitated, and looked back at Jenna. "You're definitely sure you're ready to get married?"

Jenna sighed. "Not you too. I had Zane going on about it last night. Asha and her big mouth." She hadn't thought to say to Asha that she didn't want her mentioning what Matt had said to anyone, especially not Zane. Zane was full of questions during dinner, which had been embarrassing with Steph and Buster there. In the end, she'd pulled him aside and told him to stop. "Matt's got his wires crossed, okay? I don't know what his problem is, but he tried to stir up trouble at the engagement party, and now this."

"Have you asked Brad if there's any truth to what Matt said?"

"Not yet. I'll mention it when I get home. It's not the sort of thing you ask over the phone." *You need to see their facial reaction and body language*, she thought but didn't add. She wasn't going to let on to anyone that Matt's words had rattled her. How could they not? Brad was gorgeous, charming, and successful. He could have any woman he wanted, and yes, women flirted with him and he with them. But that was all it was, flirting. She did the same herself. It was fun as long as that was all it was. While she was certain she had nothing to worry about, she would still ask him. She didn't want something like that on her mind during the wedding or any time after.

She realized her mother had said something, and she hadn't responded. "Sorry, what did you say?"

"I asked what about Asha and her big mouth?"

"Oh, nothing. It's just that everyone seems to think I'm moving too quickly. Mom, I trust my gut, and when I know

I'm doing the right thing, I go ahead and do it. And Brad is the right thing. We're going to grow old together."

Janet moved across the room and took Jenna in her arms and squeezed her. "And I'll be right here any time you need me, okay? Anything at all. Marriage is wonderful but can also have its hard moments. If you ever need to talk to me during those, you know where I am."

Jenna returned her mother's hug. "Thanks, Mom. Hopefully there won't be too many talks needed."

Janet smiled and released Jenna. "I'm happy for you, hon, I am. Deep down, we all are. We love you and want to make sure you're happy."

"I know, and I appreciate it. Now, I'll start thinking about website designs, and I'll see you at dinner."

All thoughts of website designs were pushed from Jenna's mind that afternoon as she pulled into Margie's driveway. She and Ryan were sharing a house only a short walk into town.

Margie appeared at the front door wearing her active gear and sports shoes, her straight black hair tied back.

"Hey," Margie said, flashing Jenna a smile as she slipped into the passenger seat. "Thanks for suggesting this. Ryan's right, I need to get out."

"I'm looking forward to catching up," Jenna said. "It's been ages."

"I know. And here's you, about to get married. I can't wait to hear about the plans. Asha already told me your dress is to die for."

Jenna glanced at Margie. She wasn't sure how much wedding talk was appropriate under the circumstances. "You sure you want to talk about a wedding?"

"It's your big day. It's exciting."

Jenna nodded. "I wasn't sure how you'd feel about it."

Margie was silent for a moment. "Because of Aaron?"

Jenna nodded again. "I haven't had a chance to say how sorry I am that you went through that, both of you."

"Thanks, but it's the last thing I want to talk about, and your wedding is something I do want to talk about. Tell me about Brad."

Ninety minutes later, the two women were on the return leg of their walk.

"I haven't walked this far in ages," Margie said.

"I haven't talked this much about myself in ages," Jenna said and laughed. "Sorry, I think I went from thinking it might not be okay to talk about Brad and the wedding to talking about nothing else."

"That's not true. We talked about my days as a pastry chef in France most of the way up the lake and every bit of gossip I could think of from the people in town."

Jenna laughed. "That's true." Her laughter died. "But we didn't talk about Aaron. Your fifth anniversary was yesterday. That couldn't have been easy."

"It wasn't, but..." She stopped.

"But?" Jenna probed.

Margie shook her head. "Honestly, it's not something I want to talk about. Ryan's at me to see someone for counseling, but it's not what I need. I need to forget about it. Put it all behind me and start again."

Jenna stared at Margie. It seemed like such a strange thing to say. *Forget about Aaron?*

Margie forced a smile. "You look shocked."

"A little surprised maybe, but everyone deals with death differently."

"And not everything is as it seems."

Jenna waited for her to elaborate, but she didn't. Instead, Margie changed the subject.

"I know I should butt out, but Matt's worried about you, which means I am too."

Jenna didn't respond but started walking again.

"I wasn't going to say anything, but he was upset talking to me earlier. Said he didn't know what to do. That he thinks Brad hasn't been honest with you. Brad insisted you had some kind of arrangement that ends when you get married."

"Matt's a troublemaker, Margie. We both know that. He's been jealous since day one that Brad has a girlfriend. His friend has something he wants—a relationship, that is. He's not interested in me."

"And you think he'd make this up?"

"Definitely. Look, I'll ask Brad tomorrow when I get home about what he said to Matt. But as we don't have any kind of arrangement, he'd be silly to say something like that and risk me finding out. And I had a text yesterday from one of his friends who was out with him on Thursday night saying he hoped Brad's head was okay and that they'd all had a great night. Brad definitely wasn't out with a woman on his own."

"Phew." Margie pretended to wipe her brow. "Okay, that's all good. I thought I wouldn't be much of a friend if I didn't say something. I got the impression from Matt that that was his feeling too, but you know him better than I do."

"No one knows Matt Law," Jenna said. "He's one of a kind and not one you want to spend too much time around. Ask Charlie, or Asha, or pretty much anyone in the town."

Margie frowned. "I thought all of those issues were

resolved. Steph said he's been amazing on the development for the wellness retreat."

"Wait and see," Jenna said. "There will be another issue with Matt. He'll burn someone or lie about something. Remember the lies he told trying to manipulate the situation with Charlie? When he wants to achieve something, he'll go to any length. Petty jealousy isn't going to ruin my relationship, I can assure you."

Matt puffed as his feet pounded the dirt trail that ran along the side of Lake Hopeful. He'd started running a few weeks earlier to complement the gym workouts he did and was already noticing the difference in his cardio fitness. He'd spent the morning going over his books, trying to work out if there was equity in his investments that he could leverage for new business. He'd come to the conclusion that there wasn't. That was okay for the moment. Once the wellness retreat was up and running and he began to recoup his investment there, things would change. He smiled to himself as he thought of Holly's and of Steph's face the day before. She'd been like a little kid at Christmas when the excavator took the first scoop of earth, breaking ground for the new pool.

Matt slowed as he saw two women walking a short distance in front. The swing of her blonde ponytail told him that one of the women was Jenna. She was the last person he wanted to run into today. Laughter from the other woman was instantly recognizable as Margie. He hesitated for a moment, his eyes focusing on Jenna as he appreciated her slim, athletic build. He shook himself, turned, and ran back in the direction from which he'd come. What was he thinking? He'd been disgusted at Brad's behavior, and now he was checking Jenna out? *Jenna, who was about to marry that dog.*

Thirty minutes later, he circled back and made his way to the Sandstone Cafe. It was Margie's afternoon off, so he hoped that she and Jenna wouldn't be there. He walked along the outside of the building, casually peering in through the large windows. There was no sign of them. He stopped as he recognized the familiar dark curls and recognizable face of Susan Lewis. *What is she doing in Hope's Ridge?* Matt frowned, turned toward the front door of the cafe, and went inside. The cafe was busy for a Saturday afternoon, and he noticed most tables had wine glasses on them rather than coffee cups. The liquor license was changing the weekend dynamic of the cafe. The rooftop bar was proving a huge success, especially on a beautiful afternoon like today. He imagined it was at capacity as people enjoyed the afternoon sunshine and settled in for the afternoon and evening to watch the sunset.

His eyes scanned the cafe and locked on Susan Lewis. She sat at one of the booths, across from a man whose back was to Matt. He'd recognize the back of that head of thinning gray hair anywhere. He crossed over to them and stopped by the table. "Dad? What are you doing here?"

Walter smiled at Matt. "I wanted to show Susan around. She's never been to Hope's Ridge." He let out a laugh. "Hard to believe, isn't it?"

Not really, Matt wanted to say but didn't. If she was a city person, then what reason would she have to come out to the ridge?

Susan tapped her carefully manicured nails on the

table. "It's a lovely little town," she said. "The main street's quite charming, and you've done an excellent job with the apartments attached to the cafe."

"Thank you," Matt said.

"Sit down with us," Walter said, moving along the booth seat to make room for Matt. "What we've been discussing affects you too."

Matt slid into the seat beside his father. "In what respect?"

Walter exchanged a glance with Susan. "In the respect that changes to my investment portfolio could impact some of your projects."

Matt stared at his father. "How?"

"Financially. I have ownership in most of the developments you're currently undertaking, and I'd like to convert that ownership into cash."

Matt shook his head. "That's not possible without selling."

Walter nodded. "I realize that."

Heat rushed to Matt's face. "What? You expect me to sell the developments?"

"If that's what it takes to get my money out of Hope's Ridge, then yes. Susan and I have an opportunity that I want to sink most of my capital into."

"But even if I agreed, which is unlikely, it would take ages to sell the properties."

"It's time to change things up," Walter said, "and I'm confident we can shift the properties quickly."

Matt shook his head slowly. "Not if we want them to be profitable."

Walter sighed. "Look, son, Susan and I had further discussions since we had dinner on Thursday, and I've made the decision that I want to sell off properties in Hope's Ridge and Drayson's Landing and shift all future projects to the city."

Matt's mouth dropped open. "You've made that decision in the space of a couple of days? But we own a reasonable percentage of both towns." He turned to Susan. "Is this your advice?"

Susan nodded. "It is, but it isn't something Walter wasn't already considering."

Matt looked from Susan to his father. What was going on between them that would make his father act so impulsively?

"I think you and I should meet, Dad, and discuss this matter privately." He turned to Susan. "I'm sorry, but Dad's been investing in this town for over forty years. You've suddenly appeared, and now we're selling everything? I'm not sure what's going on between the two of you, but I don't want it affecting the business I've worked hard to build."

Susan stood. "I think a walk by the lake would be a nice way to get a feel for Hope's Ridge. How about I go and do that and leave you two to talk."

Matt waited until she'd left the cafe before turning back to his father.

"Are you nuts?"

Walter leaned back and studied Matt. "Yes, I'd say I probably am."

Matt managed a wry smile. "This is a joke? Or are you having a relationship with Susan and trying to impress her?"

"Neither. I meant I was nuts leaving my money tied up in this deadbeat town for so long. I was practically run out of here with the town objecting to my ideas and constantly protesting. You've had a bit more luck recently getting this place done up, plus the apartments next door, but that's not enough—the town's too small, Matt. We'll never do well here or in Drayson's Landing. We need to put our money where the opportunities are limitless."

"And Susan has limitless opportunities for you?"

"She does. Look, I'm not stupid. I know a good investment when I see it and what Susan's offering is. A conservative estimate would provide us a fifteen percent return in six months. If we invest a large amount, we'll be laughing."

Matt shook his head. "But putting everything into one investment? You've always said you'd never do that. That it's important to spread risk."

"I'm happy to *look* at doing that," Walter said, "it doesn't mean I'll go ahead. But I don't want my money tied up here or in Drayson's Landing." He sighed. "I'm sick of this town benefiting from my success. Look at all of the money we've poured into this place and the Landing for people who try to stop our developments and constantly complain. Yet they love it when the projects are complete, and they're enjoying the upgrades. You only have to go up to your rooftop bar to see that. We couldn't get a seat up there; it's so busy, yet I seem to recall numerous objections to the development."

His father was right, but they'd been expected and fairly easily overcome. "It's doing really well," Matt said, "which is why I can't understand why you'd want to sell."

Walter shook his head and stood. "Then you haven't been listening to me. I'm sick of financing a better lifestyle for people who don't appreciate you or me. Sure, we profit from the developments, but they protest and complain and make it all too difficult. They don't deserve what we do.

This place is toxic, son. They'll burn you and spit you out. You mark my words. It doesn't matter how much good you do in Hope's Ridge; there's always someone after you, even when you're not to blame. I'd sell everything off and move to the city. There are so many opportunities there. Now, I'm going to go find Susan. She was intrigued to see the place, but now that she has, we can leave. I'll send over some paperwork during the week to confirm what I want to sell and at what price. You can let me know what you're able to buy and what needs to go on the market."

Matt watched his father walk to the counter, pay, then leave the cafe and cross the road toward the lake. What had happened? Sure, the people in the town benefited when a development was complete, but that was the whole point of doing it. The town benefited, and Matt and Walter profited. This change of heart didn't make any sense. His father was not someone who made rash decisions or quick decisions when it came to money.

He watched through the window as his father walked toward the lake trail and Susan. Who was she? And why did she have such a hold over his father? Matt pulled himself up from the booth and walked over to the counter. Without his father's investments, he wasn't sure he'd be able to retain ownership of any of the properties in Hope's Ridge. The bank was unlikely to finance him further as the apartments and the wellness retreat had stretched his lending capacity to the maximum. He pushed the thought from his head. For now, there were two things he needed. One, to find out who Susan Lewis was and why she was so influential when it came to his father, and two, a drink.

Jenna returned to her parents' house after her walk with Margie, feeling invigorated. It had been so good to catch up, although she did worry that she'd monopolized the conversation. Margie had, however, assured her that no, Jenna wasn't overly talkative, and yes, she wanted to hear about the wedding and didn't want to talk about her husband or what they'd been through. Jenna hesitated as she passed her parents' mailbox and stepped onto the flower-lined path that led to the front door. Something about Margie's reluctance to talk about Aaron and his illness didn't sit quite right. Jenna understood that it might be too painful to talk about, but she wasn't sure that was the problem. She wasn't sure what it was, but her gut said there was more going on with Margie than the obvious.

The thought returned to her an hour later when Asha and Zane arrived at the house for dinner. Her parents were busy out on the back deck firing up the grill when her best friend and brother arrived.

"Have either of you noticed anything weird going on with Margie?" she asked as the three of them worked together in the kitchen to prepare a salad.

Asha looked up from the carrot she was chopping. "Like what?"

"I'm not sure," Jenna said. "We went for a walk this afternoon, and she clammed up when the conversation turned to her and her husband."

"It's probably too painful to talk about," Zane said. "I know if I lost Ash, I would disappear into a dark hole of depression."

"No, it wasn't that." Jenna shrugged. "I don't know, something didn't sit right, that's all. I know she's sad and no doubt devastated, but there was this hesitancy about her. Like there was something she wanted to say but couldn't."

"I guess you'll find out, if she wants to talk," Asha said.

Jenna nodded, her frown quickly replaced with a sly grin. "What about you two? I've already grilled Ash about this, Zane, but now it's your turn. Are you even aware that there's a betting system at Traders?"

"For what?" Zane asked.

"For when you're going to do the right thing and ask Ash to marry you. A lot of people are already out of the running as the dates they selected have come and gone. You're keeping everyone in suspense."

Zane's cheeks reddened, and Jenna wished she'd kept her mouth shut. What if this was some kind of issue between the two of them? Asha had mentioned her *plan*. Maybe there really was one. "Sorry," she added. "None of my business."

"You're right," Asha said with a twinkle in her eye. "It's not." She nudged Zane. "You tell her."

Jenna's eyes widened. "You're not engaged?"

"We could be," Zane said, "but someone is very clear that they need to have dated for at least twelve months before they'd consider accepting my hand in marriage. It's all part of her grand plan."

"Really?" Jenna turned to Asha. "That's the plan?"

Asha nodded.

"Wow, no wonder you thought I was rushing," Jenna said. "But twelve months must be coming up," she said. "You've been together nearly twelve months, haven't you?"

"Not quite," Zane said. "But I'm hoping to find a loophole." He grinned as Asha swatted at him with some paper towel.

"How's the salad coming along?" Janet asked, entering the kitchen. "The chicken and burgers are almost ready if you want to take everything out back."

A few minutes later, the five of them sat around the outdoor table, the evening air warm with the promise of summer.

"This will be your last family meal without Brad here," Janet commented. She smiled at Jenna. "To think next time you're home, it will be as part of a married couple."

Roy snorted, causing all heads to turn his way.

"Roy?" Janet said. "What was that for?"

He looked around the small group. "Sorry. It slipped out." He picked up the garden salad and offered it to Asha, who took it from him at the same time Jenna's cutlery crashed onto her plate.

"What slipped out?" Jenna demanded. "Come on. This is your last chance. If you've got something to say about Brad and me, then say it now."

"Calm down," Roy said, causing Jenna's annoyance to rise even higher. "I think it's unlikely that the next time you're here it will be with Brad by your side. He's been here, what, once since you started dating? I think your mother's expectations are unrealistic if she thinks marriage is going to change anything."

Jenna stared at her father. "Once we're married, a lot will change. When I come home for the weekend, Brad will come with me. The same when he visits his family."

Roy shrugged. "Fine. That's great, hon. I look forward to spending time with him."

"What else is going to change?" Zane asked.

Jenna turned to her brother.

"What do you mean?"

"You said that once you were married, *a lot will change*. I'm wondering what else and whether Brad's aware of these changes."

A jittery feeling started in Jenna's stomach. Why couldn't her family accept that she was getting married and leave it alone? There were always questions. "I meant that being husband and wife changes things, that's all." She picked up her cutlery. "Now, can we eat and not talk about my relationship? You're always pointing out negatives about it."

"What about this arrangement you and Brad have," Zane continued. "Does that stop once you're married?"

Jenna turned to Asha. "I asked you not to say anything."

"She didn't," Zane was quick to interject. "Matt spoke to me. He's worried about you and said he wouldn't be able to sleep if he didn't say something."

"Say something about what?" Roy asked, placing his beer down on the table.

Jenna let out a long, slow breath, doing her best to calm her increasingly rapid heart rate. "Nothing. Matt saw Brad out with Nadia and others from work on Thursday night and is convinced Brad's having a relationship with Nadia."

"And is he?" Roy asked.

"No!" Jenna leaped to her fiancé's defense. "Matt's jealous, and he's trying to cause trouble."

Roy looked to Janet, and a silent communication took place between them. Jenna shook her head. "Now what?"

"We're all worried about you, Jen," her father said. "We don't know Brad well, and some of the stories we're hearing are concerning us. We care about you, that's all. I want you to get married to your best friend, someone who will be there by your side, supporting you for the rest of your life.

If Brad's playing around before you get married, then that's not going to change once you marry."

Asha reached under the table and squeezed her knee. Jenna turned to her friend. "Do you think he's playing around?"

Asha hesitated for a split second, long enough for Jenna to have her answer.

"You don't even know him, Ash."

"No, but I know Matt, and while he has a history of causing trouble, he's moved beyond that. Working with Charlie and Steph has changed him a lot. I definitely can't see him stirring up trouble between you and Brad without a good reason."

Jenna looked around at the faces of her family and best friend. Their expressions were all ones of concern. She knew they were looking out for her, but it hurt. That they doubted Brad, the man she loved so much. She pushed her chair back and stood.

"Honestly, after what Matt Law did only a few months ago to you, Asha, and then his treatment of both Charlie and Zane, I can't believe you'd let him change your opinions of Brad. I'm going to pack and drive back to the city tonight. I don't want to be in a house full of people who aren't supportive of me or my marriage."

She turned amid protests from her mother and strode from the room.

Matt climbed out of the pickup; the pit of his stomach filled with dread as Steph waved from the door of the yoga studio. How was he going to tell her that if his father's plans went ahead, then Holly's might have to be sold?

She hurried toward him as he did his best to return her smile. "I can't believe it," Steph said. "They got most of the pool dug out yesterday. I thought it would take them days to get that done. Come and have a look."

Matt followed Steph past a recently landscaped garden bed to the back of the retreat and was greeted by a large hole with a huge pile of dirt beside it. It started quite shallow and grew deeper as it moved away from the buildings.

"It's going to be amazing," Steph said. "Dillon, the physical therapist we interviewed, was saying how good the shallow entry design would be for clients who need it for rehabilitation. They'll be able to walk in gradually or be wheeled in in one of the aquatic wheelchairs. It will still have the look and feel of a resort pool but will have that added wellness aspect."

"It will." Matt's lack of enthusiasm didn't go unnoticed.

Steph frowned. "Are you okay?"

Matt sighed. "Some unexpected stress from my dad yesterday."

"Oh no, is he okay? It's not his heart, is it?"

Matt opened his mouth, then closed it again and smiled. "You're too nice."

"What do you mean?"

"You automatically think about my dad's health, rather than what a cold and selfish businessman he can be. I almost wish the issue was his health."

Steph's eyes widened. "You don't mean that."

He shook his head. "Sorry, I shouldn't wish something like that on him, especially after the heart attack. It's not his health; it's his business decisions. He's making some changes to the way he operates, and it may impact some of my developments in Hope's Ridge."

Steph's eyebrows drew together. "Not Holly's?"

Matt sighed. "I hope not. This is my passion project. Buster owns the majority share, so the question is whether he'd be in a position to buy me out if I did have to sell. I wouldn't want a stranger buying in."

Steph lay a hand on his arm. "Oh, Matt. I'm so sorry. After all of the work you've done on Holly's, it would be awful if you had to sell."

They both looked up as a white pickup pulled into sight along the winding driveway that led from the main road.

"Is there a class this morning?" Matt asked.

Steph shook her head. "That looks like Roy Larsen's vehicle. Did you have a meeting with him scheduled?"

"Not for today. It's Sunday, and I assume he takes the weekend off. I was planning to meet with him early in the week to discuss the types of wood for the railings of the boardwalk, and I was going to meet with Zane, too, to see if he'd be interested in doing some carvings for us. I guess we can discuss this now." He moved toward the pickup as Roy drew to a stop about fifty feet from where they stood.

Matt smiled as the older man stepped from his vehicle, the signage for Larsen's mill now clearly visible on the side door of the truck. He held out his hand. "Roy, great to see you. I was hoping to talk to you about some special wood for our boardwalk and carvings. If you've got the time, I'd love to show you around and get your input on what you'd recommend."

Roy didn't take Matt's hand. Instead, he folded his arms across his chest and stared at him. The feeling of dread

Matt had arrived with returned with full vengeance. Whatever Roy wanted, it didn't look like a friendly visit or a chance to discuss wood. "Everything okay?"

"You tell me, Matt. We had Jenna storm off last night and drive back to the city a day early due to accusations you've made about Brad. This was supposed to be our last weekend with her before she gets married. A family affair to be remembered and enjoyed. Thanks to you, it didn't turn out that way, and my wife's not happy. Not happy at all."

Matt took a step backward. "I haven't made any accusations, Roy. I told both Jenna and Zane what I saw in the city on Thursday night. Jenna's chosen not to believe me, whereas Zane was going to have a chat with her. I was looking out for her, that's all."

Roy's eyes narrowed. "You saw Brad with another woman?"

Matt nodded. "I did, and there was nothing innocent about it. Brad was all over her. I didn't tell Jenna that. All I said was that Brad told me they have an arrangement that would stop once they were married. I shared more detail with Zane."

"Did you have anyone with you who can confirm what you saw?"

Matt shook his head. "No, I was meeting Dad, but he hadn't arrived yet."

"Why would I believe you? Jenna's convinced this is you playing your usual games. Jealousy, perhaps?"

Matt shook his head. "Not at all. I'm looking out for her as I'd expect Zane or any of my friends to do if I had a sister. Nothing more, nothing less."

Roy's face darkened. "If I thought I could believe one

word that came out of your mouth, then I'd be grateful for you stepping in. But with what you did to Asha, then Zane and Charlie, I can't." He stepped closer to Matt and held up his hand in a fist. "What I will say to you, Matt Law, is if I find out you're deliberately trying to sabotage Jenna's relationship or wedding, then there will be trouble. Big trouble." He locked eyes with Matt for a long moment before turning and walking back to his pickup.

Steph stepped up next to Matt as they watched Roy back out of his parking spot, turn, and drive down the driveway toward the main road. "That was awful."

Matt nodded, managing a wry smile for Steph's benefit. "A regular day in Hope's Ridge. I'm used to verbal attacks. It would be a slow day without one."

Steph shook her head. "The way he spoke to you is not okay, Matt. I can't believe you'd deliberately stir up trouble for Jenna."

"Really? You honestly wouldn't believe I'd do that?"

Steph's hesitation caused Matt to sigh. "I don't know why I'm surprised at anyone's reaction when even you have your doubts. You know better than anyone how much I've changed, yet there's still a small part of you that wonders if I've got some ulterior motive. Isn't there?"

Pink splotches appeared on Steph's cheeks. "I'm sorry. I do want to believe you. Honestly, I do."

"It's okay. I get it. My reputation isn't going away anytime soon. But in this instance, I'm purely the messenger. The messenger who, by the reactions from the Larsen family, is the one that's going to be shot." He turned toward Holly's. "Come on. There is a lot to go over here with regards to the construction that needs to be done this week. I need to make sure we're both on the same page and that the crew will have one of us overseeing their work each day. Let's forget about Jenna. Her wedding's still two weeks away, and all I can say is I hope she wakes up between now and then and doesn't make the biggest mistake of her life."

———

Jenna didn't drive back to the city on Saturday night as she'd led her family and Asha to believe. She'd contacted Isaak at Traders and booked a room, asking him to keep her stay discreet as she didn't want it getting back to her family that she was still in Hope's Ridge. She wanted time to think before she saw Brad. As much as she didn't want to believe Matt or the doubts that her family or anyone else had with regards to her relationship, she would be lying if she said the comments hadn't affected her. What if it turned out Brad was cheating on her, and she had ignored Matt?

She woke the next morning with the same thought playing in her mind. She needed to distract herself and, rather than rush home to Brad, decided some retail therapy was in order. She'd hurried to pack her bag and leave Hope's Ridge, not wanting to bump into Asha or anyone she knew.

By the time she arrived back in the city four hours later, she was ready to shop. She went straight to the Premium Outlets district on the edge of the city and found that the day, and a good chunk of her credit card limit, disappeared quickly.

Hours later, Jenna was surprised to find nerves flitting in her stomach as she pushed open the door to the third-floor apartment she shared with Brad. The city lights were already twinkling as the weekend drew to a close.

"That you, babe?" Brad's voice drifted down the hallway from the bathroom. Jenna could hear the water running.

She dropped her bags and made her way along the hallway to the bathroom. The door was open, and Brad grinned at her from the shower, droplets of water running down his lean, muscular body. "Care to join me?"

An hour later, Jenna sat across from Brad with a glass of wine in hand. The nerves she'd arrived home with returned as she thought about how to broach the Matt Law issue.

"Everything okay?" Brad asked, nudging her foot with his.

"Mm, thinking about something someone said, that's all."

Brad raised an eyebrow. "Anything interesting?"

Jenna's heart beat faster. What if Matt was right? What if she did have something to worry about? She pushed the thought away as quickly as she had it. "It was Matt. He saw you on Thursday night."

Brad nodded. "He did. At O'Reilly's. Nadia and I were having a drink waiting for the others before we went on to the Manson Bar."

"He suggested you were—"

Brad leaned forward in his chair. "I was what?"

"Cheating on me."

Brad fell back against the couch and laughed. "Let me guess. I was all over Nadia, and that was okay because you and I have an arrangement."

Jenna nodded. "Pretty much what he said."

"And you believed him?"

"No. I didn't. But I thought I'd be stupid not to ask. It's a pretty big accusation."

Brad laughed again, reached into his back pocket, and pulled out his wallet. He flicked through it and took out some money. "One hundred dollars going to Matt Law."

"What?"

"Matt made me a bet. Said there's no way a woman like you could trust me. He said he was going to make something up so you'd think I'd been unfaithful, and you'd ask me."

"It was a bet?"

Brad nodded. "Not one that I thought he'd act on. He always has to feel like he's got the upper hand. Remember how jealous he was that I'd found you? Well, I guess this is his way of making himself feel better."

"Why would you agree to a bet like that?"

Brad moved forward on the couch and took Jenna's hands. "Because I never thought I'd lose. I thought you knew how much I love you, Jen. I'd never risk losing you. And anyway, why would I even look at another woman? You're gorgeous, smart, and adventurous." He winked with this last description. "I've never been with anyone like you. I can't wait to share my life with you. I hope that over time you'll trust me one hundred percent, and if Matt Law, or anyone else, makes a stupid bet or comment, you'll know not to believe them."

Tears pricked the back of Jenna's eyes. She'd allowed Matt Law to get under her skin, ruin her weekend, and make it look like she didn't trust Brad.

"Hey, don't get upset."

"I do trust you. I said as much to Matt. I'm upset that I let that creep get to me."

"He's an expert manipulator. Don't even worry about it."
He moved onto the couch and slipped an arm around her.
"All that's important is that we have each other, and in less
than two weeks, we will be husband and wife. I can hardly
believe I'm so lucky."

Jenna pulled Brad toward her and kissed him, all
thoughts of Matt Law dissolving as she did.

*a*s Matt stood next to Charlie looking up at the apartments, he realized how relieved he'd been to have heard nothing from his father for two weeks. Knowing how his father operated, he'd expected the documents outlining his plans to sell his investments to arrive within a day or two of their chance meeting in the Sandstone Cafe. He was relieved they hadn't. He'd done his own investigations into who Susan Lewis was but had only discovered what he already knew—that she was a successful venture capitalist working for a small but reputable firm in the city. The fact that he hadn't heard from his father as quickly as he'd suggested was a little unusual, but for now, something he was grateful for. He was also grateful that he hadn't heard anything else about Jenna and her wedding. By the end of the day she'd be married to Brad, and he, for one, was not going to be there to witness it.

"They're looking good, Matthew," Charlie said, raising his hands toward the apartments.

"They are," Matt agreed. "You and the team have done an amazing job."

Charlie moved his gaze from the building to the street and rubbed his hands together. "Here she is," he said. "The woman who will make the transformation complete."

Matt smiled as Steph joined them. "Thanks so much for doing this."

"I'm not sure I'll be of much help."

Matt had asked Steph to give him her opinion on how the apartments should be furnished. They were to be rented to vacationers, so they would need full furnishing. "I want them to be modern but inviting. The type of place you walk into and feel completely at home."

"I have made suggestions," Charlie said, "but Matthew says no, we need an expert."

Steph laughed. "Then you've definitely come to the wrong person. But I'm sure between the three of us, we can come up with some ideas."

Between Charlie and Steph, Matt knew he was lucky. He had two people in his life and involved in his business whom he could learn from. Steph's humility was one of her most admirable qualities.

An hour later, Matt knew he'd made the right decision to involve Steph. She'd had ideas on everything, from the window furnishings to furniture, bed linen, and accessories and even how she would present the kitchen and other areas.

"Have you thought of asking Ryan whether you can use his artwork?" Steph said. "I believe he offers prints of some of his pieces. You could even commission him to do something specific for this development."

Matt smacked his head. "I can't believe I didn't think of that earlier."

"He's been doing a lot of work since he's been here," Steph said. "Margie was telling me that he's trying to work out how to sell them. He has an online gallery, but he thinks you need to get pieces in front of customers. You might be able to purchase some for the apartments."

"Possibly," Matt said. "Although I wonder if Ryan would consider leasing them. He'd have a lot of potential buyers among the clients who rent the apartments from us. They'd see them for the days they're staying here, and we could put small tags next to them with prices."

"I'm not sure how that would compare to his exhibition at the Met a few years ago," Charlie said.

Matt laughed. "It wouldn't. I'm trying to think of a win-win situation, that's all."

Steph checked her watch. "I'd better get going. Buster and I are leaving soon for the city. We want to check in to the hotel before the wedding this afternoon." She turned to Charlie. "Now, are you sure we can't give you a ride?"

Charlie clapped Matt on the back. "No, my ride is here."

Matt looked at Charlie. "Hold on. You never mentioned a ride. I'm not going."

Charlie shook his head. "No, that won't work, Matthew. You are my ride. Why would you not come?"

"I don't think Jenna would want me there. She was pretty mad at me last time I saw her and is probably even madder now."

He went on to briefly fill Charlie in on the situation.

"Another woman? Does Zane know?"

Matt nodded. "And Asha. Ash was the one who told me

what Brad said to Jenna. Something about a bet I made to try to prove that Jenna doesn't trust him."

"Are you a betting man, Matthew?" Charlie asked.

"Absolutely not. I think Jenna might get hurt badly down the road. Anyway, I thought I'd give the wedding a miss. I don't think I want to see her marrying that lowlife."

"You have feelings for Jenna?"

Matt's cheeks heated at the older man's question. "No. She's a friend. Although probably not even that anymore."

Charlie nodded, his face serious. "You will need to drive me, Matthew. I am a good judge of character. If I meet this Brad and decide he is not good enough, I will ensure the bride knows."

"You can't do that moments before the wedding, Charlie. It will ruin Jenna's day." Steph looked horrified at Charlie's suggestion.

"Better today be ruined than many years ahead. Although, Jenna is unlikely to listen to an old man. Now, I will go home and change. Pick me up in one hour, Matthew."

Matt watched as Charlie exited the apartment block and turned right toward his house, which was only a few doors down.

"Looks like you're coming," Steph said.

Matt sighed. "Looks like I am."

Jenna, her mother, and Asha arrived at the Miller's Country Estate at nine and were greeted with a beautiful spread of cakes to start their morning of pampering. After a walk around the grounds to double-check the area where the ceremony would be held and then inspect the marquee to be used for the reception, they'd been brought into the estate's day spa, where they'd enjoyed massages before having their hair and makeup done. It had been a wonderful way to spend the morning.

Now, dressed in her Anna Kara gown, Jenna turned away from the full-length mirror to face Asha and her mother.

She smiled as Asha handed her mother a tissue. "Don't ruin your makeup, Mom."

"Oh honey, you look so beautiful. Dad and I are so proud of you."

"You're stunning, Jen," Asha added. "Absolutely stunning."

Jenna squeezed her friend's arm. "So are you."

Asha was dressed in a deep emerald-green off-the-shoulder midi dress that complemented her curly auburn hair perfectly. While over four hundred guests were attending the wedding, Jenna was intent on keeping the bridal party small. Brad had wanted his brother as best man, and Jenna wanted Asha as her maid of honor. She'd given Asha the job of finding her own dress, with only one stipulation. *No upstaging the bride.*

"I can't believe today's finally come," Janet said. "That we're saying goodbye to our little girl."

"It's not goodbye," Jenna said.

"I know, but it's a big step. I've always seen you as my little girl, and now I'm looking at a beautiful woman on her wedding day."

Jenna moved across to her mother and hugged her, careful not to squash either of their dresses. A movement on the lawn below caught her eye, and she gave her mother a quick squeeze before moving across to the window.

She looked down where she could see Brad mingling among the guests who'd already arrived. Her father had insisted they serve drinks on the front lawn of the country house prior to the wedding. Jenna's heart contracted as Brad laughed, and his face lit up. He was so handsome and in his wedding suit could be straight off the cover of GQ.

"Did you invite the whole town?" Asha asked, standing next to her.

Janet laughed. "Roy can be blamed for the number of guests. Brad's parents too. It's only once you get to give your daughter away, and Jenna's father insisted it be done in style."

"And it's lovely of him," Jenna said. Her father had surprised her after she'd announced her engagement to Brad when he'd shown her a special bank account he'd contributed to every year since she was born. "What can I say," Roy had said. "I love weddings, and I want yours to be special. Extra special."

The money had paid for her dress and the majority of the wedding expenses. Brad's parents had offered to pay half, but Roy was having none of that. He'd relented only at John's, Brad's father's, insistence that he at least pay for their guests at the reception. It was a token amount compared to the overall expense.

"There's Charlie," Asha said, her fondness for the older man clear in her tone.

"And Matt," Jenna said. "I didn't think he'd dare show his face. Came to collect his money, I guess."

"Money?" Janet asked.

Jenna looked from Asha to her mother. "I'll tell you

later. But put it this way, he'll want to stay out of my way today."

"What's he doing?" Asha pointed as Matt suddenly hurried across the lawn and out of sight. "He's practically run in the direction of the parking lot."

"Leaving, hopefully. Now, watching all of the guests below drinking champagne makes me think we should start the celebrations. Let's forget about Matt, open a bottle, and people-watch. Check out Margie! She looks like Audrey Hepburn in that vintage piece. It's absolutely stunning. Ryan scrubs up pretty nicely too."

Asha took the bottle of Cristal champagne she'd had chilling in an ice bucket and poured three glasses. She handed one to Jenna, who walked away from the window to join their trio, and one to Janet before raising her own. "To my best friend in the world. May today be the most magical day filled with love and happiness." The three women clinked glasses before turning their attention back to the window.

"Matt's back," Jenna said. "Talking to Brad by the looks of it."

"They look like they're arguing," Janet said. "Surely they wouldn't argue on a wedding day."

Jenna sighed. "You don't know Matt, Mom. He'd argue at his own funeral. I should have told him not to come. I guess I didn't think he'd dare." She put her drink down and moved back to the window. Matt had stepped closer to Brad and was up in his face. He looked like he was shouting. Other guests were turning to watch. As Jenna was about to ask her mother to tell him to leave, Matt brought his fist up and smashed it straight into Brad's face.

Matt shook his hand. He wouldn't be surprised if he'd broken something. He'd definitely broken Brad's nose by the look of the groom splayed across the grass, blood pouring onto his suit and white shirt from his now crooked nose.

Screams had broken out from the other guests, and both Zane and Roy Larsen had raced over, immediately bending over to help Brad.

Zane looked up at Matt. "What have you done? This is my sister's wedding day!"

Matt stared at him. "Hopefully, she'll rethink that idea."

"Brad!" Jenna's high-pitched scream caused all heads to turn as she raced across the perfectly manicured lawn, her wedding dress no longer a surprise. She shoved Matt as hard as she could as she reached them. "Leave. You never should have come."

"Come on, Matthew," Charlie took his arm and led him away. "Let's get our jackets and go."

Matt jolted out of his dazed state. He'd done that. He'd thought about it, but he didn't think he'd go through with it. But after what he'd learned, he'd seen red. He could not let Brad get away with this. "No, you stay, Charlie. I'm sure someone will give you a lift home."

"No, Matthew. I know you'll have a good reason for what you've done. I'm proud of you."

"I'm not sure anyone else will consider my actions something to be proud of."

"If your actions are honorable, then the truth will be heard."

Matt doubted even if it did that Jenna would ever

forgive him. He could hardly believe what had happened himself.

He'd been standing with Steph and Buster sipping his drink when a movement to the side of the large wedding tent distracted him. A woman with wavy red hair was standing on her own, her curls bouncing to and fro as her head turned, searching the gathering groups of people for someone.

Matt squinted. *No way. She wouldn't turn up today.* "Excuse me for a minute," he'd said to Steph and Buster. "There's someone I need to speak to." He hurried across the lawn to where the woman was still standing.

"Nadia?"

She smiled. "Matt, right?"

He nodded. "What are you doing here?"

"Brad invited me."

Matt took a step backward. That was not the answer he was expecting. "Really?"

She blushed. "Well, no. But I knew he was coming without a date, so I thought I'd surprise him."

Matt stared at her for a moment. She must know that this was Brad's wedding. Was this another of her jokes?

"You're kidding right?"

Nadia frowned. "No. Do you know where he is?" Her eyes continued searching among the guests.

Matt took her by the arm and led her away from the area where drinks were being served. "Can I talk to you for a moment?"

"Sure. What is it?"

"It's about Brad." Matt took a deep breath. "Look, I'm sorry. There's no easy way to tell you this, but—"

Nadia's eyes filled with concern. "But what?"

"But this is Brad's wedding."

"What?"

"Brad. He's getting married today. To Jenna. They've been together for a year or so and have been living together for some of that."

Nadia shook her head. "This is some kind of sick joke, right? Brad told me when you met us in the bar the other week that you were a troublemaker. He and Jenna broke up ages ago."

"So you know about her?"

Nadia nodded. "She's his ex. He ended their relationship a few weeks before we met and we've been going out for two months."

Surely she'd overhead plans for the wedding at work? Although if she wasn't invited, perhaps it hadn't been discussed with her.

"It's not a joke, Nadia, and Jenna's not Brad's ex. He's getting married to Jenna today." Matt looked over his shoulder, searching the growing crowd enjoying their pre-wedding drinks. "Look, there he is, over by the fountain, talking to the lady in the aqua dress."

Nadia's face paled as her eyes landed on Brad. "He might be part of the bridal party." She turned back to Matt. "You're a horrible person."

"Nadia, I'm not, and I don't want to see Jenna's day ruined. He's not part of the bridal party. He's the groom. Please, come and sit down for a minute, and I'll prove it to you."

Nadia allowed Matt to direct her to some chairs. "I'll be back in a minute." Matt hurried to the table where he'd seen the wedding program. The front page featured a photo of Jenna and Brad. He picked up a copy and raced back to Nadia. He handed it to her.

Her face paled. "Does the bride know about me?"

Matt shook his head. "I tried to tell her after I saw you and Brad together. She didn't want to believe me, and then Brad lied to her. Said I made it up to win a bet. That you were just work colleagues."

Nadia sucked in a breath. "He was in my bed earlier this morning. Where does she think he goes? He's been seeing me for two months and staying quite often."

"I have no idea what he's told her," Matt said, "but it appears he's a convincing liar."

"I have to talk to him. He can't marry her."

"Would you want him back now that you know what type of person he is?" Matt asked.

Tears rolled down Nadia's cheeks. "I thought we had a future together. He made all sorts of promises. I should talk to Jenna at least. Let her know what she's marrying."

Matt looked from Nadia back to the chaotic scene surrounding Brad, fury raging through him. This should not be happening. No one should be at this wedding today. He felt anger toward Jenna. Why had she instantly decided he was lying? What did he have to gain from this?

"Are you okay, Matt?" Nadia asked.

Matt shook his head. "No, I'm not. Stay here. I'll be right back."

Matt looked from guest to guest until his eyes landed on Brad. He'd moved away from the woman in the aqua dress and was now talking to a man with a bald head and rounded face. The man clapped Brad on the back and threw his head back and roared with laughter at whatever Brad had said.

Matt didn't allow himself to think. He took large strides across the lawn until he was in front of him.

Brad's smile turned to a scowl. "What do you want? You shouldn't even be here after what you did."

"What I did? Are you kidding me?" He took a deep breath, doing his best to control himself. "Nadia's here."

The color drained from Brad's face. "What? Did you invite her?"

"No, I suggested she leave."

"Where is she?"

"Over by the tent. I told her that it was your wedding and she got upset. You're a real dog. You know that?"

"Get rid of her," he hissed. "That's your only job for today, okay? I don't need a lecture or your opinion of me. I need you to do that one thing."

"You need to tell Jenna."

Brad took Matt's arm and moved him away from the other guests. "I'm not telling Jenna anything. This is our wedding day. Like I told you. From today forward, she's the only woman for me."

"You also told me you were breaking up with Nadia the night I met her, yet she tells me you were in her bed this morning."

Brad shrugged. "Figured I deserved to enjoy my last moments of freedom before I'm chained to Jenna."

"Chained? Are you kidding me? Why are you even marrying her if you feel like that?" Matt's eyes traveled to where Brad's focus had shifted to Roy Larsen. "The mill? Are you marrying her for the mill? She's not even interested in it."

"I'm marrying her because I love her. And no, I'm not interested in the mill any more than she is."

Matt stared at Brad. "But she'll inherit it at some stage."

"And that will be a bonus."

Anger tore through Matt. This lowlife was marrying Jenna because her family's mill was worth millions, and one day it would be passed to Jenna and Zane. He'd probably cheat on her all through their marriage, waiting for that payday.

Matt moved closer to Brad. "You need to go and tell her right now, or I will."

"And I'll deny everything. Say you're setting me up."

"Nadia will tell her it's real."

"Doubt it," Brad said smugly and nodded toward the driveway, where Nadia was climbing into a taxi.

Red flashed in front of Matt's eyes, and he'd raised his hand and punched Brad as hard as he could in the face.

4

$\mathcal{I}$t was like living in a bad dream. Jenna couldn't believe she was looking at the mangled face of her husband-to-be rather than standing at the altar about to marry him. They'd moved inside and Brad's uncle who was a doctor and had confirmed the nose was broken and would need medical treatment.

"I'm going to kill Matt Law," Jenna hissed. "Does he have any idea what today meant to us and how much it cost?"

Brad closed his eyes.

"Sorry," Jenna added, laying her hand on his arm. "None of that matters. What does matter is getting you fixed up. We'll postpone the wedding to another time."

"No." It was the first word Brad had spoken since Matt knocked him down.

Jenna's heart contracted. He was battered, bruised, and in pain and still wanted the wedding to go ahead. "Oh babe, I love you for suggesting we go ahead, but we can't. You need to go to the emergency room. We'll do it another day."

Brad's eyes opened. "I meant no, we won't postpone it, we'll cancel it. Matt's right. This isn't meant to be. I think he's saved us both a lot of heartache down the road."

Jenna drew her hand back from Brad. "What? Why would you even say that?"

"Because it's true. I'm sorry, Jenna. Maybe Matt's punch knocked some sense into me, I'm not sure, but I am certain that I don't want to marry you."

Jenna stared at Brad. "You've probably got a concussion. You're not thinking straight."

Brad pulled himself up. "I am, and I know for sure that I don't want to be married to someone whose friends and family don't think I'm good enough for them."

"Is that what Matt said to you?"

Brad nodded. "And it's what Zane and Asha think and your dad. He's probably ready to rewrite his will so that none of the mill comes to us when he eventually dies."

"It wouldn't anyway. It's left to Zane."

"What?" Brad's eyes widened.

"I said it's left to Zane. But that's not important right now. What is important is that we love each other, and this should be the happiest day of our lives."

"Hold on, back up for a minute. You're not inheriting the mill?"

"No. It will go to Zane to run or to outsource to someone else to run. I'll get some other assets, but the mill goes to him."

"It's worth millions."

"It's—" Jenna stopped, a cold shiver running through her. "Hold on, is this why you were marrying me? For the mill?"

Brad shook his head. "No, but down the road it would have been a bonus."

"I thought you loved me. That you wanted to marry me."

"I thought I did too, but right now, having been smashed in the face by your friend and being told that I'm not good enough for you when you're financially worthless makes marriage less appealing. If I could turn back the clock, I never would have proposed, and we'd never be in this position."

Jenna's legs began to tremble. She reached for a chair to steady herself. "Then why did you?"

"Because you pressured me. You wanted this to happen as quickly as possible, and it almost did. Jenna, the runaway train. Everyone tried to slow you down; Asha, your mom, your friends at work, but no, you decided you wanted me, and it had to be now. You hadn't counted on Matt's intervention. And while I'm not going to thank him for breaking my face, I am going to thank him for waking me up. We're done. I'll spend the weekend with my parents, so I'd appreciate it if you could move your belongings from the apartment before Monday."

Jenna fell into the chair and put her head between her knees, trying to take deep breaths. Surely she'd wake up from this nightmare at any minute. But she didn't. She was conscious of Brad leaving the room and, a few minutes later, heard footsteps. A hand gently rested on her back.

"Jen, it's me," Asha said. "What can I do to help?"

Jenna shook her head, the tears she'd been holding back finally releasing. She lifted her head and, through tear-filled eyes, looked at Asha. "He ended it. Said I pushed it too fast from the start, and he's grateful to Matt for waking him up to the fact that no one thinks he's good enough for me. He wants me out of the apartment by Monday."

"Oh hon, I'm so sorry." Asha crouched down and put her arms around Jenna.

"I'll never forgive Matt," Jenna said through her tears. "If he'd stayed away, none of this would have happened."

Asha didn't respond.

"What? You don't agree?"

"I think Matt's actions were despicable," Asha said. "But I'm surprised at Brad's response. I'm sorry, Jen, but if he truly loved you, nothing and no one would stop him from marrying you. Maybe not today with the broken nose, but certainly in the future. Unless there's more to it."

"What do you mean?"

"I mean unless Matt threatened him. We know how manipulative Matt can be when he wants something. But what would he want from you? You're obviously not going to fall in love with a guy who ruined your wedding day."

Jenna shook her head slowly. "No, but he's been interested in the mill. He's spoken to Dad in the past about working together, but Dad's been hesitant. The Laws don't have a great reputation, so I think he wants to keep him at a distance. Matt might be looking for ways around that."

Asha's eyes were wide as she listened to Jenna. "How?"

"I have no idea," Jenna said. "Except Brad thought one day I would inherit the mill, so maybe Matt does too."

Asha looked skeptical. "That's a long-term plan. Your parents are only in their sixties. They could be around for another thirty years, hopefully longer."

Jenna did her best to fight back another onslaught of tears. "I have no idea, Ash. All I know is Matt's outburst resulted in Brad dumping me on my wedding day, and there are four hundred guests downstairs gossiping about what happened. What am I going to do? Dad's going to kill me. He spent a fortune on today."

"No, he's not." Roy Larsen stood in the open doorway. "Can I come in?"

Jenna nodded.

Roy moved into the room and put his arms around his daughter. "I'm not sure whether I should kill Matt, Brad, or both of them."

"Both," Asha and Jenna said in unison. Jenna would have laughed if the situation weren't so dire.

"I told everyone downstairs that the wedding's been called off, and we'll let them know in the near future if a date will be rescheduled. In the interim, I suggested they enjoy the night. It's been paid for, and they might as well have a party to thank them for coming all this way."

The music volume increased at that moment, and the sounds of laughter drifted up through the windows.

"You can do whatever you like now, Jen. You can leave if you want, or you can hold your head high and join the party."

"Leave." Jenna's answer was immediate. "This is the most mortifying day of my life. I want to go home, curl up in a ball and never resurface."

"Are you sure you want to go back to the apartment?" Asha asked.

"I said home," Jenna said. "To Hope's Ridge. I doubt I'll ever show my face in the city again. That okay with you, Dad?"

Roy pulled Jenna closer to him. "You can stay as long as you need to."

"And I want to sneak out of here. Out a back door or something. I don't want to see anyone."

Roy looked to Asha. "Think you can make that happen?"

Asha nodded. "I'll drive Jenna home. You and Janet should stay. You have so much family here. It would be a shame not to enjoy the party with them."

Roy sighed. "I don't think Janet or I will be enjoying much tonight. But you're right. We should stay. I'd appreciate it if you could take Jenna home. Get Zane to go with you. It's a long drive back."

Fifteen minutes later, Jenna had changed out of her wedding dress into jeans and a casual top she'd packed in her luggage for her honeymoon, and she sat in the back seat of Zane's pickup. She closed her eyes, a vivid image of Matt punching Brad replaying in her mind. Regardless of anything that might have happened between her and Brad in the future, the one thing she knew for sure was she would never forgive Matt Law. Not only would she not forgive him, but her return to Hope's Ridge gave her a mission. A mission to do what he did to her—destroy him.

Matt lay low for the remainder of the weekend, not setting foot outside his house. He sent Steph a brief text letting her know he was unlikely to be available during the week and needed her to look after any issues that might arise with the wellness retreat. He sent a similar text to Ryan that he wouldn't be at the cafe, and Ryan was to manage it. He already knew Charlie was on top of the Lake Drive apartments, so he could leave that in his capable hands.

It was late Sunday afternoon when Matt finally allowed himself time to think about what had happened. He'd done the right thing; deep down, he knew that. Although perhaps he could have gone about it differently. He was half expecting the police to arrive and assumed they still might if Brad pressed charges. He had plenty of witnesses to the assault, so there would be no way of getting out of any consequences around that.

Matt lay sprawled out on the couch, empty beer cans littering the coffee table. He'd hardly eaten since returning with Charlie but had done his best to empty the fridge of beer. He wondered what he should do next. Maybe he should ask Nadia to speak to Jenna, explain what had happened. He dismissed that idea as quickly as he had it. Surely Jenna would have realized by now that she was better off without Brad.

A knock on the front door drew him out of his thoughts. He pulled himself up off the couch, wishing he'd put on some better clothes. If it was the police, he'd prefer not to be taken to jail in his sweatpants. But it wasn't the police; it was Steph. She held out a small box to him.

"My vegetarian laksa with freshly baked bread and some fresh muffins from the food truck."

Matt's eyes filled with tears. He was exhausted and emotional, and Steph's kindness was too much.

"Hey," Steph said, "it's only laksa. My southern Indian vegetable curry is worth crying over, but not laksa."

Matt gave a strangled laugh and motioned for Steph to come in. He led her through to the kitchen, where he placed the box on the bench.

"Thank you. This is so kind."

"What happened, Matt? I know you better than anyone,

and I know what you did could only have been for Jenna's benefit. I'm hoping that's the case at least."

"He was cheating on her, Steph. I caught him a couple of weeks earlier with a girl who knew nothing about Jenna and thought she was falling for Brad. He told me he and Jenna had an arrangement and he would be faithful after the wedding. I took this information to Jenna when she was back home a couple of weeks ago, and she got angry and didn't believe me. I took some advice from someone to leave Jenna to find out what Brad was like down the road, but then Nadia, the woman I saw him with, turned up at the wedding."

"What?"

Matt nodded. "She turned up, hoping to be his plus one. She had no idea it was his wedding. She assumed he was a guest."

Steph's hand flew up to her mouth. "Oh my."

"Oh my, alright. This would make a great scene in a movie or a romance book. It's so awful. She turned up to be the date of the groom."

Matt's lips twitched as he saw Steph trying to suppress a smile.

"We shouldn't be finding this funny," Steph said, her smile widening.

Matt started to laugh. "Until this exact moment, I didn't think it was funny, but it's so awful, it is. Poor Nadia. Imagine how she feels. She was falling in love with him and then found out Jenna wasn't his ex at all and he was getting married to her."

"And poor Jenna."

"If only *poor Jenna* had listened," Matt said. "How is she?"

"Devastated. She went home to her parents' place. From what Asha said, she's threatening to kill you."

Matt sighed. "Thought that might be the case. I guess I have to explain what happened. I'm not sure whether she'll believe me. Charlie will back up my story, although he didn't see Nadia, so that's probably no help. I feel like I can't show my face around town. Again," he added. "I thought I'd moved on from the town hating me."

"I'm not sure they all hate you, Matt. They're curious about why you punched Brad."

"What do I tell them?"

"I think you need to speak to Jenna. You can't go telling people the real reason until she knows. And then she might not want that revealed as it's humiliating. Jenna Larsen dealing with mortification and humiliation is something no one in this town has seen before. They know her as the head cheerleader, the homecoming queen. Miss Confidence. She won't want anyone's pity."

"I'm surprised she came back to Hope's Ridge," Matt said. "Hiding in the city would be easier. Everyone here knows her, and most of them were at the wedding."

"Ash said Brad kicked her out. He told her to move her stuff from the apartment by Monday. Asha's going with Zane and Roy tomorrow morning to get everything. If I were you, I'd lay low for the next day or two and then go see Jenna. Explain what happened. I'm sure once she hears the truth, she'll not only forgive you, but she'll probably thank you. I know I would."

Jenna lay in her childhood bedroom staring at the ceiling. The events of Saturday felt like another lifetime ago, not three days. She closed her eyes, wishing she could shut them and never wake up. She'd had several relationships before Brad, none of them serious, and she'd been the one to end them. She'd never been on the receiving end of rejection, and she'd never known what a broken heart felt like.

A gigantic sob wracked her body. She wasn't sure she even knew who the Brad of Saturday was. He'd ended their relationship so easily, during their wedding day. Who did that? She would have preferred he not turn up at all and leave her at the alter than to do what he did. But what he'd said to her, that she'd pushed the relationship too quickly and that in hindsight he never would have proposed, was what hurt the most. Mostly because she knew it was true. She had pushed Brad, but it was because she loved him. She'd known from their first date that they'd be good together. And it wasn't as if she'd twisted his arm or manipulated him into proposing. He was a man. He could make his own decisions. A niggle of doubt crept over her as she had this thought. Yes, he was a man, but she was also persuasive. He'd often laughed that her body and adventurousness in bed gave her an unfair advantage.

She'd only left her room since they'd arrived back on Saturday night to use the bathroom and hadn't had the energy to shower. She must look a mess with her wedding makeup now smeared on the bedsheets and her hair twisted in knots. Eventually, she'd pull herself together, but today was not going to be that day. Thankfully she was supposed to be on her honeymoon, so she didn't need to worry about work for another two weeks.

She wondered vaguely as to what Brad had done with the honeymoon. Had he canceled the trip to Poipu on Kauai? She'd been so looking forward to ten days of sun, surf, and sex. They had planned scuba diving, kayaking, and cliff walks, and Jenna had been eager to explore the markets of Old Koloa Town. Now it, along with everything else for the wedding, had gone to waste. At least from what her mother had said, her friends and relatives had made the most of the wedding venue and party and had eaten and drunk well into the night. The thought of what it had cost her father made her shudder. But she had to admit, he'd been a bigger support than she ever would have imagined, and for that, she was truly grateful.

A harsh cry from the garden below her bedroom jolted her from her misery. It was her mother.

"No, Roy, don't do that."

"Get out of here," her father was yelling, the rage in his voice sending a shiver through Jenna. "You'd do anything to get your hands on the mill, wouldn't you, boy? Well, I can tell you right now, you'll feel the sting from this gun before you ever set foot on that premises again."

Jenna leaped out of bed and dashed to the window. She gasped. Her father was pointing his shotgun at Matt.

"I need to talk to Jenna, Roy," Matt said. "She needs to know what happened on Saturday. I didn't set out to ruin her wedding. Jenna's my friend. I only want to see her happy."

"Happy? If it weren't for you, she'd be riding cloud nine right now. You stole every bit of joy from my daughter on Saturday. To humiliate her on such an important day is something she, us, and the town will never forgive you for."

"Let me talk to her, please. There's a lot more to this than you realize. Brad was cheating on her."

"So you tried to tell her before the wedding. All part of a bet, from what we understand. And what was this, another bet? Breaking up a wedding day? Did you get a hundred dollars for that too? 'Cause you cost me thousands, absolutely thousands."

"I'd be happy to reimburse you. As I said, I didn't do this to hurt Jenna. I found out something on Saturday that made me see red, which is why I punched Brad, and in all honesty, if he was here right now, I'd do it again. Jenna deserves someone with honor and integrity, and that is not Brad."

"And it's not you either, Matthew," Jenna's mother said. "You've proven yourself time and time again to be the same as your father—manipulative, egotistical, and out for your own gain. Look what you did to Zane when he returned to Hope's Ridge. You had him working on your developments when you were doing all sorts of illegal dealings behind his back. And now this. My family seems to be a target for you, and I won't have it. The town forgives you, and then you do it again. This time I don't think forgiveness will come so easily. It's a shame for Steph, Margie, and Ryan. That's all I can say."

Jenna could see the confusion on Matt's face. "I'm not sure I understand."

"I'm sure it will become clear in the coming days. Now get off my property." Roy walked toward Matt with his gun pointed at him.

Matt didn't move. Instead, he moved his focus from Roy to Jenna's window. She stared straight at him.

"Please come and see me, Jenna. I need to talk to you. I

need to explain. I'm not the bad guy here. Honestly, I'm not."

Jenna stepped back from the window out of sight. She might not know what her next steps were in relation to her life plans, but the one thing she did know was that she had no intention of speaking to Matt Law—ever.

Matt left the Larsen residence shaking. He didn't think Roy would actually shoot him, but then again, he'd never expected Asha to hurl a rock at his car four months earlier either. The wedding would have cost at least fifty grand, he expected. No expense seemed to have been spared, and there was a huge guest list. He didn't see why he should pay for it, he'd done Jenna a huge favor, not that she could see that right now, but he would if it would help change Roy Larsen's perspective. He had hoped to partner with Roy in the future as he saw huge opportunities for the mill, but it had nothing to do with this situation with Jenna and Brad.

Matt was still shaky a few minutes later when he drove through the gates to Holly's and parked outside the yoga studio. Steph had left the Heat Wave signage on the studio, deciding it would be good to keep the branding of the yoga studio. "Holly's can be the overall name of the retreat," she'd said. "But if we keep Heat Wave for yoga, then we can give other areas specific names too. The pool, for instance, might have its own name, as might each of the residences. I thought we could choose inspirational words, like hope and faith and joy."

He glanced at the clock in his car. It was five-thirty, which meant the parking lot should be full of clients attending the five o'clock hot yoga class. It was empty. He climbed out of his pickup. Perhaps Steph had gone home sick and canceled the class. It was unusual that she hadn't contacted him if this was the case.

He pushed on the entrance door to the studio, expecting it to be locked, but it wasn't. "Steph?" He stepped inside the reception area. A moment later, Steph appeared out of the yoga studio. Matt instantly realized his mistake. She might have been teaching. Occasionally a client arrived on foot. "Sorry, I thought you weren't here. There were no cars out front. Please tell me I didn't pull you out of a class?"

"No, it's just me. I was doing some cleaning and was about to head off."

"What happened to the five o'clock class?"

"You don't want to know."

Matt stared at Steph. "Please tell me this has nothing to do with Jenna."

"Afraid so. It appears Roy Larsen has been doing the rounds in town. He's asked everyone to boycott your businesses."

A weight settled on Matt's shoulders. "The cafe too?"

Steph nodded. "I called Ryan, and he said that the only customer today was Charlie coming for his free lunch. Apparently, Asha's been run off her feet all day."

Matt shook his head. "What do I do?"

"You need to speak to Jenna."

Matt laughed and walked over to the small sitting area and sat down heavily on the couch. He explained to Steph what had happened.

"He pointed a gun at you?"

"And threatened to pull the trigger. I'm not sure if he would have done that, but you never know. He's pretty mad.

That's a lot of money down the drain as far as the wedding goes, and then there's Jenna, who's a mess."

"Would you like me to talk to her?"

"I'd love you to," Matt said. "Please ask her to come and see me. I need her to understand the truth."

"I'll go over there now," Steph said. "Hopefully, we can get this sorted out, and the town can return to normal. I'm amazed so many people are going along with Roy. I thought people could think for themselves."

"He's the biggest employer in town," Matt reminded her. "He has a lot of power, and people know it. He's never put his foot down before. Lucky me to be his first victim."

Steph covered her mouth with her hand. "Sorry, trying not to laugh. I'm thinking of how much drama you've managed to create in the last year or so. It's quite an achievement. If someone wrote a book about you, no one would believe it."

"Well, they often say real life is stranger than fiction. I'll go home. If you could ask Jenna to call me or to come over tonight or tomorrow, I'd appreciate it."

"Will do, and I'll let you know what she says so you're not waiting around if she's not coming."

They stood and moved toward the studio door.

"And Matt," Steph added, "it'll work out. Things always do. Not as quickly as we'd like sometimes, but what's meant to happen will. It's like Jenna and Brad. While it feels messy the way it all happened, they were never meant to get married. If Nadia hadn't turned up at the wedding, it would have gone ahead, and Jenna would now be living with a guy who doesn't love her and would break her heart at some point. The universe is doing its thing as we need it to, even if we don't understand why it works the way it does."

Matt stepped up to Steph and hugged her. "You are the wisest person I've ever met. Thank you. Your friendship and trust in me mean so much."

"You're a good egg, Matt. I know that, and Jenna and the rest of the town will see it. Give everyone some time."

After the dramatic scenes between Matt and her father, Jenna had returned to her bed and slept. She was relieved that her father hadn't shot Matt and gotten himself into trouble, but she was also grateful for the support he was showing her. He, Asha, and Zane had left for the city to collect her belongings shortly after the run-in with Matt. She'd hoped she'd have the strength to go herself, but didn't. Now hours later, she lay on top of the bed covers, her back to the door.

A gentle knock caused her to groan. While she appreciated her mother's kindness, the regular check-ins and insistence that she eat were getting annoying.

"I'm fine, Mom, and I'm not hungry," she called.

The door creaked as it was pushed open. "It's me, Steph."

Jenna turned over. Steph? What was she doing here? She didn't think Steph had ever been in her bedroom. It had to be bad news. "Is everything alright? Asha? Zane?"

Steph moved closer and sat down on the edge of Jenna's bed. "They're fine. It's you that we're all worried about."

Jenna closed her eyes briefly. "Thank goodness. Sorry, I don't think you've ever been to my house, so I wasn't expecting you."

"I came once or twice to pick up Asha when we were at

school, but no, you wouldn't be expecting me. I've come for two reasons, and the first is to see if there's anything I can do to help."

Jenna groaned. "Turn back the clock twelve months and don't let me meet Brad would be a good start."

Steph smiled. "Can't do that, but I'd be happy to do some meditation with you or some private yoga classes if you want to do something that provides a mental escape."

"Thanks, that's lovely of you. Right now, I don't want to leave my bed, but if I ever step foot outside again, I'll consider it. What was the other reason you're here?"

"I'm here as a messenger."

"As long as it's not on behalf of Brad or Matt, I'm listening."

Steph frowned. "I thought that might be your reaction, but I'm going to ask you to listen anyway. I'm here for Matt. He needs to speak to you."

"I'm not speaking to Matt, which I would think he'd be pretty clear about, considering Dad threatened to shoot him earlier today."

"I heard. Look, there's more to what Matt did on Saturday than you're aware of. While he could have perhaps handled the situation better, I think he did the right thing."

"Smashing Brad in the face half an hour before our wedding ceremony was the right thing to do?" *Is Steph out of her mind?*

"As I said, the way he went about it wasn't ideal, but stopping you from marrying Brad, yes, that was definitely the right thing to do."

"Are you going to tell me why?"

Steph shook her head. "You need to hear it from Matt.

He asked if you could call him or drop around and see him. I'd be happy to walk with you now if you wanted to go. Please, Jenna, it's important."

Jenna stared at Steph. She was different from Asha, serious and intense in many ways. Asha always spoke highly of her, saying how intuitive Steph was. "You see the good side in everyone, don't you, Steph? Not many people would give Matt a second chance after everything he's done."

"He's redeemed himself on a lot of levels, Jen. You should remember that. And yes, I do like to think that deep down everyone has it in them to be a good person. I'm proven wrong from time to time, but I don't think this is the case with Matt. Charlie believes in him too."

"Charlie Li?"

Steph nodded. "He told me he would have punched Brad himself knowing what he now knows, and he says he's very proud of Matt."

Jenna shook her head. "Proud of him? Well, I guess he's on Matt's payroll, so perhaps being proud of his boss is part of the job requirement."

"Charlie's not like that. He's full of integrity, and if he believes in Matt, then I think it's worth hearing what Matt has to say."

Jenna closed her eyes. Her head was beginning to throb.

"Why don't you have a nice hot shower," Steph suggested. "Freshen yourself up, and then we'll go see him."

Jenna couldn't help but smile. "I look terrible, don't I?"

"I wouldn't say terrible, but you do look like you've slept in the same clothes the last few days and possibly didn't remove your wedding makeup."

Jenna opened her eyes. "You're right. I want to curl up in a ball and die. What's the point to anything?"

"Oh hon, you'll get through this. You'll find love again one day, except next time it will be with someone who loves you back even harder than you love them. Now, go and get cleaned up, and I'll wait for you."

Jenna dragged herself up off the bed, surprised moments later to find herself standing in the shower. Asha had always said how persuasive Steph was. How it caught you off guard, and you found yourself saying yes when you definitely didn't want to. And leaving her house to visit Matt Law was right on the top of her to NOT do list.

5

*M*att was sitting at his kitchen counter responding to emails when Steph's text arrived.

On our way over. Jenna's a mess, so tread carefully.

Nervous energy flitted through Matt. As much as he needed to talk to Jenna, the reality of doing it was another thing altogether. He finished his email and went over in his head again what he needed to say.

Less than ten minutes later, he was nervously tapping his foot against the leg of the coffee table in the living room when he heard footsteps on the driveway. He leaped up and opened the front door before they reached it.

He gave Jenna a tentative smile. "Thank you for coming. I appreciate you giving me a chance to explain."

"No lies, Matt, I mean it." Jenna pushed past him and

made her way into the living room. She sat down on a chair on the far side of the room.

"Did you want me to stay?" Steph asked.

"It's probably a good idea," Jenna said, "that way if I decide to kill Matt, you can attempt to stop me."

Matt swallowed. He knew Jenna wasn't joking. He cleared his throat. "Would you like a drink before we start?"

"No. I want to hear what you've got to say so I can leave and go home."

"Okay. So, I saw Brad a couple of weeks before the wedding at O'Reilly's in the city. He was with a woman."

"Yes, we've all established that fact. You then had a bet with him, which you won."

"There was never any bet, Jenna. He told you that to try to get out of what he did. Brad lied to you. There's no way I'd suggest a bet like that to him or anyone else. Anyway, the woman I saw him with turned up to your wedding."

"Which, conveniently, you were the only to witness."

Matt let out a frustrated sigh. "Yes, because I asked her to leave. She thought she was going to be his date. She had no idea it was Brad's wedding, and she didn't know about you."

"If any of this is true, why is it that no one else saw any of this? And considering Brad broke up with me, why would he even bother trying to hide this? What difference would it make now?"

"I guess he didn't want to admit to being such a dog," Matt said. "He can blame the breakup on me punching him rather than admitting what he's been doing."

Jenna shook her head. "This is a waste of time. It boils down to being your word against Brad's. Both of you are dogs, as you like to call him, and I'm not sure it makes any difference as to who is telling the truth. You're both as bad as each other."

"It makes a huge difference," Matt said, pushing a hand through his hair. "I did this *for* you, Jenna. Marrying him would have been the worst mistake of your life."

"Why, because I should be marrying you?"

Matt's mouth went dry. Where had that come from? He opened his mouth to speak, but nothing came out.

"Because that's what people are saying. That Dad's rejected your offers to buy into the mill time and time again, and this is how you thought you could get your hands on it."

Were people saying that? Bile rose in Matt's throat. "That's not true." His voice was hoarse, the words hard to get out. He threw his hands up in the air. "I'm not sure what I can say to make you believe that I was honestly looking out for you."

Jenna stood. "There's nothing you can say. You're not someone I could ever trust, Matt, or ever believe to be looking out for someone other than yourself. There's always a hidden agenda, and if it's not getting your hands on the mill, then I'm not sure what you have planned. The one thing I can say to you is stay away from me." She walked from the living room back to the front door and let it bang behind her as she left.

"You okay?" Steph asked.

Matt shook his head, a pain creeping into his chest. "She's never going to believe me. Never."

"I'm sorry, really I am," Steph said. "Give it time, Matt. I know you're sick of hearing me say it, but life does work out how it's supposed to. The truth will come out at some stage.

Unfortunately, you'll have to ride the waves with Jenna and her family until it does."

"Ride the waves?" Matt dropped his face into his hands. "Right now, I feel like I'm drowning."

After her run-in with Matt the previous day, Jenna was tempted to continue to hibernate in her parents' house, but a text from Margie drew her back out.

Hey Jen, meet me at the lake for a walk tomorrow at three. I'm thinking you could use an ear to listen, and even if you don't want it, I'd like some company for a walk. See you there. Ryan says no arguments - not sure if he was talking to me or you. xx

It was a direct, no arguments type of text, which wasn't like Margie. Jenna wondered if Ryan had sent it. While on the one hand, she wished everyone would stay out of her business, on the other, she was grateful that she had friends who cared. The added bonus of talking with Margie was that anything she said wouldn't be filtered back to Zane and her parents like it seemed to be each time she confided in Asha. Her best friend and brother getting together wasn't working so well for her.

"Hey," Jenna said as Margie met her on the lake path.

Margie's smile was edged with sympathy. "Hey yourself. Same walk as last time?"

"No, let's go in the other direction," Jenna said. "Walk around to the old boat sheds by Ricket's Point. I haven't been that way in years."

"Perfect."

The two women fell into step at a reasonably fast pace.

"This is what I need," Jenna said, breathing in the warm

mountain air.

"Who owns the house on the lake?" Margie asked as they passed a white and gray wood cladding house. Its garden was immaculately maintained, and it looked like it had been recently painted.

"The mysterious Lake House," Jenna said. "No one knows. When we found out Charlie owned most of the land around town, Asha asked him if this was one of his properties, but he said no. It's weird, as it's been empty for as long as I can remember."

"Maybe the owner plans to sell it, so they're keeping it looking nice."

Jenna laughed. "You'd think they would have sold it years ago if that was the case. I guess it will remain a mystery."

"For now, I guess it will." Margie took a sideways glance at Jenna. "Change of subject, but am I allowed to ask how you're doing, or would you rather talk about something else?"

Jenna sighed. "Not sure I have a lot else to talk about right now. It all feels surreal. I still don't understand why Brad ever pursued a relationship. It's ridiculous to turn around now and say that he felt pressured and that I pushed it too fast. There were only two of us in the relationship, he could have said slow down, or that he didn't want to do what I suggested. It's not like I asked him to propose either. That was a huge surprise for me."

"Sometimes things happen that make you realize you don't know someone as well as you thought you did."

Jenna snuck a sideways glance at Margie. She looked a million miles away. "You've had that experience?"

Margie nodded. "Yes."

"With Aaron?" Jenna wasn't sure what the protocol was about asking questions about someone's dead husband.

Margie didn't answer immediately. Her eyes were focused on the path. "Aaron wasn't the man I thought he was. We had a wonderful relationship before we got married, but after we were married, it was like he had two personalities. The one I loved, and then this darker, angry guy that I honestly didn't recognize."

"I'm so sorry. I had no idea."

Margie shrugged. "No reason you would have. No one does—I never told anyone, not even Ryan."

"Did he...did he hurt you?"

Margie nodded, her eyes focused on the track again.

"Oh hon, suddenly my situation is put in perspective. It's nothing compared to that. Can I ask you something?"

"Sure."

"Why did you stay?"

Margie gave a wry laugh. "You know how you hear of those women who stay in abusive relationships, and you shake your head and wonder why they'd do that?"

Jenna nodded.

"Well, you're looking at one. I honestly hoped he'd change. The side of him I'd fallen in love with was there about ninety percent of the time, and the unrecognizable version of Aaron only about ten percent, so I figured that the percentages were in my favor. He was always so apologetic, said it was an illness. That when a certain mood or energy overtook him, he had no control."

They continued walking, the smell of freshly cut grass wafting through the air. The crew hired by the township had been out with the mower earlier, and the lakefront was looking neat and tidy.

"Did he seek help?"

"He told me he did, but after he died and I went through the finances, I discovered the weekly psychologist appointment he told me he was attending was a weekly massage. So he lied about that."

"I don't know what to say, Margie. I don't want to speak ill of the dead, but he sounds like a real ass."

Margie stopped walking, threw her head back, and started laughing. She laughed so hard she ended up doubling over holding her side. Jenna stood and watched, unsure as to what Margie found so funny.

Margie stopped laughing and wiped her eyes. "Sorry. I needed that. Finally, someone calling Aaron what he was rather than tiptoeing around me, worried that I'm the grieving widow. Come on, let's keep walking."

Jenna couldn't help but smile as they picked up the pace. Margie's unexpected revelation and laughter had certainly distracted her from her own thoughts. "I guess no one would have called him anything if they didn't know he was abusing you."

"I know," Margie said. "I tick all the boxes for the cliché abused woman. Too ashamed to tell anyone. Too in love with him to leave. If he hadn't died, I'd hate to think where I'd be right now. Probably still believing his lies that he was getting help and risking my own life in the process."

"This might sound like an awful thing to ask," Jenna said. "But how did you feel when he died?"

"Relieved."

Margie stopped again and looked at Jenna, her eyes full of horror. "I can't believe I said that. I'm sorry. I was devastated that he'd died."

Jenna stepped forward and pulled Margie into a hug.

"Don't apologize. I think anyone in your position would have been relieved. I know I would have been. I'm sure you grieved the man you loved, but knowing he could no longer hurt you would have been a huge relief."

Margie pulled away from Jenna. "Thank you. You don't know what it means to me to be able to talk about this." She gave a little laugh. "My technique for cheering you up is a little unorthodox."

Jenna gave a genuine laugh. "It's definitely working, distracting me at least and putting my problems in perspective. My boyfriend broke up with me, whereas your husband abused you and then died. I shouldn't be giving my issues another thought."

"He wasn't your boyfriend, Jen, and it was on your wedding day with a lot of friends and family around. Not exactly a normal breakup. You've got every right to feel sad. It doesn't matter what happened to me or anyone else who's going through a hard time. This is *your* hard time, and you have to feel it and grieve it. Even though Brad's still alive, there is a kind of grief that accompanies breakups. Don't dismiss it, but don't let it take over either. Other than Brad, nothing else in your life has to change. You've got a great family, a good job, and you're intelligent and gorgeous. When you're ready for another relationship, you'll have your pick of guys."

"The thing I keep wondering is if Matt hadn't punched Brad, whether Brad would have gone through with the ceremony. Would I be married to someone right now who didn't want to be married to me or had a hidden agenda?"

"Hidden agenda?"

"It seems that Brad assumed I'd be inheriting the mill one day and would be worth a lot."

"That seems a bit odd. It would be different if you had millions now, but an inheritance like that is probably twenty or thirty years away, possibly longer."

"I know, it's strange. Anyway, it seems like I'm better off without him."

"You might need to thank Matt rather than be angry with him."

Jenna's hands drew into fists at the mention of Matt's name. "I will never thank Matt Law for what he did. I don't know that I'll ever understand it either. He didn't know that Brad was feeling pressured and looking for a way out. He wanted us broken up for his own benefit. But as he's going to find out, that's backfired spectacularly on him."

"What do you mean?"

Jenna stopped as they reached the first of the boathouses. "Wait and see. I don't think you'll find Matt's too happy this week."

***

After a night of tossing and turning, Matt woke, realizing that he was going to have to move on as if the wedding nightmare had never happened. Jenna refused to believe him, which he had to admit seemed strange. In the middle of the night, he'd had the epiphany that perhaps her denial was self-preservation. Who wants to learn that their partner is cheating on them? Was it easier for her to blame Matt for the end of her relationship rather than question why her partner would stray? Matt wasn't sure whether this was at all relevant, but he did know that appearances were important to Jenna, and it certainly could be part of the reason.

He pulled himself up out of bed and headed to his rustic kitchen to make coffee before getting ready for the day. Initially, he'd planned to lay low this week. Keep out of the sight of most of the townsfolk, but overnight he'd realized this was probably the worst thing he could do. He needed to get back to business as usual.

He put a K-cup in the coffee chamber of his machine, hit the brew button, and sat down on the wooden bar stool at the kitchen counter. He ran his hand over the redwood countertop. It was a beautiful piece of wood he'd hand-selected from the mill and reminded him every day as to why he loved what he did. Renovation and tasteful improvements were in his blood.

He took his coffee from the machine and set it in front of him, realizing that he'd yet to work out what he'd say if anyone asked him why he punched Brad. Jenna was refusing to believe he'd cheated, and it was probably the last thing she'd want circulating around town. He certainly didn't want to create further angst for her by spreading rumors of that sort. He decided it was best to say nothing.

Having made that decision, he took a sip of his coffee, mentally planning the day ahead. He needed to check in with Charlie and then get over to Holly's. The construction crew would be starting on the internal walls of the residences that morning. An unexpected jolt of excitement ran through him. This was the one part of the development he knew his mother would have approved of, and he couldn't wait to see it come to fruition.

His phone pinged as his thoughts briefly digressed to his mother and what life might be like now if she hadn't become sick. He slid it across the counter and checked the message. It was from Buster.

. . .

Can you come into the office this morning to meet with Travis and me? We have a major problem. Any time that suits you is good for us.

Matt stared at his phone. He hadn't planned to travel to Drayson's Landing today. It was thirty minutes each way, and he didn't want to waste time traveling. He pressed Buster's number on his phone and put the phone to his ear. Buster picked up on the second ring.

"Hey, Matt, we've got a problem."

"I gathered. Look, I wasn't planning on coming to the Landing today. Is it urgent?"

"That's an understatement. The mill has put an embargo on any wood being used for your projects. They're refusing to supply."

"What? You've got to be kidding!"

"Afraid not. Travis wanted to speak to you about alternative suppliers and the impact of the delays on the projects."

Matt ran a hand through his hair, his fury rising. "Leave it with me for an hour, okay? I'll go see Roy Larsen and try to talk some sense into him. If I can't, I'll come over and meet with you."

"Okay, sounds good. I was expecting to be out at Holly's this morning for the start of the internal build of the residences, but they're not supplying drywall or any other building supplies either. I've let the contracting team know the start's been delayed. Hopefully, we can source it elsewhere and get it going tomorrow."

Matt ended the call and slammed his fist down on the countertop. The one thing his dad had always taught him was to keep business and personal affairs separate. It appeared Roy Larsen didn't get the same memo.

Twenty minutes later, he sat in the waiting area at the mill. Zane had greeted him and said it was unlikely Roy would see him, but he'd check.

"He'll see you in about half an hour," Zane said. "You can wait if you like or come back then."

"Have you got a minute?" Matt asked. "I need someone to listen to me about why I hit Brad. I tried to talk to Jenna, but she won't believe what I have to say. He's fed her so many lies, Zane."

Zane held his hands up in the air. "I don't want anything to do with it. I've heard so many different explanations as to why Matt Law ruined my sister's wedding that I don't want to hear another."

"Not even one that's the truth?"

Zane frowned. "See, that's the problem, Matt. How would I know it *is* the truth? When I worked for you, you lied constantly and did a ton of underhanded and manipulative things. And then there was the Charlie situation, trying to get him declared unfit to care for himself. Why would I believe you've changed?"

"Because I have. Ask Steph or Charlie. I've been a different person ever since I bought the yoga studio. Charlie's been an amazing mentor, and I can honestly say I'm different as a result. Zane, I was looking out for Jenna. Brad's a cheat and a liar. That's why I punched him. He doesn't deserve someone like Jenna."

"And you do?"

Heat flooded Matt's cheeks. "What?"

"Rumor has it that the attack was brought on by jealousy on your behalf. That you've always had a thing for Jenna and couldn't watch the wedding happen."

"I haven't had a thing for Jenna."

Zane raised an eyebrow.

"I've always thought she was pretty amazing, but I never believed she'd be interested in someone like me, so I never even asked her out. My attack, as you call it, had nothing to do with jealousy. The girl Brad's been seeing turned up at the wedding. It would have been a disaster if I hadn't done something."

A deep laugh caused both Zane and Matt to turn.

"And you think it wasn't a disaster?" Roy Larsen asked.

"I'd say the biggest disaster was averted," Matt said. "Jenna marrying that lowlife would have been the real disaster."

"That was her decision to make, not yours," Roy said. "But I assume you're here for something else."

Matt cleared his throat. "Yes, Buster called me this morning. He told me of the supply issue he's having for my jobs."

Roy folded his arms across his chest. "Yes, we no longer supply to any business you're associated with. I'd appreciate outstanding invoices being paid today, so we don't have to pursue legal action."

"Roy, I'm a large client. I've spent hundreds of thousands of dollars with your business over the years."

"And now you're no longer a client. Stay away from all of us, Matt. You're bad news."

Matt's stomach churned. The nearest timber supplier was in Tall Oaks, three hours away, and not only was it more expensive, but the added freight charges would blow Matt's budgets.

"Roy, let's settle this. We both have a big stake in the town with development and employees. We need to be seen to be getting along. How about I pay the bill for the wedding, and we move on."

Roy shook his head slowly. "That's all it is to you, isn't it? Money will fix everything. Well, not this time. Yes, I'm furious about the wasted money, but my bigger concern is my daughter, who's heartbroken and, thanks to you, humiliated."

Matt took a deep breath. "Do none of you care that Brad was cheating on Jenna with multiple women?"

"Here's the thing, Matt. You keep saying this, yet both Jenna and Brad have a different story. Your interference pushed Brad into deciding it was all too hard, and he decided to walk away."

"Listen to yourself, Roy. Is that the kind of man you'd want for your daughter? One who gives up when life gets hard? Wouldn't you want someone who wanted to fight for her? Who would put Jenna before anything? Surely that's the type of son-in-law you want. The type of man you'd want as a husband for your daughter."

Roy gave a wry laugh. "And what, are you auditioning for the role?"

Matt shook his head. He wasn't going to justify that question with a response. "Okay. I'll source my timber elsewhere. But don't come running back begging for my business when you find out the truth about Brad."

Roy locked eyes with Matt, and Matt could almost see the cogs ticking over in his mind. "You care about her, don't you?"

Matt's anger turned to embarrassment. "I care about all of my friends, Roy. That's what no one seems to be able to understand. If you'd seen and heard what I had, I can guarantee that shotgun of yours would have had a good workout. Brad would be nursing more than a broken nose. I had no ulterior motive, I promise you."

Roy sighed. "And that's the problem, Matt. Your promise means nothing in this part of the woods. We've all been burned too many times before. Now, please leave."

"I'll walk you out." Zane, who'd remained silent throughout the exchange, stepped forward and opened the door for Matt.

"That went well," Matt said, unable to hide his sarcasm.

"I guess you messed with the wrong family. Dad's opinion of you was pretty low before I started working for you and then even lower after. Then the business with Asha and Charlie made it unlikely you'd redeem yourself in his eyes."

"I'm surprised he was okay with doing business with me if that's how he felt."

Zane shrugged. "Up until now, he hasn't been personally affected by anything you've done. Now he has. My father is like an elephant. He never forgets, and he never forgives."

Matt nodded. "Okay, well, I'll find an alternative supplier for my jobs and look forward to an apology from all of you down the road." He opened the door of the pickup, not waiting for Zane's response. It wasn't until he'd driven back out onto the main road that his father's words from their dinner came back to him.

This place is toxic, son. They'll burn you and spit you out. You mark my words. It doesn't matter how much good you do in

Hope's Ridge; there's always someone after you, even when you're not to blame. I'd sell everything off and move to the city. There are so many opportunities there.

Matt turned out to the street leading up the winding road out of Hope's Ridge toward Drayson's Landing. He needed to meet with Buster and Travis, and he was beginning to think that for once, he needed to listen to his father.

———

The walk with Margie the previous day lifted Jenna's spirits. Margie had insisted Jenna join her for coffee at the Sandstone Cafe after they'd finished, and while initially reluctant, Jenna was glad she had. Rather than the whispers and looks she expected to happen behind her back, she was offered sympathetic smiles, and old Lori Johnson, who many people were convinced could predict the future, gave her a squeeze on the arm and whispered in her ear.

"There's a better one on the horizon, love. Give it time, and you'll be surprised at how much love you'll feel for someone you never would have imagined spending your life with."

She'd disappeared out of the cafe before Jenna had had a chance to ask any more. But she'd quickly dismissed the message. Lori had an interesting reputation, but as she'd also predicted a creature to emerge from Lake Hopeful, and twenty years later, they were still waiting for that to happen, it was unlikely.

Now, Wednesday morning, Jenna pushed off the covers the moment she woke up. She needed to get her act together. Margie was right; she might have dodged a bullet not marrying Brad. She'd never know for sure, but she was only twenty-nine, and she had her whole life ahead of her. She needed to make a decision. If she was going back to the city, then she'd need to find a new place to live. Not *if* she was going back to the city. *When*. She loved her job at Graphix, and there was no one on staff who was friends with Brad, so there was no reason to feel awkward. Her boss, Maya, had called a few times, but she hadn't had the headspace to call her back. Maya was one of the many witnesses to her humiliation, and while she appreciated her concern, she didn't feel like talking to her.

She sat down at the small desk by the bay window and powered up her laptop. She'd email Maya to thank her and let her know she'd be back on Monday next week as planned.

Having sent the email, she dressed and hurried downstairs to the kitchen. Her father and Zane had already left for the mill, but her mother was sitting at the kitchen table drinking a cup of tea. She smiled as Jenna entered the room.

"Hey hon, how are you feeling?"

"Good!"

Janet's eyebrows raised. "Really? Why?"

Jenna laughed and sat down across from her mother. "What do you mean, *why*? I had a good talk with Margie yesterday, and I'm ready to move on. Moping around isn't part of my make-up. I'll probably still have my moments, but I'm ready to work out what I'm doing next. I'll need to find a new place in the city, so I'd better jump online and start looking. I want to be settled before I go back to work."

"Oh." Her mother's eyes dropped to her tea.

"Mom?"

"I hoped you might come back to live here, that's all. It's

been so nice having Zane back in Hope's Ridge. Having you here would be wonderful."

"What would I do? And don't say the mill because that's never going to happen."

"That's what Zane said," her mother said with a smile. "And look, he's gone from only wanting to work for a month to being a permanent fixture there."

"Yes, well, miracles do happen, but it's not for me."

"That's fine, but there are plenty of opportunities around town. The whole of Main Street needs new signage, and I'm sure there are brochures and all sorts of things, particularly with the tourism side of the town's business."

Jenna shook her head. "No, Mom, city life is for me."

Her mother gave her a weak smile. "I kind of hoped you coming home might be the silver lining to what happened with Brad."

Jenna pushed the chair back from the table and leaned over to hug her mother. "I'll still visit lots, but I love my job too much to give it up. Sorry."

"You don't need to apologize, Jen. I love having you around, that's all. Now, where are you off too?"

"I'm going to walk down and see Asha. I'll be home a bit later."

Jenna did her best to push the image of her mother's forced smile and disappointment from her mind as she walked along Emerald Bay Drive until she reached Lake Drive. She crossed over to the lake side of the road and joined the lake trail that led to Irresistibles. It was only a few minutes before the pavilion and food truck came into view. She was pleased for Asha. While her dream of running a cafe hadn't turned out, the lakefront location and extended pavilion seating area had made a huge difference to the business. Asha's bottom line had doubled, which was amazing.

Asha waved to her from the pavilion where she was clearing tables as Jenna, hands stuffed in her pockets, reached Irresistibles.

Jenna smiled at her friend. "I think I need something hot to drink. It's cold again. What's happened to the summer weather?"

"No idea, but it's much warmer up here," Asha said, pointing to outdoor heaters that were dotted around the pavilion. "I can't believe I have to put them on at this time of the year, but that's just how it is. Come on up, and I'll get you a coffee or a hot chocolate."

"Hot chocolate sounds great," Jenna said. "Can you take a break and join me?"

"Sure can. Orla's working for me this morning. She should be able to handle the orders unless there's a mad rush. Give me a couple of minutes, and I'll join you."

Jenna eased herself onto one of the stools that lined the edge of the pavilion and looked out over the lake. Having grown up in Hope's Ridge, it was so familiar that she sometimes forgot how beautiful it was. She took a deep breath and did her best to clear her mind. Today she was going to think of the future and think positively.

A few minutes later, Asha joined her, placing a tray with apple and raspberry muffins and two hot chocolates down on the counter.

"Yum," Jenna said, adding one of the marshmallows Asha had placed in a separate bowl into her hot chocolate. "Comfort eating at its best. This is one upside of no longer being with Brad; I can enjoy real food again."

Asha raised an eyebrow. "I remember you telling me that it was your choice to eat like a rabbit around him and that it wasn't his influence."

"I might have exaggerated that a bit. He definitely wasn't keen on a woman with fat on her. I still ate, just not quite as many treats as I usually like." She picked up a muffin and took a bite, licking the crumbs from her lips as she replaced it on the plate. "Delicious." She grinned at Asha, who looked at her warily. "What?"

"Are you drunk?"

Jenna laughed. "No!"

"You're much happier than I was expecting. Zane led me to believe you were a basket case, and each time I called your mom, since you wouldn't answer the phone, she said you weren't taking calls and not to come by."

Jenna shrugged. "I've decided that I can't change what happened, and I need to get on with life. Something Margie said resonated with me. It made me realize I'd been a bit blind to Brad and who he really was."

"Margie? You saw Margie, but you wouldn't see me?" Hurt flashed in Asha's eyes.

"I wanted to speak to someone who didn't know Brad and wouldn't report anything back to Zane. We hardly spoke about Brad. The discussion was mainly about Margie and what she's been through. Put a few things in perspective, that's all."

Asha nodded. "Poor Margie. Ryan mentioned that the anniversary of her husband's death is coming up. He's planning something special for her."

Jenna frowned. "What?"

"I'm not sure, but he did say he wanted to show Margie

how much we all care about her. I imagine he'll ask us to be involved in whatever it is."

"Mm," Jenna said. "I'm not sure she'll want to do anything."

"Ryan said the same, but he also said that he thinks she needs to feel like she can talk to us about him. That she's keeping everything bottled up and needs to talk about it."

"Honestly, that's the last thing she needs. I think she'd rather forget about him and move on."

Shock flashed in Asha's eyes. "That's an awful thing to say. You weren't here when she arrived back in the Ridge, Jen. She was a mess. Absolutely devastated. Ask Ryan."

"I will definitely have a chat with Ryan," Jenna said. "But enough about that, tell me about you and what's happening here. Mom said she thought Charlie was considering doing another development on the lakefront."

"He's talking about turning this into a proper cafe, but I'm not sure it's what I want. Expanding Irresistibles to have the pavilion has turned out well." Asha's eyes moved from Jenna and focused on something over Jenna's shoulder. "Don't turn around."

Jenna swung around to see why not. Matt's pickup had pulled up across the road, and he was stepping out. Charlie was waiting for him and clapped him on the back.

"I'm surprised Charlie's having anything to do with him," Jenna said. "He's probably meeting with him to let him know the bad news. Although that development might not be impacted."

"Bad news?"

Jenna went on to tell Asha about her father's decision to cut Matt off from the mill.

"Zane didn't mention it," Asha said. "Steph believes

Matt's done nothing wrong. That he was looking out for you, and one day we'll all see what a good guy he is. I hate to even ask this, but do you think there's any chance at all that Brad could have cheated?"

"With Nadia?" Jenna shook her head. "No. Matt's whole story didn't make any sense. Why would Nadia from Brad's work turn up at the wedding thinking she was Brad's date? She knows I exist, and she knows Brad and I were about to get married. She wasn't invited to the wedding as Brad only invited a few people from work. I'm also sure she's in a relationship, possibly with a woman."

Asha didn't look convinced. "Steph's usually spot on about people, that's all. Maybe this time she made a mistake."

"There's one way to find out," Jenna said. "Come with me to the city tomorrow and we'll go see Nadia. See what she has to say for herself. Brad's denied having anything to do with her. Let's see if she'll tell me the truth or not. It's also my only opportunity to do it while he's still out of the office, supposedly on his honeymoon. It will give me a chance to have a look for a new apartment too. Please say you can get away?"

"Give me a sec," Asha said, standing. She walked over to the food truck and spoke briefly with Orla before returning. "Okay, Orla can take over for the day. What time do you want to leave?"

They arranged that Jenna would pick up Asha at six the next morning.

"That will give us the full day in the city," Jenna said. "Plenty of time to visit Nadia and then go apartment hunting."

6

Matt pushed open the door to the Sandstone Cafe, pleased to see a smiling face. He returned Ryan's smile and made his way over to a stool at the counter. He was hoping for a day with fewer dramas than the previous day when news that the mill was no longer supplying his projects had broken. He'd met with Buster and Travis, and they'd been able to source a new supplier in Tall Oaks. It wasn't ideal at all but would do for the interim.

"Coffee?" Ryan asked.

"A latte would be great. How's business?"

Ryan glanced up at Matt as he began preparing the coffee. "It's been almost dead since Saturday."

Matt groaned and put his head in his hands. "Roy's boycott?"

"Appears to be. I thought maybe we need to do some kind of promo to get people back through the door. Buy one get one free, or something like that."

Matt nodded. "Whatever it takes. I'm sorry. Has it affected your workshop bookings?"

A month earlier, Ryan had asked Matt whether he could use the cafe after hours to run some painting classes.

"I'll find out tonight," Ryan said. "I haven't had any cancellations, but people might not turn up. It's only the second week of the course."

"Hopefully, they'll realize the classes are your thing and in no way related to me." He gave a wry laugh. "Ironically, I was thinking of coming along, but I guess I'll stay away."

"Until this blows over, I think that's a good idea. Now, there's something I wanted to talk to you about." He placed Matt's latte on the counter in front of him.

Matt raised an eyebrow. "Sounds interesting. To do with the cafe?"

"Kind of. I was hoping to hold a private function here in a few weeks' time."

"That shouldn't be a problem. What's it for?"

"It's the one-year anniversary of Aaron's passing. Margie's husband. Margie's had a pretty hard time dealing with her grief since he died, and while she does her best to act like she's coping, I'm not convinced she is. I hoped if we did something special to acknowledge Aaron, it would let her know that it's okay to talk about it. That it's okay to grieve and be sad, and she doesn't need to feel like she has to hide it all the time."

"Sounds like a great idea, and definitely use the space. Let me know if there's anything I can do to help. And don't worry, I won't expect an invite."

"I'm sure Margie would want you there," Ryan said. "But again, under the circumstances, it might be better to see how things are closer to the time." He hesitated for a moment and looked at Matt as if he was weighing whether or not he could say whatever it was he was thinking. "Can I show you something?"

Matt nodded.

"Hold on a minute," Ryan said, "and I'll get it." He disappeared into the storage area that led off the industrial kitchen and returned moments later with a large canvas. The back of it was facing Matt.

"I've spent a bit of time the last few weeks creating this painting," Ryan said. "I thought it would be nice for Margie to have." He turned it to face Matt. Matt put his coffee down and studied the detail in the portrait. Ryan had captured Margie perfectly. Next to her, with his arm around her shoulders, was a man Matt assumed was Aaron.

"It's amazing," Matt said. "It could almost be a photo it's so lifelike. I imagine she'll love it."

"I was thinking I could wrap it and have it hanging on the wall on the night, and then after giving a nice speech about Aaron, it could be unwrapped, and Margie could see it and decide whether she takes it home or whether she displays it here."

"It's a beautiful idea. Extremely kind of you, Ryan."

Ryan shrugged. "I feel like I need to do something for her. She's not the same person anymore, and I'd love to get a glimpse of the old Margie."

"Whatever the reason, I'm definitely behind it. As I said, let me know if you need any help with anything. I'll do whatever I can." He sipped his coffee. "Thanks to Roy Larsen, all of my projects are delayed. I have sourced a new supplier at least."

Matt's phone rang, and he hesitated before accepting the call.

"Hey, Dad."

"Matt, I heard what happened at the Larsen girl's wedding."

Matt sighed. "I don't know what version of the story you heard, but I can tell you that yes, I punched the groom in the face and ruined the wedding. I can also tell you that he was cheating on Jenna, and neither she nor her family wanted to listen to me."

Matt held his breath, expecting his father's anger to gallop down the line. Instead, he held the phone away from his ear, his father's laughter penetrating the air. Confused, Matt put the phone back to his ear. "It's not that funny."

Walter continued to laugh. "Sorry, son, it's the best story I've heard in ages. Those stuck-up Larsens needed a shock like that. Someone stirring up their perfect existence."

Matt remained silent. He'd forgotten how much his father hated Roy Larsen. *Always interfering with my projects, trying to get me shut down. Roy Larsen is the number one reason I left Hope's Ridge. There was no point trying to develop the town with him in charge. He might as well have been the mayor with the power he has over everyone.*

"I'm proud of you, Matt."

"For ruining the wedding of a family you hate, or for standing up for what's right?"

Roy laughed again. "Both, definitely both. With an emphasis on the first one." He cleared his throat. "Okay, now the serious part of the conversation. Larsen's stopped supplying the apartment project in Drayson's Landing."

"And everything I'm doing in Hope's Ridge," Matt said. "I've sourced a new supplier in Tall Oaks. It's going to cost a little more with transportation, but it's our only option. I'm going to have to hope that I can get the Larsens back on our side."

"No, forget them," Walter said. "I'd rather pay extra than let Roy Larsen think he can have any power over our business. It's completely unprofessional. Susan suggested we take him to court, but I don't want to give him the satisfaction that he got to me either."

"Susan?"

"Yes, we were discussing the situation last night. There are a few other issues I want to speak to you about too. Is now a good time?"

Matt looked up at Ryan, who was keeping himself busy cleaning the coffee machine. While he was sure Ryan wasn't listening, he didn't want him hearing and worrying about anything his father might say about selling the Sandstone Cafe. "Dad, I call you back in five minutes if that's okay."

Matt ended the call and walked back over to the cafe's counter. "Sorry about that. Now, I need to take off."

"Everything okay?"

Matt nodded. "Few issues with my dad I need to sort out." He forced a smile. "I'd better go. But let me know how the class goes tonight. If no one turns up, I'll have a chat with Roy. He can't punish you for what he thinks I've done."

Ryan smiled. "Will do. And Matt, I'm sorry that this happened. I know you've been trying to turn things around for yourself."

Matt shrugged. "As Steph always says, what's meant to be will be." He turned and strode to the exit of the café, wishing he could feel as confident about Steph's words as he sounded.

Jenna glanced in the mirror and smiled. Her face was made up, her hair freshly washed, and her black skinny jeans hugged her in all the right places. She felt more like herself than she had since before the wedding: no more sweatpants or active gear. A day in the city was what she needed. She was so glad Asha had agreed to come with her. It was an opportunity to look for a new apartment as well as drop into her workplace. She'd received a reply to her email to Maya, her boss at Graphix, which had left her intrigued.

I'm glad you're doing okay. My messages were partly to check on you, but also I need to discuss some changes in the company. Could you get in touch when you are up to talking? If you're coming into town at all, I'd like to discuss the details in person.

Was it possible the creative director job had opened up? A tremor of excitement raced through Jenna as she considered this possibility. It would mean greater responsibility and a raise and would be a fast-tracked way to move on from the wedding disaster. She'd arranged a meeting for one p.m. with Maya and planned to stop at Bold Realty to see Nadia before that.

It was close to ten by the time she and Asha pulled into the underground parking lot of Bold Realty.

"Come with me to this one," Jenna said. "I'd like your vibe on whether you feel Nadia's lying."

Asha nodded. "Does she know you're coming?"

"No. I didn't want to give her any warning. We'll put her on the spot and see how she reacts."

Nadia's reaction was nothing like Jenna expected. Jenna had been relieved when they walked into the reception area of Brad's workplace to find a new receptionist. One who didn't know who she was so had no reason to alert the other staff or have someone contact Brad.

"We're here to see Nadia," Jenna said. "If you could let her know that Jenna Larsen and Asha Jones are here."

"Certainly, Ms. Larsen."

The receptionist spoke briefly with Nadia, her friendly smile quickly replaced with a worried glance at Jenna. "Are you sure it's Nadia you need to see? She said she didn't have a meeting with you and wondered if it was someone else you meant to visit? She said to remind you that Brad's on leave if it's anything to do with him."

"Definitely Nadia," Jenna said. "Tell her it will only take a few minutes."

The receptionist relayed the message. "She'll be right out. You can take a seat if you wish."

Jenna and Asha moved over to the waiting room and sat down. They were only kept waiting a few minutes before Nadia appeared. Her red hair was piled high on her head in a French twist, and her perfectly made-up face was a blend of sympathy and concern. It was hard not to feel intimidated by her flawless complexion and towering height. It wasn't hard to imagine Brad being tempted.

She embraced Jenna. "I'm so sorry about Saturday. I hope you're okay."

Jenna pulled out of the embrace and stared at the other woman. "What do you mean you're sorry?"

Nadia frowned. "I'm sorry for what you went through. That your day was ruined the way it was. Come down to my office, and we can talk."

They followed Nadia along the narrow corridor and into her small office. Two meeting chairs sat in front of

Nadia's desk, and a sparsely filled bookshelf filled one wall. The view out over the busy city streets, however, brought a vibrancy into the room.

"Take a seat," Nadia said. "Can I get you anything? Tea? Coffee?"

"No," Jenna said. "I needed to talk to you, that's all."

"Okay." Nadia sat down across the desk from Jenna and Asha. "I'm a little confused. I assume this is related to Brad?"

Jenna nodded. "It is." She took a deep breath. "I'm asking this for no other reason than it will help me to move on. There's some confusion over this matter, and I guess I need an answer."

"Jen," Ash murmured. "Get to the point."

Heat flooded Jenna's cheeks. Even to her, her question had sounded stilted and unnatural. She was nervous. She wasn't sure what she wanted Nadia to say. It was one thing for Brad to end their relationship because he felt pressured and wasn't ready. It was another altogether to discover he'd been cheating.

She took a deep breath. "Were you and Brad having a relationship?" The words came rushing out and hung in the silence of the office.

Nadia looked from Jenna to Asha. "Is she serious?"

Asha nodded.

"I'd hardly have driven here from Hope's Ridge if I wasn't. I need a yes or no, and then we'll leave."

"Can I ask why you'd think I was having a relationship with your fiancé?"

"I was told that you were seen with Brad two weeks before the wedding at O'Reilly's and that you were all over each other."

"And you did turn up at the wedding," Asha added. "That seems a little strange when you weren't invited."

Nadia put her hands up to stop Asha. "Hold on. I didn't come to the wedding. And in answer to your question, no, I'm not having a relationship with Brad and never have. Other than a professional one, in that we work together. I can't begin to think why you'd believe that we were."

Jenna glanced at Asha. She knew her friend well enough to know that she believed Nadia. "But you were out drinking with Brad a couple of weeks before the wedding. A Thursday night at O'Reilly's."

Confusion clouded Nadia's eyes. "The whole office joined him for drinks as a send-off. But it was Friday night, and it wasn't at O'Reilly's, it was at the Manson Bar."

Jenna hesitated and turned to Asha. "It was definitely Thursday night, wasn't it?"

Asha nodded. "You arrived at the Ridge on a Friday morning, so yes, definitely Thursday."

"Let's assume I've got the day mixed up," Jenna said. "Were you with Brad by yourself that night?"

"No, Mike from accounting gave me a ride and we were the last two to arrive." She locked eyes with Jenna. "Jenna, I'm not involved with Brad. If that's why you canceled the wedding, I'm sorry, but you were mistaken." She picked up a photo frame from her desk and passed it across the desk. "I got married last year. It was before you met Brad, so I guess there's no reason you'd be aware of that."

Jenna stared at the wedding photo. Nadia looked gorgeous in a slim-fitting lace dress, and her partner equally as beautiful in a white pants suit. Her partner was unmistakably female. She looked up at Nadia. "I'm so sorry. I feel like such a fool."

Nadia gave a small smile, her eyes full of sympathy. "No, you're not, Jenna. Whatever happened obviously is a shock, and I'm sorry if you've been hurt by Brad. If he has been doing the wrong thing, it certainly wasn't with me."

Jenna stood. "We'll leave you to your day. Once again, I'm so sorry. I hope you'll forgive me."

Nadia laughed. "Nothing to forgive. Although, I am curious. Why did you think I came to the wedding?"

It was a good question and one that Jenna and Asha discussed as they drove from the meeting to an apartment Jenna wanted to look at.

"I'm so sorry, Ash, I've completely wasted your day. I should have called her."

"No, you needed to see her reaction. I do wonder why Matt said she turned up. Did anyone else see her?"

"Not that I know of." Jenna shook her head. "I have to admit it's a relief to know he wasn't cheating. I can live with the relationship being over, but the extra humiliation isn't something I need right now."

"Agreed," Asha said. "I tell you what, it's my turn to tell Matt off when we get back. This web of lies of his is ridiculous."

Jenna pulled to a stop outside a modern apartment block. She took a deep breath and turn the car off. "Let's look at this apartment and put everything to do with Brad behind us. I got my answer—he didn't cheat—which means Matt is a despicable human, and right now, I need to move on. She opened the car door and stepped out onto the sidewalk. The white flowers on the Beach Plums that lined the path were incredibly inviting and hopefully a sign that this apartment would be part of her new start. She linked arms with Asha, and together they walked to the apartment building.

Matt crossed the road, deciding to sit by the lake and call his father back. He followed the path that wove around the side of Irresistibles, returning Orla's wave. He wondered where Asha was—possibly collecting supplies or having an unheard-of day off. She'd become a fixture on the lakefront. He wished he could turn back the clock to before Jenna's wedding, not get involved, and not lose Asha's friendship as well.

He pushed the thought from his mind, took a deep breath, and looked out across the lake. It was a beautiful day. A few white puffy clouds floated on the horizon, but otherwise a blue sky with sunlight glinting off the water. He could see a small fishing boat off in the distance. It must be nice to put your worries aside and do something so relaxing on what was a workday for most others.

He sighed as he reached the lakeshore, wishing he had no worries. Listening to his father's laughter suggested Walter was in a good mood, but that didn't stop Matt from dreading the conversation he knew he needed to initiate. He needed to get to the bottom of what was happening and why Susan Lewis had such a hold over him.

He made his way over to a group of rocks that jutted into the lake and sat down on a flat one. He took his phone from his pocket and pressed the call button for his dad.

"Matt. Good, thanks for getting back to me so quickly," Walter's deep voice reverberated down the phone line. "I'm still laughing picturing Roy Larsen's face. I wish I'd been at that wedding. I told Susan about it and she said—"

Matt cut him off. He wasn't interested in what Susan Lewis had to say. "What's going on, Dad? Susan seems to have a strong hold over you. Who is she?"

Silence greeted him.

"If she's someone you're dating, then I'm fine with that." In reality, he was anything but fine with his father dating someone his age, but that wasn't the point. "What I'm not fine with is her having such a hold over you when it comes to your business decisions. What's going on?"

"Look," Walter said, "I have a history with Susan's family that I don't want to get into right now. She contacted me wanting to talk, and I felt that I owed it to her to do that. When we got to talking and she presented her ideas, I realized I'd be a fool not to listen. There are some great opportunities available to us, Matt."

"Which I'd be happy to discuss with you. But from the way you've spoken so far, it sounds like you've made your decisions. Decisions that affect me."

"I own fifty-one percent of our joint ventures, son. I suggest moving forward you don't give the majority share to someone else. As it is, you don't have a say when it comes to the decision-making."

"You're my father," Matt said. "You said I would always have a say, and you'd always listen." Matt knew these were his father's empty words but thought he'd remind him that this was something he'd said.

"And I will listen. But when we don't agree, then I have to do what I think is best. Look at the situation you've gotten yourself into over the wedding. You stood up to protect Jenna Larsen, and look at the thanks you get, Roy

Larsen throwing his weight around, hoping to cripple your business because he can. What's the point of trying to work in a small town when you've got someone in a position of power like Roy? Between the two of us, we've spent hundreds of thousands of dollars with that mill. He doesn't deserve our business, and the town doesn't deserve the improvements you're trying to make. I wanted out of there years ago and have only stayed involved as I know you wanted to stay in the area. But why, Matt? What's Hope's Ridge got to offer you? Both you and I have made enemies of nearly everyone. I don't understand the appeal."

Matt fell silent. His father was right. He'd managed to put nearly everybody off at one point or another. Why did he want to stay? An image of his mother appeared in his mind. She'd loved Hope's Ridge, absolutely adored it. *It's everything, Matty. The lake, the hills, and the people. They make it special. I could never leave Hope's Ridge.* He agreed with her. It had a special feel to it, but that was often marred by the problems he encountered with the people. His mother had never had those problems. No one could understand why she'd married Walter, and when the town was protesting against one of his developments, they didn't blame Holly. She continued her volunteer work and had plenty of friends dropping in to see her. She was a huge part of the community, which was completely at odds with the way his father was perceived. But neither Walter nor Matt had ever been accepted in the same way. Matt hoped one day he would be, but he wasn't going to tell his father that. He also wasn't going to tell him that being in Hope's Ridge kept his mother's memory close. Walter would laugh at his sentimentality.

"Matt? Why would you want to stay in that awful town?

Is it a girl? That one you're doing the retreat with. Is she the drawing card?"

"I've told you before that Steph's a friend," Matt said. "I consider Hope's Ridge home. I know you don't get it, but I do. I don't want to live in the city. I've got friends here," *those who are still speaking to me*, "and it's where I see my future."

"I'm afraid that you're going to have to work out a way to make that future happen without my money. I'll be sending over some documents in the next week or two outlining what I want to sell and what it's been valued at. If you can buy my share, then you'll be able to do whatever you want. I'm going to send the investment prospectus over, too. Have a look at it. You might regret not coming in with me."

Matt ended the call and sat staring out across the lake. If he regretted anything, it was going into business with his father to begin with. He realized he hadn't found out any more in relation to why his father was so invested in Susan. His father had *a history* with her and her family. What kind of history would cause you to sell everything you'd worked so hard to develop?

Jenna left Asha drinking her coffee in the small cafe they'd spent the last hour lunching in. Asha had done her best to steer the conversation away from Brad and Matt's lies regarding Nadia, and instead they'd spent their lunchtime discussing the apartment they'd looked at and speculating as to what Maya wanted to discuss with Jenna.

The one-bedroom apartment they'd looked at was perfect. It was only a short distance from her job and was set back a few streets from the main downtown cafe and restaurant strip. It was a little expensive for one, but if the meeting with Maya went how she assumed it might, her raise would definitely help cover the cost.

Nerves flitted in the pit of Jenna's stomach as the elevator door opened and she stepped into the reception area of Graphix, the company where she'd worked for the past eight years. August, the receptionist, was on the phone but looked up and waved to Jenna, pointing to a seat in the waiting area. Jenna sat down, finding it hard to believe she felt nervous about being at work. If she was honest, she wasn't sure if the nerves were in anticipation of her upcoming discussion with Maya or whether they were her worrying about what the staff would say about her wedding. She had her answer to that as the elevator doors opened and three staff members walked out. They stopped when they saw her in the waiting area.

"Jenna!" Angela's face clouded in concern. "Are you okay? You must be feeling so humiliated."

"Oh, you poor thing," Pam added. "I can't believe you're showing your face. I think I'd have to hide for at least a year."

Jenna hoped her face didn't reflect her sudden need to vomit. While she'd never class these women in the same league as Asha or Margie, she'd thought Pam and Angela were her friends. Was everyone else laughing at her?

"Ignore them," Justin said as he walked toward her. "It's good to see you." He frowned. "Although what are you doing out here? Shouldn't you be at your desk?"

Jenna forced a smile, grateful for his kindness. "I'm on leave for another few days. Maya wanted to meet with me." She lowered her voice. "I'm hoping it's about the creative director position."

Justin's eyes widened. "You're in the running for it?"

Jenna nodded. "I hope so."

Justin's forehead creased. "Okay, well, good luck."

His good luck wishes seemed anything but genuine. "Are you applying too?"

Justin shook his head before glancing at his watch. "No, but I thought it was filled. Dana was going on about it yesterday. Nothing official, so she probably has her wires crossed. I'd better get moving. I've got a meeting in a few minutes. Let me know how it turns out."

Jenna watched as he, Pam, and Angela walked through to the open-plan cubicle area. Heat tingled her cheeks as she heard Angela's snigger. "And she thought she was so high and mighty marrying that guy."

"Yeah, I heard he was cheating on her. What a loser."

"Who, her or him?"

The answer was blocked out by their laughter.

"Jenna?"

Jenna turned at the sound of Maya's voice. She stood, accepting the hug Maya stepped forward and gave her.

"I'm sorry about everything that's happened recently."

"Thank you."

"Come down to my office so we can talk."

Jenna followed her boss through the open-plan area, her eyes firmly on Maya's back. She didn't dare catch the eye of anyone she worked with. Were they all laughing at her? If it had happened to one of them, she'd like to think she'd be compassionate and not making jokes at their expense.

"Coffee?" Maya asked as she shut her office door and motioned for Jenna to sit at the small meeting table.

"No, I'm good," Jenna said. She sat and did her best to

smile. She needed to get this conversation back to a professional level. "I'm looking forward to coming back next week. I've had some ideas for the Onyati campaign. Beyond the artwork, I think the overall branding needs some changes."

Maya nodded. "Possibly. Look, Jenna, it's the bigger picture I wanted to talk to you about today. The company's looking to make some staffing changes."

Jenna smiled. "Yes, and I'm excited about them. The creative director's role is a great opportunity and one I'm definitely ready to take on."

"Oh." Maya looked taken aback.

"I'm assuming that's what we're here to discuss?"

Maya glanced down at her notes, not meeting Jenna's eyes. "Not exactly."

Jenna's previous nervous excitement was replaced by dread.

"Jenna, the changes affect you and three others. Graphix has bought out Leeds Martin Designs. We're merging the two companies, keeping some staff from Graphix and some from Leeds Martin, but not everyone. And I'm afraid you're one of the staff members we need to let go."

Jenna's mouth dropped open. "What? Are you kidding?"

"I'm sorry, but we have some amazing talent coming over from Leeds Martin, and we're only keeping Justin in your department. Nick and Abbey have also been given notice."

"You're keeping Justin over me? Justin, who's only had four years' experience and usually gets my help on his projects?"

"It was a hard decision, Jenna. Very hard. But the

management felt that in light of recent events it was probably best that you take a break."

"Hold on. You're letting me go because of my disastrous wedding?"

Maya flushed bright pink. "That would be illegal and unethical."

"When was the decision made to let me go instead of Justin?"

"A few days ago."

"After my wedding?"

Maya nodded. "But again, I reiterate, it had nothing to do with your personal life. Now, a package will be provided to you." She took an envelope from her pile of papers. "All of the information is in here."

Jenna stared at Maya. She couldn't think of anything to say. They'd chosen an inferior designer over her because what, they thought she was going to have a meltdown?

She picked up the envelope and pushed her chair back. "I need to speak to a lawyer."

Maya's face paled. "Jenna, the conversations about who was going to be let go started well before your wedding. There's documentation showing that Justin was always the first choice of the company."

"If that's true," Jenna said, half spitting the words, "then the company should be safe if I decide to sue. If it's not, you'll definitely pay for this." *As will Matt Law.*

She did her best to hold herself together as the elevator made its way to the ground floor. She'd been fired because they thought the failed wedding would make her unstable. Tears filled her eyes, and she roughly wiped them. Matt Law had not only ruined her relationship. With no job and nowhere to live, he'd taken everything from her.

7

*M*att wiped his face with his towel before bending down and rolling up his yoga mat. He'd become addicted to the hot yoga class Steph ran at Heat Wave and found himself attending at least three times a week. Steph's calming energy, coupled with the heat of the room and intense stretch, was what he needed right now. Anything to calm his mind. He'd been relieved to find three others turn up for the class, a sign that not everyone was following Roy Larsen's instructions to boycott his businesses. But three was hardly the same as the usual thirty who would attend. He quietly stepped around another student who was lying on her mat, enjoying the final relaxation, and made his way out of the studio.

Steph was in the reception area, a frown on her face as she read a message on her phone. She looked up as Matt approached. "Feeling better?"

"Yes, but you look worried. Is everything okay?"

"I'm worried about Buster, that's all. He went to visit Eve today. It's her birthday, and he felt bad for her still being in prison. He was sure that the judge would agree to her appeal, and she'd be out by now. But as she's serving the full three years, he feels he should be there for her, even if only occasionally."

"Does it bother you that he stays in touch with his ex-wife?"

Steph shook her head. "She seems to have changed from what he's told me, and they will always be linked by Holly and their grief for her. This is the first time he's seen her in months, so it isn't a regular thing. It's more that it's a long and emotionally draining day when he goes. For both of us as I worry about him so much. How about you?" Steph said, changing the subject. "Everything okay?"

"I'm still waiting for the documents from my dad," Matt said. "It's driving me crazy realizing that there might not be much I can do about it. I want to see the prices he's putting on his investments before approaching anyone."

"Buster said he should be able to help out with Holly's if you can't hold onto it," Steph said. "He said he'd speak to you when he sees you next but definitely said not to worry. That the retreat will go ahead as you and I have planned, and even if you give up some ownership, he'd still want you involved. This is our dream, Matt. You can't suddenly not be part of it."

A lump formed in Matt's throat. He was sure Steph's continued kindness was one of the only things keeping him going. He cleared his throat. "Please tell Buster I appreciate that. Hopefully, I'll be able to figure something out. Well, I'd better go and shower and get on with the day. I'm going to have to go over to Tall Oaks and look at the wood the new supplier's suggesting we use. I don't want a truck turning up if it's not quite right."

"Tall Oaks? But that's a six-hour return trip."

"Thanks to Roy Larsen, there's nothing I can do about that."

"Is it worth speaking to Jenna again? Surely there's some way to have her believe you?"

"With no witnesses and Brad lying, I don't think there is."

"What about the woman, Nadia, who you say came to the wedding. She'd be able to convince Jenna."

"She would. I did think about contacting her, and probably should have. I don't know how open she'll be to admitting to Jenna that she was having a relationship with Brad."

"If she thought he'd broken up with Jenna then she wasn't doing anything wrong. How about I find out the name of Brad's company and get her details. It would be worth talking to her at least."

"That would be fantastic, thank you." Matt smiled his thanks before walking out of the studio and into the parking lot. He was grateful for Steph's support.

He sighed as he opened the door of his pickup. He had a huge drive ahead of him today, thanks to Brad. He could blame Roy Larsen, but if anything, he had great respect for him. His own father had never put the family in front of profit, which was what Roy was doing. His loyalty to his daughter was commendable. Matt wondered what Roy would do if he discovered Matt had acted out of loyalty for Jenna too. Would he apologize? Do business with Matt again?

He started the pickup and drove slowly from the retreat to the main road. Wondering what Roy Larsen *might* do was irrelevant. It was what he *had* done that was affecting Matt's day. He'd go home, shower, then stop at the Sandstone Cafe and pick up coffee and supplies for the road before commencing the long drive to Tall Oaks.

Jenna had returned to Hope's Ridge the previous night in a state of shock. Asha had done her best to assure her that everything would work out, but even she hadn't been all that convincing. Asha was as shocked by Jenna's dismissal as she was.

Now, as she sat at the carved counter in the pavilion of Irresistibles, the one positive she needed to focus on was the support she'd received from her family, particularly her father. Her mother was always there for her, but her father was less predictable. She wasn't sure he'd ever forgiven her for moving to the city straight after college and rejecting his offer for her to work at the mill. He'd been resentful of both her and Zane, but in the last few months, since Zane had moved back home and had started working at the mill, he'd definitely softened. His unwavering support since the wedding disaster had been unexpected. She thought he'd be more concerned about the loss of money than the impact everything had had on her, but she'd been wrong. He'd made a point of telling her that money was money, whereas a broken heart was something he'd never wish on her. When she'd returned last night with the news that she'd been fired, he'd immediately called his lawyer.

"They can't get away with that, Jen, absolutely no way. We'll take them to court and make them pay."

Jenna wasn't sure she wanted to go through anything like that, but the fact that her father had her back meant a lot. He'd offered her some project work at the mill, redesigning signage and the website, which she was grateful for.

"You okay?" Asha asked, placing a plate with a double chocolate fudge muffin in front of her.

Jenna smiled. "I won't be if I eat too many of those."

Asha shrugged. "Comfort food. You're looking too skinny, by the way, so you should eat a few of them."

Jenna picked up the muffin and took a big bite. "You're right. My pants needed a belt this morning, which definitely means it's time to indulge." She put the muffin back on the plate. As delicious as it was, she didn't want to admit to Asha that she didn't have an appetite.

"What's on the agenda for today?" Asha asked as a flash of silver caught Jenna's eye. She glanced over to the parking area in front of the Sandstone Cafe as a silver pickup stopped, and the door opened.

"Is that Matt?"

Asha nodded. "New vehicle."

Jenna pushed back her stool and stood.

"Jen," Ash put a hand on her shoulder. "Don't do anything you'll regret."

Jenna turned and stared at Asha. "That I'll regret? Are you kidding? There's absolutely nothing I could do to Matt Law, including killing him, that I'd regret right now."

"Don't bring yourself down to his level. That's all I'm saying."

But Jenna was no longer listening. She pushed past Asha and hurried across the road to the Sandstone Cafe.

Matt did his best to push his concerns away as Ryan greeted him as he entered the cafe. It was ten o'clock on a Friday morning, and usually, the cafe would be full of customers, some having a late breakfast, others enjoying coffee and cake. But other than Ryan and Margie behind the counter, it was empty.

"We're not sure whether to continue producing the baked goods," Ryan said as Margie placed a carrot cake in the display cabinet. "We've hardly had any customers this week. It's getting ridiculous donating them to Lake View every afternoon."

Margie closed the cabinet and looked up. "Not that the residents of Lake View are complaining. I think they assume the retirement home's won the baked goods lottery."

Matt shook his head. "I'm so sorry. I can't believe the town would boycott the cafe over what happened at the wedding."

"Too many people here are on Roy Larsen's payroll," Margie said. "I heard that he stopped production at the mill the other morning. Apparently, he supplied morning tea that he got from the bakery and asked the staff to support him in this. He wants you run out of town."

Matt smiled, causing Margie to raise her eyebrows. "What's to smile about?"

"I'm imagining what he'd do to Brad if the truth ever came out. He's doing his best to ruin my businesses in his revenge, and I stood up for his daughter. I think Brad would want good hospital insurance, that's all."

"There's also talk that you've always had a thing for Jenna," Ryan said. "That you couldn't handle that she was getting married, and it was a jealous rage."

Heat flooded Matt's cheeks. "I liked Jenna in high school. Who wouldn't? She's gorgeous, smart, sexy. But she's been away for ten years. I've hardly seen her and certainly never thought about making a move." That wasn't completely true. He'd thought about it, assumed she would reject him, so he had never put himself in that position. "It definitely wasn't a *jealous rage*. Let's talk about something else. As for the cafe, if you want to shut down early or close completely, that's fine by me."

"The wine bar was still busy last Friday and over the weekend," Ryan said. "We could think about only opening in the afternoons."

Matt considered this. "No, on second thought, let's shut completely from this afternoon. I need to get the town behind me again. I'll go into Traders over the weekend and see if I can convince people to come back. Hopefully, by closing, they'll miss the cafe and start realizing it will shut down permanently if they don't start coming back."

Ryan and Margie exchanged a look.

"Don't worry," Matt added. "I'm not planning on closing it. Absolute worst case, I'll sell it so the town sees a change of ownership and comes back."

"Sell it?"

Matt nodded. "Now, I need to go. Can you pack me up some food for the day? Sandwiches or anything that's made up. Thanks to Roy Larsen I have to waste my day going to Tall Oaks to talk with a new supplier."

"And thanks to Matt Law, I'm single and unemployed."

Matt, Margie, and Ryan all turned at the sound of Jenna's voice. She stood in the doorway of the cafe, her arms folded.

"As sorry as I'm sure you'd like people to feel for you,

Matt," Jenna continued, "I'm hoping Dad can get the supplier at Tall Oaks to stop doing business with you too."

Matt stared at Jenna. She'd been angry at the wedding, furious afterward, but the deep lines of hatred in her face brought her rage to a whole new level.

"Jen," Margie said, coming around from the serving area and walking over to her friend. "Are you okay?"

It was obvious to all of them that Jenna was not okay. She looked ready to burst. But Matt couldn't understand why she was this worked up now. Shouldn't she be calming down? It had been almost a week since the wedding.

"No, I'm not okay, thanks to him," Jenna said, stabbing an accusatory finger in Matt's direction. "I was fired yesterday, and it's your fault."

"What?" Matt said. "You were fired? But you're amazing at your job. Are they crazy?"

Jenna's expression softened and she took a step backward, appearing surprised by Matt's words. "The company merged with another, and they decided to let three of us go. The guy they're keeping is my junior and someone I've helped complete projects. It was made clear that recent incidents meant they were worried I needed time off and might be unstable. In other words, my disastrous wedding and breakup also cost me my job."

"Oh, Jen," Margie said. "I'm so sorry. Can you fight it?"

Jenna nodded. "Dad's lawyer's going to see what he can do. I wouldn't want to go back there now anyway, but they shouldn't be allowed to get away with that."

"They definitely shouldn't," Matt agreed.

Jenna's expression hardened once again and she stepped toward him. "And neither should you. You've done this awful, awful thing, yet you're here living your normal life."

Matt snorted. "Normal, are you kidding? Most of the town won't talk to me, and your father's doing his best to ruin me. That's hardly normal."

Jenna shook her head. "It's not enough. You've messed with people's lives many times and walked away. I hope karma comes back to bite you, Matt. You deserve every horrible thing that could ever possibly happen to you."

"Jenna!"

Remorse flashed across Jenna's face at Margie's reprimand, but it didn't erase the image of pure hatred he'd seen in her eyes only moments before. He'd had his issues with people, but he didn't think anyone had openly despised him like this. It was unsettling and upsetting, especially when it was Jenna. A woman he'd admired, even if it was at a distance, for so long.

"I wish..." He was cut off by his phone ringing. He took it from his pocket and glanced at the screen. It was his aunt. He frowned. She rarely called him, believing the phone was only for emergencies. "Sorry, I need to take this," he said, turning from the group and walking toward the large glass window that looked out to the southern end of the lake.

"Auntie Kate?"

"Matt, honey, I'm so sorry to have to call."

The wobble in her voice caused goosebumps to appear on Matt's arms. He stopped walking, steadying himself with one of the cafe's chairs. "What happened?"

"It's your father. He's had another health issue. I'm with him at the hospital."

"An issue?"

"Heart attack, Matt. The doorman of his apartment found him in the elevator. He started CPR while someone called the paramedics, and they continued once they arrived."

"Is he okay?"

His aunt let out a gentle sob. "It's not looking good. They've got him on life support and are doing brain imaging scans to see whether damage has been done. You need to come, Matt. I have a bad feeling."

"Okay. I'll leave now. I'll be there as soon as I can. Call me if there's any change, please."

He ended the call, slipped the phone back into his pocket, his gaze still fixed on the lake.

"Matt?" Ryan's voice was soft. "Is everything okay?"

He turned to find concern etched on Ryan, Margie, and even Jenna's face.

He shook his head. "It's Dad. Another heart attack. He's on life support, but it doesn't sound good. I have to go." He turned, about to walk out of the cafe, when a hand on his shoulder stopped him. He turned, his eyes blurry with tears, to find Jenna in front of him.

"I'll take you."

Matt shook his head. "I could never ask you to do that. I'll be fine. Thank you." He turned again, but Jenna pulled him back.

"Matt, I feel awful. What I said about you deserving karma...I was angry and upset. If I could take every word back, I would."

Matt nodded. He didn't have the time or energy for this. He needed to get to the city.

Ryan approached them, a large paper bag in his hands. He handed it to Jenna. "Food for the road."

Matt shook his head again. "Thanks, but I'll be fine." Tears escaped his eyes and ran down his cheeks.

Jenna put a hand on his back and gently pushed him toward the door. "My car's out front. It's full of fuel, and I'm driving you. No arguments."

Matt didn't have the strength to debate with her and, as directed, climbed into the passenger seat of Jenna's white Jeep.

———

The four-hour drive to the city passed with minimal conversation. Jenna glanced at the passenger seat on numerous occasions to check on Matt, but his face was turned to the window, so she couldn't tell if he was okay or not. She knew she wouldn't be if the situation were reversed. She reached behind her to where she'd put the bag Ryan had given her and pulled it through to the front seat. She placed it on Matt's lap.

"You should eat something. We both should. It could be a long day, and you'll need your energy."

Matt nodded and opened the bag. He took out a cookie and handed it to Jenna before taking out a second one for himself.

"I know this is a stupid question," Jenna said. "But are you okay?"

Matt shook his head. "I can't stop thinking that he's going to die, and then what do I do? Regardless of what you or anybody else thinks of him, he's still my dad. I won't have anyone other than my aunt, but she and I aren't close."

"You'll have your friends, Matt. They'll be there for you."

Matt gave her a wry smile. "I don't have many of those right now."

Jenna had to bite her tongue. This was not the time or place to remind Matt why that might be. "Regardless of anything that's happened between us, I'm sorry you're going through this. Family's everything and is far more important than anything else."

Matt nodded, taking a small bite of his cookie.

They traveled in silence for the remainder of the trip. Jenna pulled up outside the front entrance of the hospital. "You go in," she said. "I'll park and come and find you."

Matt unbuckled his seat belt and pushed open the door. "No, don't be silly. You head back to the Ridge. And thank you, Jenna. You've done more for me today than I would ever expect you to. I don't know what's going to happen with Dad or how long I need to stay here. It'd be crazy for you to stay."

"No, Matt. I'd like to."

He shook his head. "I'll let you know how he is. I'd better go, and thanks again. Drive safely." He closed the door and strode toward the hospital entrance before she had a chance to respond.

She sat for a moment, debating what she should do. A honk from a vehicle behind her startled her into putting the Jeep in gear and driving out. An uncomfortable feeling swirled in her gut. She felt awful that she'd spoken so viciously to Matt only moments before he received the phone call, but it wasn't only that. If Walter died, Matt would be alone. As much as she said she hated Matt, it wasn't true. She hated what he'd cost her in the last week, but she didn't hate him. Anyone who'd seen the look on Matt's face when he'd ended the call with his aunt would know that he wasn't the cold, uncaring person Jenna had tried to paint him as.

She pulled away from the hospital's entrance and followed the signs to the visitor parking lot.

Matt was given instructions to the ICU when he entered the hospital and was quick to find his father's room. His Aunt Kate was sitting in a chair outside the room. She stood as soon as she saw him. Her eyes were red, and his gut clenched as tears trickled down her cheeks as he approached. Was he too late?

She held out her arms as he got closer and enclosed him in a hug.

He pulled back as soon as he felt was appropriate. "How is he?"

"Not good," Kate said. "The doctor will be back to talk to us soon, but the scans are showing no brain activity."

Matt sucked in a breath. "He's brain-dead?"

Tears flowed down Kate's cheeks. "It's quite likely, Matt."

Matt nodded. "Can we see him?"

"Yes, but you need to try to prepare yourself. He's surrounded by tubes and machines and is on a ventilator. It's quite overwhelming."

Kate was right. Matt felt light-headed as he watched his father's chest rise and fall as they entered the room.

"He's breathing?"

Kate shook her head. "Not on his own. That's being done by the machine."

"What if they turned off the machine?

Kate closed her eyes. "I think we'd need to say goodbye."

Matt stood staring at his father. His skin was pale, and he looked lifeless, nothing like the easily riled-up Walter Law.

"I called Susan," Kate said. "She's on her way."

Matt's forehead creased as he frowned. "Susan? Why tell her? She's a business acquaintance."

"Walter said to me about three weeks ago that if anything ever happened to him, I was to contact you and Susan. He didn't say why, and I didn't think to question him."

Matt nodded and sat down on one of the chairs by his father's bed. Whatever Walter's reasons were for including Susan really didn't matter now. He watched his father's chest as it continued to rise and fall, his head jolting up as a female doctor entered the room.

"I'm Dr. Young," she introduced herself. "Stay seated," she said to Matt as he went to stand.

She checked some of Walter's machines before turning to face Matt and his aunt. "I'm sorry to be the one to bring this news to you, but Walter has suffered a major cardiac arrest. We've run an apnea test and a thorough physical examination that suggested his brain has stopped function-ing. I'm afraid that this, coupled with an EEG, has confirmed there is no brain activity."

"He's brain-dead?" Matt's voice was a whisper.

The doctor nodded. "I'm sorry, but yes."

Matt stared back at his father. It was hard to believe

there was nothing going on inside of him. "And the machines are keeping him alive?"

"Yes," Dr. Young confirmed. "Were you aware that your father was a registered organ donor?"

Matt shook his head. "No. What does that mean?"

"It means that your father can give the gift of life to someone in need. We have his authority but do need his next of kin, which we believe is you, to sign some documents so that we can get the process started."

Matt looked to his aunt. "Did you know he was an organ donor?"

She nodded. "We both are, Matt. After Bob's lung transplant, we both registered knowing that one day we'd have a chance to give back."

Ten years prior to his death in a car accident, Matt's uncle had been the recipient of a donor's lung. "I'd forgotten," Matt said. "If I sign the documents, what happens?"

"We'd ask you to say your goodbyes to your father, and then we'll take over. His body will be released to the coroner after his organs have been harvested to enable you to prepare for a funeral or whatever send-off you choose to have."

"What about his heart? Surely that's no use to someone else."

"No, it won't be. Vital organs rarely are after cardiac death, but bone, skin, heart valves, and corneas can all be harvested."

Matt lowered his head into his hands, nausea churning in his gut. This was far too overwhelming.

"I'll leave you," the doctor said, "so that you can think through everything. We know it's a lot to ask, Matthew.

Please take your time, and I'd be happy to answer any questions you have."

Matt nodded without looking up. She murmured something to his aunt, and the door closed as she left the room.

Kate moved closer to the bed and took Walter's hand. "We didn't always see eye to eye, Walt, but I need you to know that you were a wonderful big brother. You looked out for me so well after Bob died. Thank you. I love you very much." Matt watched as his aunt leaned down and kissed her brother on the cheek. She brushed back a stray piece of hair that had fallen across his forehead before turning to Matt.

"I'll wait outside the room for you," his aunt said. "In case there's anything you want to say to your father in private."

Matt nodded as she left the room. What should he say? His father couldn't hear him, but he felt like there was so much he did need to say. He opened his mouth, but the door to the room reopened.

Susan Lewis stepped inside tentatively. "Is it okay if I sit?"

He nodded.

They sat in silence for a few minutes before Susan spoke. "I'm sorry, Matt. Very sorry." She choked on the last word. "I only got to spend a few months with him. It wasn't long enough."

Matt wasn't sure how to respond. He still had no idea as to the exact nature of their relationship. Walter had suggested he wasn't seeing her in a romantic way, but the way Susan was acting suggested he definitely was.

"I won't stay," Susan said. "I'd like to say my goodbyes if you don't mind?"

"Would you like me to leave?" Matt asked, standing.

"No, stay, please." Susan stood and took Walter's hand. "I'm not sure what to say, other than I wish we'd had longer. It's so unfair that this has happened when we just met." As his aunt had done, Susan leaned forward and kissed Walter's cheek. "Goodbye and thank you. I know that meeting you has changed my life and my future, and I'll be forever grateful for that." She turned to Matt. "Thank you."

He nodded as tears welled in her eyes, and she left the room.

He returned his focus to his father. "You might not think so, but that was strange. I'm not sure whether to be impressed or disgusted that you've been dating someone my age. I guess it doesn't matter now." Matt took a deep breath and continued talking. The main thing he said was goodbye and that he loved Walter, even if their relationship hadn't been a particularly smooth one. Matt doubted Walter had ever had a smooth relationship with anyone.

He had no idea how long it had been when there was a gentle knock on the door.

Dr. Young entered the room. "I hope I'm not interrupting."

"No, I said everything I wanted to."

Dr. Young sat down beside Matt with a file full of papers in her hands. "If you'd like your father's lawyer, or your own, to discuss any of this with you, we'd be happy to contact them on your behalf. It's quite normal for families to delay this process."

"Don't you need the organs as soon as possible?"

"Ideally, but we can keep your father's organs alive through life support until we are ready to harvest them. The most important thing right now is you. We don't want you to feel rushed or pressured and want to make sure you're fully informed of how the process works."

"All that matters is Dad registered for organ donation, and my aunt was able to confirm that." He reached for the paperwork. "I'm happy to sign anything you need."

It took a few minutes for Dr. Young to explain everything Matt was signing and for the paperwork to be complete. She stood once they'd finished. "Your aunt told me she said her final goodbye, so I'll leave you to do the same. And thank you, Matthew. It's not an easy thing to do, and please know that it's incredibly selfless of your father and something that will always be appreciated."

Incredibly selfless wasn't a phrase that Matt imagined had ever been used to describe his father before. He stood as the doctor left the room and did what Susan had done before him—he took his father's hand. An overwhelming sense of sadness overcame him as he did. This was it. The final goodbye. He would never see his father again. Never hear his laugh or his pointed, and often annoying, comments. He'd never hear him disparaging the residents of Hope's Ridge or Drayson's Landing again. He almost smiled as he had this thought, but a wave of grief caused a crushing pain to weigh down on his chest. He'd give anything right now to be infuriated by his father rather than saying his final goodbye. Tears ran freely down his cheeks, and he found he was unable to make himself walk away. But eventually, he knew it was time. "I love you," were his final words as he let go of Walter's hand and turned and left the room.

He stepped out into the corridor, wiping his eyes with his sleeve. He expected his aunt to be there, but he didn't expect to see Jenna. She stepped forward, her eyes full of compassion and sadness, and took him in her arms. "I'm so sorry, Matt."

He wrapped his arms around her, unable to stop himself, and sobbed uncontrollably against her shoulder.

Jenna pulled the Jeep off the highway and into a roadside stop two hours into the drive back to Hope's Ridge. Matt's Aunt Kate, who he'd introduced her to, had suggested he stay in the city with her, but he'd said no, he wanted to go home. He needed time by himself to digest what had happened but would be in touch with her and come back into the city to make arrangements for the funeral.

"I'm going to stop and get us some coffee," Jenna said before Matt could ask why they were stopping. "It's been a long day, Matt. Why don't we get something to eat too? I know you probably don't feel like it, but you should eat something."

"Yes, Mom." His response was automatic, and for a moment, Jenna thought he was going to smile, but instead, his eyes filled with tears. "Sorry," he said, wiping them roughly. "It's just, well, they're both gone now."

Jenna pulled into a parking spot and switched off the Jeep's engine. "I'm so sorry, really I am. I'm also sorry that I don't seem to know of anything else I can say to make this any easier on you."

"Jenna, you being here for me is far beyond anything I would expect of you. I know it's probably the last place you want to be, and I'm the last person in the world you'd want to be with, but it's made a difference."

A lump formed in Jenna's throat. This vulnerable side

of Matt was something she'd never seen before, and she wanted to throw her arms around him and hold him tight. But then a little voice would remind her, *It's Matt.*

She pushed open her door and walked around to Matt's side, opening his for him. "Come on, let's get something to eat." She hesitated for a moment. "And Matt, I'm glad I can be here for you today. What you're going through isn't something I'd wish on anyone." Her cheeks heated as the words left her lips. If only she hadn't said what she'd said in the Sandstone Cafe earlier. It was unforgivable.

The smell of fried food hit them as they entered the truck stop.

"I doubt they're going to serve anything you'd eat here, Jen," Matt said. "I'm assuming deep-fried isn't high on your list of preferred cuisines."

Jenna smiled. "Up until recently, I've been living off lettuce leaves."

Matt frowned. "That's not healthy. Why would you do that?"

"Brad. He didn't like fat on women."

"That's ridiculous," Matt said. "You can be fit and healthy and eat. I'm surprised you have the level of energy you do if you've been eating like a rabbit."

Jenna smiled. "The level of energy that allows me to go crazy at you?"

He blushed. "I think you should eat some real food."

She raised an eyebrow, causing him to smile.

"Granted, we're not going to find that here, but some comfort food would go down really well right now. Why don't we share a big bowl of fries and get some milkshakes? That's my ultimate comfort food."

"Deal," Jenna said and walked over to the counter to place their order.

Ten minutes later, they sat opposite each other, an overflowing bowl of fries between them. Matt held his milkshake out to Jenna, and she knocked hers against his. "Just saying thanks again."

"No need," Jenna said and took a sip of her Butterscotch Whirl shake. Her eyes widened with delight. She hadn't indulged in a milkshake in years.

"Good?" Matt asked, helping himself to the fries.

"Amazing," Jenna said, taking another sip before reaching for the fries.

"For a girl who lives off lettuce, you're adapting pretty quickly."

Jenna laughed. "I'll be the size of a house within a few weeks. You wait and see. You'll be walking down Main Street thinking, 'Wow, who's that blimp in front of me?'"

Matt shook his head. "You're gorgeous, Jenna. You were gorgeous when we were kids, even more gorgeous in high school when I suddenly noticed the female species, and beyond gorgeous now. And I'm not talking about what you look like. I'm talking about who you are. You're an incredibly kind and lovely person."

Jenna blushed, surprised and flattered by his praise. "Thank you," she finally managed. Jenna found herself dealing with mixed emotions as she watched Matt sip his chocolate milkshake. If she could erase everything she knew about Matt Law and only have this moment with him, not only would she think he was a decent guy, he was someone she'd quite likely be attracted to. She quickly sucked on her milkshake, horrified that she'd had that thought. He was still Matt.

"There's one thing I don't understand," Matt said, "and that's what Susan Lewis was doing there today."

"Who is she?" Matt's Aunt had introduced Susan, and Jenna had spoken to her briefly while waiting for Matt.

"I have no idea. I've met her twice before today, and Dad was completely under her spell. She's a venture capitalist and had convinced him to move a lot of his investments from where they currently are and invest in some schemes she's got going."

"Had he done that?"

"No, not yet. Well, not the investments that he's part-nered with me in. I was waiting to receive documents from him on what he wanted to do with our joint projects, as he wanted to sell out."

"And you'd buy his share?"

"Ideally, yes, but realistically no. I'm fairly stretched with my current projects and doubt the bank would loan me additional funds." He sighed. "I guess it's probably not relevant now. I'm assuming I'll inherit Dad's estate including his shares in my businesses."

"It's strange," Jenna said, "that Susan would come to the hospital if it was a business relationship."

"I know. I think there was something going on between them."

Jenna cringed, causing Matt to smile.

"I should probably be offended on behalf of my father, but that's how I feel too. It's so gross. She's our age, and he's sixty-five. Was sixty-five."

Jenna's eyes filled with tears as Matt wiped his eyes. She'd always thought of him as tough and emotionless and was now learning that she didn't know him at all.

"I'll have to go back to the city on Sunday or early next

week," Matt said, seeming to be thinking out loud. "I have no idea how to plan a funeral. I went to Mom's, and I went to Buster's little girl's, but that's it. I can't imagine where I even start."

"You should speak to your father's lawyer," Jenna suggested. "See if your dad had anything planned. If he did, then that makes it easier, but if he didn't, whatever funeral home you use will be able to help you with everything. I can help you too, Matt. If you've got photos of your father or can access them, I can put together a slideshow for you. I could also put together a flyer or something with details of Walter on it for people to take with them. I've designed a few items for funerals before."

Matt shook his head. "I couldn't ask you to do anything else, Jenna. Imagine what your dad would say. It wasn't long ago he had a gun pointed at me."

Jenna blushed. "Dad would feel the same as I do about this, Matt. Family's more important than anything else that's gone on. I'm not saying he'll go back to supplying your businesses or being nice to you, but I'm sure you'll find he, and the rest of the town, will show you the compassion and kindness they would expect in the same circumstances."

Matt nodded, his eyes once again filled with tears. They finished their milkshakes and fries and made their way back out to the Jeep.

Two hours later, they arrived back in Hope's Ridge.

"My car's at the cafe," Matt said. "Would you mind dropping me off there?"

"Sure," Jenna said. It was close to nine, and the sun had set some time ago. It was a clear night, and the moon was shining on the lake. Jenna pulled into the parking spot next to Matt's car and got out of the Jeep. She walked around to him and put her arms around him. "I'm here if you need anything, okay?"

Matt nodded and squeezed her in thanks, pulling away as they heard someone clear their throat.

Both Jenna and Matt turned to find Charlie standing in the shadows. He smiled at them. "I'm so glad to see you've learned the truth, Jenna, and you and Matt are on good terms once again."

Jenna looked to Matt, who spoke.

"Can you not mention that you saw us to anyone please, Charlie? Jenna's been a big help to me today, but it has nothing to do with what happened. That situation hasn't changed."

"Then I shall set the record straight," Charlie said, turning to Jenna.

"No," Matt said. "Charlie, today's been awful, and Jenna's been a good friend to me. Neither of us wants to discuss anything else.

Charlie turned back to Matt. "Matthew, are you okay?"

Matt's face crumpled at the innocent question. He buried his face in his hands, shaking his head. Jenna moved to him and rubbed his back.

"Charlie, Matt's dad had another heart attack today. He...he didn't make it. Matt's been at the hospital saying goodbye."

"Oh, Matthew. I'm so sorry," the older man said. He moved forward and did his best to put an arm around the larger man's waist. "Come with me. You will come to my home, and I will look after you."

"I think Matt wants to be alone," Jenna said, thinking

back to Matt's response when his aunt had suggested he stay with her.

"Nonsense," Charlie said, leading Matt away. "I live only a few doors down, and Matthew needs comfort now, not solitude. Thank you, Jenna."

Jenna had to stop her mouth from falling open as the older man led Matt away.

8

*M*att pulled into the underground parking lot of Z.P. Legal ten minutes before his scheduled appointment with Zeek Potts, his father's lawyer. They'd met three weeks earlier, a few days before the funeral, to go over Walter's instructions. Today, however, was to meet and discuss how Walter's estate had been left.

It was hard to believe that two weeks had passed since Matt had said his final goodbye to his father. The funeral had been a huge surprise. Over four hundred people had attended, many of them from Hope's Ridge. He hadn't expected any of the town to go and had been overwhelmed by the support and kind words. Even Roy Larsen had shaken his hand and offered his condolences. "Sometimes we need to put our differences aside and pay our respects, son," he'd said to Matt. "It might not change how we coexist on a day-to-day basis, but for today it matters."

Matt had learned within a week of burying his father that Roy had no intention of burying the past and moving forward. Matt was still banned from ordering from the mill, although his customers had returned to the Sandstone Cafe, and bookings at the Sandstone Apartments had recommenced. He was grateful for that, at least.

Matt had been surprised at how disappointed he'd been when Jenna only spoke to him briefly at the funeral. She'd given him a quick hug and then gone to sit with Asha, Zane, and Steph. He knew he shouldn't expect anything else from her, but he had. The day of his father's death had been a bonding one. If only the whole wedding debacle with Brad had never happened. But then, if it hadn't, Jenna wouldn't have been in Hope's Ridge and in a position to take him to the hospital either.

Susan Lewis had arrived with her mother, Veronica, who she'd introduced to Matt after the service. Veronica was wiping away tears, which surprised Matt. After all, she'd probably never even met Walter. "Funerals do this to me," she'd explained. "Walter's death brings up many memories for me of my late husband."

"I'm sorry for your loss," Matt had said. "Did you know my father?"

Veronica had stared at him, seemingly unable to answer the question. In the end Susan had dragged her mother away, saying this was not the time or the place. He hadn't spoken to Susan since, so he couldn't imagine when the time and place would be. He doubted he'd ever see her again.

Matt checked the time. He had five minutes before his meeting—enough time to find Zeek's office and hopefully be offered a cup of coffee.

He made his way up to the eleventh floor of the famous Hilderman Building and was ushered into a meeting room to wait for Zeek. He'd met his father's lawyer numerous times prior to Walter's death, usually at the opening of one of Walter's developments or another social function. They'd had no reason to meet on a professional level as Matt had his own lawyer.

"Matt," Zeek said, entering the room and clapping him on the back. "Good to see you, son. How have you been keeping since Walt's funeral?"

"Okay, I guess," Matt said.

Zeek sat down opposite Matt and opened a file. "You've been offered coffee?"

Matt nodded at the same time as the receptionist brought a cup in and placed it in front of him.

"Shut the door, please, Johnathon," Zeek said as the receptionist retreated from the room. "Now," Zeek said, "Walter left very specific instructions for how his estate is to be divided."

"Divided?" Matt had assumed he would be the sole heir to Walter's estate.

Zeek nodded.

"Oh, my aunt. He'd leave something to her."

Zeek looked up over the top of his glasses at Matt. "Yes, he's left her a substantial sum. I believe her estate is left to you, so Walter assumes this money will find its way back to you in due course unless she spends it."

Matt nodded. He hoped Aunt Kate would spend the money, live a little. But she'd always lived very frugally, so he doubted that would happen.

Zeek cleared his throat. "Walter's been a bit of a coward, in my opinion."

Matt spluttered on his mouthful of coffee. "That's disrespectful."

Zeek raised an eyebrow. "Sorry, but I do feel that this is

the case. He's left me to explain his will to you. I had a heated discussion with him when he made these changes that I felt this was his job, not mine."

Matt put down his coffee cup, nervous energy coursing through him. This didn't sound good.

"So," Zeek began, "Walter left his stocks and bonds to you. They make up around ten percent of his estate."

Matt nodded.

"He also left his apartment and contents to you."

"What about his property assets?" Matt asked. "They make up the bulk of his estate."

"Yes, eighty-three percent," Zeek said. "He left them to Susan Lewis."

Matt felt like he'd been slapped. "All of them?"

Zeek nodded.

"What about the projects we're partners in?"

"He left his percentage ownerships to Susan."

Matt stood and started pacing up and down the room. It was bad enough that his father had owned fifty-one percent of their joint projects, but now they were owned by a stranger. "This doesn't make any sense!"

"I'm sorry. Really, I am. I did try to talk Walter out of making these changes, but he was adamant."

"So let me get this straight." Shock had turned to anger now for Matt. "My father has some crazy affair with someone less than half his age and leaves her everything. Did she know about these changes to the will before he died? If yes, we should let the police know, check what caused this supposed heart attack."

"He wasn't having an affair with Susan," Zeek said. "Far from it."

Matt stopped pacing. "Then what possible explanation

is there for what he's done? She obviously had some hold over him."

Zeek nodded. "Yes, guilt."

"Guilt?"

"Susan was Walter's daughter, Matt. A daughter he only met for the first time about three months ago."

"What?" Matt sank back into his chair, deflating instantly.

"Veronica Lewis made contact with Walter three months ago. They'd had a relationship thirty years ago through which Susan was conceived. Their relationship ended, and from what I understand, Veronica let Susan believe that her husband, Terrance, was her father."

"Why did she contact him three months ago?"

"She heard of Walter's first heart attack and was worried that Susan might never get an opportunity to meet her biological father. She felt she should have given him the option to be part of Susan's life, for both of their sakes."

"And Dad was pleased to find out about her?"

"He had mixed feelings," Zeek said. "He said he wished he'd known earlier but also admitted that it would have ruined his marriage if he had known. He was glad to get to know her, and I believe he spent a lot of time with Susan since learning about her."

"And now he's left nearly his entire estate to her?"

"He felt that he'd given you everything he could in the last thirty years, and it was her turn."

Matt snorted. "It's hardly the same. Yes, he gave me a roof over my head and schooling and all of that, but he's handing her millions."

"I think he considered the investments he made early

on with your business to be more than giving you a roof over your head."

"The investments he kept fifty-one percent ownership in, that he's now given her? Why didn't he at least make it even? She has the decision-making power in my businesses."

"I'm sorry, Matt. I tried to talk sense into Walter, but he was adamant. He felt he owed her, having not been part of her life. To be fair, he wasn't expecting to die quite so soon either. He was only sixty-five. I think he thought he had at least another twenty years. I imagine he would have told you who she was during that time too. She is your sister, after all."

"Half-sister," Matt corrected. Although did it make any difference? He sat back. He had a sister. What a bizarre concept. A sister who was basically a stranger. A stranger who had the power to ruin him.

Jenna looked up as her father entered the office that housed the mill's administrative hub, as he liked to call it. It had certainly been improved over the last few years. What had been a small room had doubled in size and was furnished with rustic pieces her mother had lovingly searched for in antique shops throughout the Midwest. She could see why her mother thought the modern website and look her father and Zane had been considering for the business was the wrong way to go. The mill screamed historic, rustic, and charming.

"How's it going, Jen?" her father asked, coming to look over her shoulder.

Jenna placed her hands on the computer screen, blocking her designs. "I'll present it to all of you this afternoon. I don't like feedback while I'm working. It kills my creativity, especially if you don't like it, which I highly expect you might not."

Roy raised an eyebrow. "You're following the brief, right?"

"The brief Mom gave me, yes."

"What about my brief, the one Zane and I put together?"

"I've got designs for that. Don't worry. I've done something I think you'll love. I wanted to make sure Mom's ideas were represented too."

"Perfect," Roy said, "except when we have to shoot them down and choose Zane's and my concept."

Jenna smiled. "That will be your problem to deal with. I'm the supplier here." She'd agreed to work for two weeks at the mill to get the website redone and carry the new branding through to their signage, stationery, and catalogs. The biggest part of the job was getting the new branding agreed upon, and having worked on it for four days, she was ready to share it with them.

"Thanks again for doing this, Jen. We appreciate it."

"Works for both of us, Dad. I haven't worked out what I'm doing next. I don't even know if I'll go back to the city, so this buys me some time."

Roy sat on the edge of her desk. "Speaking of that, I spoke with Scott, my lawyer, again this morning. He said you've got a case against Graphix if you want to pursue it."

Jenna shook her head. "No, after everything that's happened, I don't want to stir up more drama."

"I get that, but you should be compensated, and they shouldn't be allowed to get away with illegal actions."

Jenna sighed. "And in a perfect world, my fiancé wouldn't be a cheat, and I wouldn't be living back at home. I don't want to pursue it, Dad. I've got enough to deal with right now. Okay?"

Roy's nod was reluctant. "If you change your mind, just say the word, and we'll meet with Scott. As for living back at home, your mother and I would love it if you stayed. It's been so good to have Zane back." He gave a little laugh. "Even after our rocky start. But having you here too would be perfect. We'd all be together again."

Jenna squeezed his arm. "I can't promise anything. I'm so used to the pace of the city, and I'm not sure if I'd be satisfied in Hope's Ridge."

Her father looked at her for a long moment. "What is it that would make you satisfied? If you could paint a picture of your ideal life, what would be the most important thing you?"

Jenna sat back and thought. "The most important? Family, I guess—my own family in addition to you guys. I want a good man, Dad. I thought I had that."

"It's good that you learned that you didn't," Roy said. "Before you'd married and started a family. It would have been much harder if the marriage had ended once you'd had kids."

Jenna laughed. "We should forgive Matt then?"

Roy's face clouded over. "No. I know he's been through a rough time lately, but it doesn't change anything he's done. He's not someone I can ever imagine forgiving. Let's not talk about him. What you're saying is that the right man is your priority?"

Jenna nodded. "Someone I can rely on and trust. I'm ready to have a family. Not right away, but soon. I'll be thirty in a few months and always thought I'd have three or four kids. Unless I have them all at once, I need to get started."

"Then why would you go back to the city? Raising kids out here would make sense."

"It would, except finding the right man in Hope's Ridge would be quite a challenge. Anyone decent left town when we finished school."

"What about Ryan? He's a nice guy."

Jenna pretended to give serious consideration to her father's suggestion. She knew he was trying to help, but mentioning the only eligible guy in Hope's Ridge wasn't the best selling point. "He's nice but not my type."

"Okay, then what about one of the guys who works at the mill. There are a few single ones."

Jenna smiled. "I appreciate your help, Dad, but I don't want to be set up. If the right guy happens to land at my feet in Hope's Ridge, then great. But realistically, there's a bigger pool to play in in the city, and those guys are more likely to be into the lifestyle I like. Restaurants, fine dining, and all of that."

Roy stood and sighed. "There's not a lot of that happening in Hope's Ridge, I'm afraid." He grinned. "Traders does pretty good wings and burgers."

Jenna laughed. "I'll see you this afternoon to present my concepts, okay? Mom said to be ready at four."

"Can't wait," Roy said over his shoulder as he strode out of the office.

Jenna returned her focus to the rustic version of the website she was putting the finishing touches on. She'd spent her entire teenage years longing for the day she could leave Hope's Ridge, and once she had, she'd never looked back. She'd missed her family a little and her friends, but overall, city life had suited her. Even with the right man, if he was to miraculously appear, she doubted she'd ever be content living in Hope's Ridge.

Two hours later, with the website design complete, Jenna decided to walk into town to have lunch. She needed a break from the computer screen, and she needed some exercise. The fifteen-minute walk each way would give her some fresh air and time to think. She was happy with the concepts she'd developed for the mill. She only hoped her parents would be able to agree on one. They were coming from miles apart, one wanting modern and the other wanting a historic, rustic feel.

She made her way along John's Drive and joined the lake trail. A light wind was whipping across the lake, blowing her hair back off her face. This was one thing she would miss if she went back to the city. The air was so fresh and clean. She wasn't breathing in fumes from cars or industry. She picked up her pace, deciding one of Margie's chicken and salad wraps would be the perfect lunch.

She pushed open the door of the Sandstone Cafe and grinned.

"Jenna!"

The cry from the service area was one she was getting used to each time she walked through the cafe's door. She was pretty sure Ryan didn't do it for everyone, but she had to admit it made her day.

She walked over to the counter and plopped down on one of the stools, suddenly remembering what Asha had said a couple of weeks ago about Ryan wanting to do something for the anniversary of Margie's husband's passing.

"How's life?" Ryan asked, wiping down the counter as he moved toward Jenna.

"Good," Jenna said and smiled. "Going in a positive direction, at least. Is Margie here?"

"In the kitchen," Ryan said. "Did you want me to get her?"

Jenna shook her head. "Not yet. I wanted to speak to you. Asha mentioned you were planning something to mark the anniversary of Margie's husband's death."

Ryan looked to the kitchen and back again, signaling for Jenna to keep her voice down. "It's going to be a surprise. I'll be letting everyone know this weekend and see who's available to come. It'll be small, only close friends, but I wanted to give her the opportunity to celebrate his life and feel that she can talk to us about him."

Jenna shook her head. "Don't."

Ryan's forehead creased in confusion. "What? Why?"

"She wants to move on, Ryan. She definitely won't want a party for him. If you're going to go ahead, you need to check she's okay with it. The way she's spoken to me on our walks, it would be the last thing she'd want."

"Are you sure?"

"Definitely. Speak to her if you plan to have the party. Definitely no surprises." She could only imagine how Margie would feel having to pretend for an entire evening that she had a perfect marriage.

"Maybe I won't do the party, and I'll just give her the present I made for her." Ryan sounded unsure.

"What's the present?" Jenna asked.

"A portrait of her and Aaron together." He grinned. "Don't tell her. I've been working on it in secret because I didn't want her to know."

Jenna's heart caught in her throat. She wished she could tell Ryan why this wouldn't be a good present, but it wasn't her place to do so.

"Sh," Ryan added. "I think she's coming."

As he finished his sentence, Margie appeared from the kitchen area.

"Hey, Jen, how are you?"

"Great," Jenna said.

Margie raised an eyebrow, causing Jenna to laugh.

"I do feel great," Jenna admitted. "I don't know why. It's a nice day, I guess. And I got to walk here from work. You sometimes forget how beautiful the lake is."

"Ah," Ryan said, moving over to the coffee machine, "Lake Hopeful's casting its magic spell on you. Next thing, you'll be marrying the first guy you see and having a bunch of kids."

Jenna laughed. "Have you been talking to my dad by any chance?"

Ryan shook his head. "No, why, is he saying the same thing?"

"Not only is he saying that, he suggested you'd be a good candidate for the job."

Ryan stopped wiping the steam wand and screwed his face up as if in deep thought. "I guess it's an option. I am rather good-looking and eligible, and so are you. We'd have beautiful kids. One blonde and petite like you and one tall and dark-haired like me." He flexed his muscles. "And strong."

Jenna laughed as he teased her. "But you're not feeling it, are you?"

"Sorry, I've always thought of you as a good friend."

"That's what I told Dad. He's now trying to come up with any other single man in the area. I'm sure they'll all be lined up outside the mill in the coming days."

"You two would be cute together," Margie said. "You shouldn't discount it."

Jenna met Ryan's eye, and they both laughed. There was no chemistry between them, which was surprising. Ryan was good-looking, successful, and lovely, but there wasn't a spark.

"Can I get you some lunch?" Margie asked.

"I'm thinking one of your chicken wraps, please."

"Coming up."

"Who's that?" Ryan asked, lowering his voice and nodding at one of the booths. "She's familiar, but I'm not sure from where. Walter's funeral, maybe?"

Jenna turned and snuck a glance in the direction of the woman sitting in the booth. She turned back to Ryan, frowning. "That's Susan Lewis. She had some kind of relationship with Matt's dad. I'm not sure if he's found out what the context of it was yet." She pushed herself off the stool. "I should go and say hello."

Susan looked up as Jenna approached her booth and smiled. "Jenna, hi, how are you? Join me if you'd like."

Jenna slid into the seat across from Susan. "I'm surprised to see you in Hope's Ridge. Are you meeting Matt?"

Susan shook her head. "No, although I probably should get in touch with him. If you see him before I contact him, can you let him know I'll be in touch?"

"I'm unlikely to see or speak to him."

"Really?" Susan said. "I thought you two were a couple. Did something happen?"

Jenna coughed. "A couple?"

"You looked so close at the hospital. You could tell that you care about each other." She smiled. "I'm a bit of an expert at reading body language. It's hard to disguise your feelings when your bodies give it away."

Jenna stared at Susan. "I think it was probably the situation that gave you the wrong idea. I was comforting Matt. We used to be friends, but not anymore."

Susan frowned. "Wow, sorry. I honestly thought you were one of those couples made for each other."

Margie placed Jenna's wrap down in front of her, interrupting their conversation. "Who's made for each other? Sorry," she added, "I'm incredibly nosy."

Jenna laughed. "Margie, this is Susan. Susan thought Matt and I were a couple."

Margie's hand flew to her mouth. "Oh my gosh, that's a classic. If Jenna and Matt got together, I think we'd have to declare a holiday in Hope's Ridge. A national day of disbelief."

Susan laughed as Margie made her way back to the counter. "I obviously got that wrong. Did something happen between the two of you?"

Jenna picked up her sandwich. "Something is an understatement. I'm not sure where I'd even start."

"At the beginning," Susan said. "I love a good story. I'm thinking of writing novels, so I get great inspiration from real-life stories."

"Let me assure you," Jenna said, "no one would believe this was true if you put it in a book. That someone could behave the way Matt did is probably not possible."

It was Susan staring at Jenna with her mouth open a few minutes later when she finished telling her the Matt saga.

"He did all of that?"

"Yep," Jenna took a bite of her wrap. "The town's waiting for his next marvelous accomplishment. He's got quite a reputation."

"What I don't understand," Susan said, "is why, after all that he's done to you, you were there for him when his dad died."

"That was different," Jenna said. "I happened to be here in the cafe when he got the phone call." She blushed. "I was ripping through him at the time. But his dad dying kind of trumped it all, put it in perspective, I guess."

"And you're friends now?"

Jenna shook her head. "No. I'd say we've called a truce. I'm willing to leave it all in the past, but I need him to stay well away from me. My family isn't as forgiving."

"Oh?"

"We own the mill. Dad's refusing to supply Matt's businesses, so he has to source his timber supplies from Tall Oaks, which he's not happy about."

Susan nodded as if this made complete sense. "Small town. I guess you don't want to get on anyone's bad side. What about you then, Jenna? Have you moved back here permanently?"

"I'm not sure. Probably not. I need to think about getting a new job and then decide what I want to do. I'm a graphic designer, so need to be in the city. There's not a lot of work in a small town like this."

"I don't suppose you'd be interested in a short-term project?"

"Graphic design work?"

Susan shook her head. "No, I have some research I need done in Hope's Ridge and in Drayson's Landing. I'm too busy with my day job to spend much time out here, so ideally I want to delegate it to someone. It would pay good money but would only be for a couple of months."

"What sort of research?"

"I'm a venture capitalist," Susan said. "It's mainly to do with properties and other opportunities that may exist out here. There's a fund that's become part of my portfolio that I'm deciding how to use."

"As in looking for investment?"

"Possibly. Or reallocating existing investments. I'm not completely sure, which is what the research is for." She reached into her bag and took out a card. "I can't give you additional information without signing a nondisclosure agreement. It's a small town here, so some of my research will affect existing residents and needs to be kept confidential."

Jenna took the card from her. "That makes sense. I'm definitely interested. It will buy me some time while I decide what I'm going to do."

"If it works out and you choose to come back to the city, I'm sure I can find you something else," Susan said. "I work with numerous advertising agencies who I'm sure could use a graphic designer, or even in-house where I work. I'm not sure we have a full-time role for a graphic designer, but if you were interested in learning new skills, we could combine the role with working with some of our clients in a venture capitalist capacity." She smiled. "I'm getting way ahead of myself. Sorry, I tend to do that when I come across someone I click with. I imagine a long-term working relationship and how we can benefit each other, but we probably need to get to know each other better first."

Jenna laughed. "I know the perfect way to do that. Are you staying in town tonight?"

"I thought I would," Susan said. "I was tempted to do some hiking tomorrow."

"How about a night out? Traders is a great bar, and we can get food there. I'll ask a couple of my friends along and make it a girls' night." She turned and looked back at the bar. "Margie, you up for a few drinks at Traders tonight? Show Susan a Friday night in Hope's Ridge?"

"She'll be there," Ryan called out, earning himself a punch in the arm from Margie. "What?" He rubbed his arm. "You would have said no."

Jenna laughed. "He's probably right."

Margie forced a smile. "Sure, why not. Asha and Steph might want to come too."

Jenna turned back to Susan. "Perfect. Although, I haven't even asked you what your relationship is with the Laws. You and Walter were close?" She was intrigued. She couldn't imagine this smart, successful woman having a relationship with a man in his mid-sixties, even though Matt was convinced they had.

Susan maneuvered her way out of the booth and stood. "We met a few months ago, and yes, we were close. But I can't say any more than that until I speak with Matt. I'm not sure how much he knows or how much he'll want me to share."

"That sounds secretive."

Susan tapped her nose and smiled. "Very! I'm kidding, but I wouldn't want to cause issues for Matt, so let's leave it there. Now, tonight, what time at Traders?"

"How about seven?"

Susan laughed. "You've slipped back into Hope's Ridge's clock perfectly. What time did you go out in the city?"

"About nine," Jenna admitted. "But if we go at seven, we'll be in bed before midnight, which suits me."

"Me too," Susan said. "See you there."

Matt drove back to Hope's Ridge in a state of shock. He couldn't believe his dad would hide such a monumental secret from him. He'd had another child and not told anyone? To be fair, his dad had only found out a few months ago himself, but why had he introduced Susan to him as a venture capitalist? Why hadn't he been honest? He felt like a fool. What had Walter said to Susan to have her go along with that? Hadn't she wanted to be honest with him?

He smashed his hand down on the steering wheel, fury rushing through him. His father had left him in a huge mess. Absolutely huge. If he was alive, Matt would be around there yelling at him. Demanding answers. He took a deep breath. The worst thing was, Walter wasn't alive, and Matt couldn't do that. He'd never be able to do that again.

But he did have a sister. The thought crept into his head. A sister he could get to know if he chose to. He sighed and turned up the radio, hoping to drown out his thoughts.

As he drove down the winding road that led into town, there was only one thing he was sure of. He needed a drink.

In fact, he needed many drinks. He turned onto Main Street and drove the short distance to Traders Barn. He'd call Ryan and Buster from inside and see if they'd join him. A guys' night was what he needed.

Less than an hour later, he found himself relaying the details of his day, his father's awful will, and the fact that he had a sister to his two friends.

"That's crazy," Buster said. "I'm sorry, Matt, about the will. I can't believe your dad did that to you. I guess he wasn't expecting to die so soon, but it's still awful."

"What will it mean for the cafe and the apartments?" Ryan asked.

Matt shrugged, throwing back his drink in one gulp. "I have no idea. I need to speak with Susan and find out what her plans are. Dad was already talking to me before he died about selling his percentage ownership in all of our projects in Hope's and Drayson's. I'm hoping she won't want to do that, but as it appeared to be her recommendation to Dad, I'm assuming she will."

"Can you contest the will?" Ryan asked. "It seems incredibly unfair."

"I can, but it's unlikely I'll be successful. Dad spelled out clearly the reasons for the way he left it. That he'd only recently learned of his biological daughter, and this was to even things out and ensure that she knew he considered her family. Someone he met three months ago. It's a joke, that's all I can say." He looked at his friends' glasses. "Come on, boys, drink up. I'm ordering another round."

Matt stood and walked over to the bar to order the drinks. He paid and turned to walk back to the table and saw that Asha and Steph were talking with Ryan and Buster. Disappointment flooded over him. He was in the mood for a guys' night, nothing else. Asha had been cold toward him ever since Jenna's wedding, and while he and Steph were on good terms, he didn't want her involved in their night.

"Don't worry," Asha said as he returned to the table. "We're not crashing. We're meeting Margie and Jenna. We won't be joining tables."

Matt forced a smile. "Probably a good idea." Jenna's and his paths hadn't crossed again since the funeral. He wasn't sure if that was because she was avoiding him, but regardless he knew it was for the best. Jenna was never going to forgive him.

Steph turned to Asha. "There are plenty of tables on the other side. Let's set up over there." She leaned forward and kissed Buster. "I'll see you later."

Buster smiled. "Definitely."

Jealousy stabbed at Matt. He was happy for Buster and Steph, they were two of his closest friends, but he wished it was him. He'd give anything for a relationship like they had. He sighed a loud, audible sigh.

"You okay?" Buster asked.

"Just thinking how hard life is. I'm envious of your relationship if I'm honest."

"You're into Steph?" Buster asked.

Matt laughed. "No. She's a great friend, nothing more. I'm envious of your relationship, that's all. I haven't had a girlfriend for a long time, and all of you seem to be settling down. I'm ready to do that too."

"Not all of us," Ryan said. "Mind you, that's because of a lack of available females in Hope's Ridge." He laughed. "Roy Larsen suggested to Jenna that she and I should get together. She told me, and we both laughed as if it was the stupidest idea ever."

The stab of jealousy Matt felt earlier returned, this time bigger than the first. The thought of seeing Ryan and Jenna together made his stomach turn.

"You okay?" Buster asked. "You've gone deathly pale."

Matt nodded. "Must be the alcohol." He looked at Ryan. "Are you going to ask her out?"

"Jen? No. As I said, we both laughed. I've known her forever, Matt. She's definitely in the friend zone."

"Even though she's gorgeous and a beautiful person?" he asked before he could stop himself.

Ryan raised an eyebrow. "Sounds like you're into her, even if I'm not."

"Yeah, Matt," Buster added. "What's going on?"

Matt shook his head. "Nothing at all." He forced a laugh. "Can you imagine me asking Jenna out? Her dad threatened me with a gun a few weeks back and has done his best to cripple my businesses. No, I'm definitely not interested in Jenna, and I can assure you she wouldn't touch me with a ten-foot pole even if I was."

"You could always ask her," Ryan said with a laugh. He nodded toward the side entrance of the bar. "There she is."

Matt looked over to see Jenna and Margie entering Traders with Susan Lewis right behind them.

He put his drink down, his eyes following the three women as they made their way over to Asha and Steph.

"Everything okay?" Ryan asked.

Matt shook his head. "No, that's her. Susan Lewis. The woman I've been telling you about. My half-sister."

Buster frowned. "What's she doing in Hope's Ridge, and why's she hanging out with Jenna and the others?"

Matt pushed back his chair and stood. "I have no idea, but I'm about to find out."

Jenna introduced Susan to Asha and Steph, and the women placed a drinks order with one of the wait staff before settling into a comfortable conversation.

"I heard the meeting went well with your presentation at the mill," Asha said. "Zane told me your dad was blown away with the designs."

Jenna laughed. "He was, except he can't decide which one he likes better." She went on to explain to the others her father's preference for something modern versus her mother's desire for something rustic that conveyed the feeling of history and nostalgia for the mill.

"Who makes the final decision?" Susan asked.

"Dad will think he's made it, but it will be Mom. She'll get her way; she always does. She's smart enough to make him think it's all his idea."

"How much longer are you working at the mill?" Steph asked. "It's just that there's some work we need to do for Holly's that I'd love to talk to you about. If you're doing free-lance work, that is."

"That would be great," Jenna said. "I can come meet with you on Monday if you like."

"You're certainly in demand," Susan said, raising an eyebrow. "You might not have time to move back to the city."

"Who's moving back to the city?"

The women all turned as Matt approached the table. He was smiling, what looked like a forced smile.

"Jenna," Steph said. "I was suggesting she come and chat about the signage for Holly's. There are a lot of items we need to design. The website too."

Matt nodded. "That would be great if you have the time." He blushed. "Although your dad might not be too happy with you doing work for us."

"He doesn't need to know everything I'm doing," Jenna said. "And anyway, if I work directly with Steph, there shouldn't be an issue."

Matt nodded and turned his gaze to Susan. "I didn't know you were in town."

"Arrived this morning," Susan said. "I'd planned to get in touch tomorrow if I didn't see you today. We obviously need to talk."

"I only found out the whole situation this morning," Matt said. "Did you know I was meeting with Dad's lawyer?"

Susan nodded. "I did, but I was expecting you'd spend the weekend in the city, which is why I thought it would be a good time to come out and visit Hope's Ridge."

Matt frowned. "You weren't planning to see me then?"

"I was planning to call you and see if you were in town, and if you weren't, I was going to suggest we catch up in the city on Sunday."

Jenna looked from Matt to Susan and then to Asha, Steph, and Margie, who, like her, were all watching the exchange with interest. The tension between Matt and Susan was palpable.

"What Dad's lawyer had to say was quite a shock," Matt said.

"As it was for me three months ago," Susan said.

Steph cleared her throat, causing both Matt and Susan

to look at her. "Sorry to interrupt, but I'm wondering if whatever you're talking about is private? We can leave you to chat if you like."

"No," Matt said. "You stay there. Susan, can I buy you a drink? There's a room out back that only has a few tables in it. It's much quieter, and somewhere we can talk privately." He had the good grace to blush. "Sorry, ladies, I didn't mean to interrupt your night. It's, well, it's just that Susan and I have something pretty major to discuss."

Susan stood, smiling her apologies at the others. "Matt's right. We should talk. We won't be long."

Jenna waited until they were out of earshot before turning to the others. "Does anyone know what's going on?"

"No idea," Asha said. "But then Zane and I have been on the outside of all of this. Matt's on our enemies list, so we haven't heard anything that's going on."

"Matt thought Susan and his dad were having a relationship," Jenna said. "But I find that hard to believe."

"Ugh," Asha said, causing Margie to laugh. "Sorry but imagine dating Walter Law. Even if you were the same age as him, it would be gross."

"Ash," Steph reprimanded. "That's an awful thing to say."

"Yes, but he was a pretty awful person," Asha said. "And why would someone like Susan want to have a relationship with an old guy? Do you think she's a gold digger? Maybe he left her money in his will."

"Best not to speculate," Jenna said. "Matt's got enough on his plate with everything that's happened."

Asha's stare caused Jenna to look away. She knew she was blushing.

"What's going on?" Asha asked. "Have you and Matt

made up?"

Jenna shook her head. "No, I've called a truce. He needs to grieve, and he doesn't need more angst thrown at him. At the same time, I don't want him anywhere near me, and Dad's definitely not going to forgive him. If he stays out of my way and me out of his, then we can coexist in this town."

"Charlie Li is on Matt's side with all of this," Margie said. "I was talking to him the other day when he came in for his coffee. He was worried about Matt. He was checking with me as to whether Matt was eating properly and whether there was anything he could do for him. He's got it stuck in his head that Matt's done nothing wrong. That we should all be thanking him, not alienating him."

Jenna snorted with derisive laughter. "Old age has definitely caught up with Charlie. I'm sad for Matt that his dad died, I'm sure any person with a heart would be, but that doesn't excuse his past behavior. If I was thanking Matt, I'd be thanking him for ruining my life. I don't think so."

Matt ordered drinks for himself and Susan and ushered her to a quiet table at the back of the room usually used for private functions.

A waitperson delivered their tray of drinks, and Matt lifted his in a toast. "I'm not really sure what I'm toasting."

"New beginnings," Susan suggested. "Very cliche, I know, but like you, I'm not sure how we're supposed to act either."

"I need you to fill me in, Matt said. "I only just found

out what your connection to Dad was." He forced a laugh. "I thought you were having a relationship with him."

"Oh, yuck," Susan said, her hand automatically covering her mouth. "Sorry, that slipped out."

Matt laughed. "No, it was my exact thought too. And Jenna's and Steph's."

"They all think Walter and I were dating?"

Matt nodded. "But we can tell them the real story after we've talked. How come you only saw him for the first time a few months ago?"

"My mom lied to me. Up until a few months ago, I had assumed my father was someone else. Her husband who died while she was pregnant with me."

Matt frowned. "And what, she suddenly changed the story?"

"No, she decided to be honest. She'd had a relationship with Walter, cheated on her husband, I guess, and became pregnant with me. The relationship with Walter ended around the same time her husband died. Mom scheduled DNA testing. She'd arranged for a blood sample from her husband to be freeze-dried in order to do the test when I was born."

"She knew you weren't her husband's?"

Susan nodded. "And the only other person she'd been with was Walter. He and I did another one when we first met, to be sure." She smiled. "I think he wanted to make sure I wasn't after his money."

Matt smiled. "I'd expect nothing less from Dad. But didn't your mom consider contacting my dad when she realized he was the father?"

Susan nodded. "She did but dismissed the idea pretty quickly. She was grieving her husband and was worried about how it would look to friends and family to announce he wasn't my father. She was ashamed and humiliated. She also knew that Walter's wife was pregnant, which I guess was with you."

"But thirty years later, she tells you?"

"She saw a newspaper article about his first heart attack. She felt guilty, realizing that if he'd died from the first heart attack, then she would have taken away my choice to meet him. That was when she came clean and told me everything and asked if I wanted to meet him."

Matt took a sip of his drink. "How did he react? It must have been a shock. I'm not sure I could forgive someone for keeping it from me that I had a daughter."

Matt saw Susan bristle. "I'm not sure I'd forgive a man for cheating on his wife either."

"Neither would I," Matt said. "Both of them behaved despicably."

"Fair enough," Susan said. "I guess Mom does have a lot to answer for as well. As for how Walter reacted? Shock, I believe, was his first response. But within twenty-four hours of Mom contacting him, he wanted to meet me. It was an awkward first meeting, but once the DNA test confirmed I was his daughter, we caught up a few times a week and relaxed with each other. He had a good sense of humor." She smiled.

"He did," Matt agreed. "He was also pretty pig-headed and arrogant."

"Qualities I believe you possess," Susan said.

Matt's mouth dropped open. "Who told you that?" He sighed. "Let me guess, Jenna filled you in?"

Susan nodded. "She did, but that's not any of my business."

"No, it's not," Matt agreed. "Back to Dad, did he say why he wanted to keep you quiet? Why didn't he tell me about you? After all, we're half-siblings. Why all the lies about you being a venture capitalist looking for him to invest with you?"

"Not lies. I am a venture capitalist, and I was hoping to get him to invest. There were some great opportunities that he would have done well with. As for not telling you, he was worried about your reaction. He told me how close you were to your mom, and he was worried that it would ruin your relationship with him when you found out."

"That's a surprise," Matt said. "We didn't have the best relationship in the world to start with."

"I think that was his concern, that it would make it even worse. Possibly irreparable."

"And you were okay with that?"

Susan shrugged. "Yes and no. It was strange enough finding out that this man was my father. I assumed you would be told at some stage who I was, but I wasn't in a rush for that to happen. I've gone for close to thirty years without a sibling. Another year or two wasn't going to make much difference."

"You don't feel like we have lots of years to catch up on?"

"Honestly?"

Matt nodded.

"Not especially. I would have loved to have had a brother when I was younger, but now it seems surreal. We're complete strangers who happen to share DNA."

"According to Dad's lawyer, we share more than DNA," Matt said. "I believe you now have a controlling interest in most of my developments."

"Ah, the will. Yes, I'm sure you're not happy about that."

"Understatement," Matt said. "Do you think it's fair how it's been left?"

"That's not up to me to say," Susan said. "It was our father's money and assets and for him to do with what he wished. I wouldn't want anyone telling me how to leave my estate any more than I imagine you would. You can contest it. I won't take it personally as we have already agreed that we don't know each other."

Matt nodded. "You're like Dad in that you're direct. I don't have to worry about where I stand with you. I like to be direct too. My main concern is losing the projects I care about here and in Drayson's Landing. I know Dad was talking about selling out of some of those, but he didn't understand how important they were to me. As Dad's plans didn't get a chance to eventuate, perhaps we can sit down another time and discuss them. They are profitable and a good investment."

Susan smiled. "You seem to be forgetting that I am the one who was suggesting Walter move his assets into other investments."

"And you still plan to do that?"

"Nothing's definite, Matt. I'm going to do my own research into the pros and cons of investing in the area, and then I'll get back to you. I'm not looking to upset your life or cause problems. I'm sure that if I don't want to retain ownership of any of the projects, we can come to some kind of agreement so that you can buy me out. That was Walter's plan and he had me draw up the paperwork for you. He died before I had a chance to send it. I can send it to you next week to look at if I decide it's still the way forward for me. The estate will take some time to settle, so nothing's going to happen quickly, which means there's no need to panic."

Matt nodded. He could see that she had made up her mind as to how she intended to move forward, and he was going to have to wait and see what she planned.

Susan picked up her drink and stood. "It's been nice chatting, but I'm going to get back to the girls."

Matt watched as she walked away, realizing that he hadn't asked her one of the important questions, which was why Walter had changed his will, and what had made him do that? He threw back the rest of his drink and followed her into the main bar. She was laughing as she sat back down with Jenna and the girls. He hesitated momentarily but then decided he needed an answer.

He smiled as he approached the table. "Sorry to interrupt again, there's something I forgot to ask you, Susan. Would you have another five minutes?"

Susan shook her head. "Can we leave it until next week, Matt? I don't want to discuss anything else tonight."

"Really?" Matt hadn't expected that.

"You heard her, Matt," Asha said. "Now leave us alone, please."

"Ash," Steph said, "don't be so mean. You have no idea what's going on here."

"And you do?"

Susan laughed. "Steph, and I think Margie, assume that I was having a romantic relationship with Walter Law."

Matt felt a sting as Asha laughed at the thought. "Asha, my dad died recently. You don't need to be so disrespectful."

"He's right," Steph said, glaring at her sister. "Give him a break, Ash. You're going to be on your hands and knees asking for Matt's forgiveness one day soon. You too, Jenna," she added.

"Sorry," Asha managed, returning her sister's glare. "So, you weren't having a relationship with Walter?"

"Not that type," Matt said. "It turns out Susan is my half-sister. Walter is her father." He ignored their shocked reactions and continued. "And the question I wanted Susan to answer was how it came about that my father made such a dramatic change to his will." He took a step backward, folded his arms, and stared at Susan.

Susan frowned. "Definitely not the time or place for this, Matt, but if you want to know, he told me after he did it. He said he felt incredibly guilty that I'd missed out on financial assistance during the last thirty years when you'd had so much and wanted to even things out."

"It's hardly evened things out."

Steph stood and took Matt's arm. "Come on, let's get you back to the boys so you can enjoy your night. This sounds like a private conversation that you and Susan should have another time."

Matt was about to object when he saw the kindness in Steph's eyes. He nodded and allowed her to lead him away.

"Sorry," he said as they crossed the bar. "It's all been such a shock, that's all. First Dad dies, then Susan's my sister, and he's left most of his estate to her."

"Oh Matt, I'm so sorry."

Jenna's words on the morning his dad died came back to him. *You've messed with people's lives many times and walked away. I hope karma comes back to bite you, Matt. You deserve every horrible thing that could ever possibly happen to you.* "Maybe it's karma, Steph. My past wrongdoings have finally caught up with me. Jenna will be happy at least."

Steph shook her head. "All I saw on Jenna's face during that exchange was concern, and as for karma, I don't think so. You've worked hard for months now to make things right. I can see that, and Charlie can see it, and at some point, the rest of the town will see it. Things happen for a reason, and things work out how they're meant to."

"If I believe that, then I have to believe that my dad's estate was left how it was meant to be."

"Maybe it was," Steph said.

Matt leaned forward and hugged her. "You're my voice of reason, and I appreciate it. I'm going home. Can you let the guys know for me and pass on my apologies? I can't explain what's going on tonight. I'm done. I invited them here for drinks though, so they might think I'm rude." His eyes filled with tears. "I'm not trying to be. I'm trying to be my best self, but I'm failing big time, Steph."

She pulled him to her. "Never think that, Matt. You're trying harder than anyone I know. You have to trust that the universe will give you a break and deliver."

Matt forced a smile. "If it doesn't, I'll hold you responsible."

Steph nodded. "I'm okay with that because I'm confident it will. Now go home and sleep well. It'll make a huge difference."

Matt squeezed her hand in thanks and walked out of the bar without looking back.

9

*J*enna read through the document in front of her, turned it over, and turned it back again. She must have misunderstood the context of it. She was nearing the end of her first week working for Susan and was beginning to feel uneasy about the nature of the work. It was now clear to her as to why Susan had insisted she sign a nondisclosure agreement. Her plans for Matt's businesses had the potential to cripple him. She reread the document. Susan was providing investors with detailed information on Matt's businesses with what appeared to be overinflated valuations. Would an investor fall for these false numbers? Wouldn't they get their own valuations done too?

The biggest problem with the valuations was what it meant for Matt. Susan had confirmed with Jenna that she would give Matt the first right of refusal to buy the percentage of each business she was inheriting from Walter Law, but if the valuations were overinflated, what hope would Matt have to secure finances to buy them?

And even if he did, he'd be trading at a loss for years in order to pay the money back. Jenna's stomach flip-flopped. Matt's actions had pulled Jenna's life apart. Did she care if something as awful happened to him? As much as she tried to convince herself that she didn't care, an annoying voice in her head continued to remind her that she did.

"Jenna," Margie hissed, and Jenna looked up from her document as Margie beckoned to her from the counter. "Come here."

Jenna found herself hurrying behind the counter, where Margie pushed her into the kitchen area.

"Did you know?"

Jenna frowned. "Know what?"

Margie took her hand and led her from the kitchen to the office that was attached to the cafe. Jenna stopped in the doorway, her hand flying to her mouth. "Oh no." She looked up at Margie, distressed to see tears filling Margie's eyes. The large portrait of Margie and her late husband stared back at her, the intensity of their eyes boring into Jenna. No wonder Margie looked so distraught.

"He wants me to put it on the wall here or at home," Margie said, "so I can see it every day. I can't even bear to look at it."

"Oh, hon," Jeana said, putting her arms around Margie and pulling her close. "Why don't you tell Ryan? He'd want to be there for you, and then he'll understand your feelings about the picture."

Margie shook her head, tears cascading down her cheeks. "I can't. I can't tell anyone, Jen. I'm surprised I even told you. It's so humiliating. Also, I don't want people's memories of Aaron to be tarnished with all of this. I can handle it, as long as it isn't in my face." She nodded at the painting.

Jenna's heart went out to her. She wished Margie would tell Ryan, but she did understand why she wanted the entire experience to be buried with her husband.

"Can you tell him it's too painful to see Aaron every day, and you'll leave it in storage until you're strong enough to put it on display?"

Margie wiped her eyes. "That's a good idea. He can hardly argue with that. I don't want to seem ungrateful either; I know this must have taken him a long time. The detail is exquisite."

"Exquisite, you say."

The two women jumped as Ryan entered the office. He grinned. "I'm glad you love it, Margie. But Jenna, there's a message for you." He held up a small piece of paper. "Susan Lewis called and said your cell went straight to voicemail. She needs to delay her video call with you."

"Thanks," Jenna said. She turned to Margie. "I'd better get back to work. Will you be okay?"

"Okay? What happened?" Ryan's concern confirmed he hadn't heard their conversation.

"Nothing," Margie said. "It's just the painting's so real, and every time I see it, it reduces me to tears."

Ryan put his arms around his sister. "In a good way or a bad way?"

Jenna knew the answer but wasn't surprised when Margie lied. "Good, but it's still overwhelming, Ry. It might be a little while before I can put it on the wall. I think I need to build up to looking at Aaron every day. I hope you aren't offended."

Ryan squeezed Margie. "Offended? Definitely not. I'm

sorry and not sorry that you feel such an emotional attachment to the picture. Sorry, because I know it hurts, but not sorry because I know I've captured Aaron the way he was."

"So you're okay with no party and no displaying the picture?"

Ryan nodded.

"Did you have anything else planned for me?"

Ryan blushed. "Maybe a video slideshow, but that was all. We can watch it together, or you can put it away for the future."

"Let's watch it together. It's the anniversary of Aaron's death on Saturday. Let's get a bottle of wine and some of that cheese he used to love and watch it then. The two of us. I don't want anyone else involved."

Ryan nodded. "I'd love to." He let go of his sister and turned to Jenna. "You looked pretty intense out there working on those documents. Are you enjoying the work?"

Jenna sighed, realizing the impact Susan's plans could have on the Sandstone Cafe went beyond Matt. It could also mean Margie and Ryan would be out of a job if the property was sold or if a majority owner bought in and decided to make changes. "Honestly, I'm not sure. The documents are a little confusing. I'm hoping I'm misinterpreting their meaning."

Ryan raised an eyebrow. "You're pretty smart, Jenna. I'm sure you've worked out what they mean."

Jenna smiled at what she knew was supposed to be a compliment, but inside she cringed. Unfortunately, she was fairly sure she knew precisely what they meant and knew that the consequences for Matt would be devastating.

Matt found himself sitting at a table at Traders a week after his discussion with Susan. Charlie had insisted he take Matt out to dinner, and he chose the venue. "A big juicy steak is what I need for my iron levels, Matthew," Charlie had said, "but I do not like to eat out alone. Dinner is my treat to cheer you up."

"You don't have to do that," Matt had insisted.

"I know I don't," Charlie said. "But I want to."

Now, having tackled a steak, baked potato, and vegetables, Matt leaned back in his chair, his stomach full to the point of overflowing. "I don't know where you put that," he commented to Charlie. "I'm stuffed, and you're still going."

Charlie smiled. "I pace myself, Matthew, and I will finish. Now, we have a proposition to discuss."

Matt leaned forward. This sounded interesting.

Charlie put the last forkful of steak in his mouth and chewed it with slow appreciation before putting his knife and fork together on his plate. He pushed the plate to one side and placed his hands together in front of him.

"I wish to become business partners."

Matt shook his head.

"Hear me out," Charlie said. "I am in a position to invest in any business I choose. I was thinking of developing a lakefront cafe, but Asha insists that Irresistibles is perfect the way it is." He shook his head and tutted as he said this. "I need a new project and new interests. Becoming partners with you will give me an opportunity to spread my wings into other ventures."

"I'm not looking for a partner, Charlie."

"But what if this Susan Lewis puts a high price tag on your father's share of your businesses?"

Matt shrugged. "Then I can't buy them."

Charlie tapped his nose. "Ah, but I can. Then we are partners."

Gratitude swelled in Matt's chest, and he wasn't sure how to turn Charlie down without hurting his feelings. "I'm so grateful to you, Charlie. You've taught me so much in the last few months, and I want us to continue to be great friends. I'd love your input on my projects, but as much as I truly appreciate the offer, I don't want your financial input."

Charlie was about to object when Matt continued.

"A wise man said to me recently, *Matthew, standing on your own two feet is the most important lesson a person can learn. It takes you from being a boy to being a man. It earns your respect from your peers but also yourself. Your achievements are even greater when it is your own hard work that has taken you to that point.*"

Charlie shook his head. "That wise man needs to learn to shut his mouth occasionally. Feel free to ignore him."

Matt laughed. "I hang off every word of yours, Charlie, because I believe every word. Once again, thank you for the offer, but I will decline. Another wise person constantly tells me that life will work out as it's meant to. I'll put my trust in both of you and move forward as I am supposed to."

Charlie smiled. "I am proud of you, Matthew, very proud indeed. But I do not like injustice, and when it is in my life, I feel a duty to fix it. It might not be by investing in your businesses, but it will be some other way. You mark my words. We will fix this situation."

---

10

*C*harlie sipped his coffee and looked out from the pavilion at Irresistibles over Lake Hopeful. He sighed, wishing he'd been able to help Matthew more. He knew deep in his heart that Matthew was telling the truth about Jenna's Brad. He'd known it from the moment Matt threw the punch that ruined the wedding. He couldn't say how he knew, other than he did. Ying Yue, his late wife, said he was an owl in a past life. That the spirit of the owl was still within him, meaning he could see beyond the illusions the mind creates. He wasn't sure if he believed that, but he did trust his gut.

"You look deep in thought," Asha said, placing a plate with Charlie's favorite chocolate fudge muffin in front of him.

Charlie nodded. Asha was the last person he could confide in.

"Anything I can help with?"

"No, you would not like where my thoughts are today."

Asha raised an eyebrow. "That sounds ominous."

Charlie smiled, realizing she was thinking along a different line than he was. "Nothing to do with women," he said. "I have a friend who is in trouble and who I would like to help, but I can't think of a way to do this."

Asha pulled out the chair next to Charlie and sat down. "Is your friend in financial trouble?"

Charlie shook his head. "No, it is a case of being accused of doing something she didn't do." Charlie glanced sideways at Asha, hoping the use of the pronoun "she" would hide who he was talking about.

"That's awful," Asha said. "Does the person accusing her have proof of what she did?"

Charlie nodded. "It is complicated. My friend did something that many people witnessed, but when she explained why she did it, no one believed her. They thought it was for selfish reasons when she was trying to help and protect someone she cares for."

Asha frowned. "That is complicated. If she's given her word, do they not trust her?"

Charlie shook her head. "No, she's lied before, so they feel she could be lying again."

Asha laughed. "Sounds like Matt. No one would ever believe him."

"Yes, there are similarities between young Matthew and my friend. There is, however, one person who could prove that my friend is telling the truth. I am trying to find a way to locate him."

"What do you know about him?"

"Nothing," Charlie said. "I know he attended an event. He left the event in a hurry."

"In his own car?"

"No, via taxi."

Asha stood. "Sorry, there's a line forming at the food truck, so I'd better get back. But Charlie, if he left the event in a taxi, call the taxi company, they might be able to help out. If you know where the event was and the time he left, they will know where he went."

Charlie's eyes widened. "You are very clever, Asha." His excitement died as quickly as it rose. "But privacy act. They won't tell me anything, will they?"

"Probably not. Tell them your friend left something in the taxi, and you were hoping to speak to the taxi driver or something like that."

"How would that help?"

"If you can speak to the taxi driver you might be able to offer him compensation to drive you to the same location where he dropped your friend off. It's only an idea, but you never know."

"Bribe the taxi driver?"

Asha nodded and a wide smile formed on Charlie's lips as Asha hurried over to the food truck to help serve.

Jenna was sitting at a table at Irresistibles working on a proposal for Susan when Charlie stopped by her table. She'd been tempted to work out of the Sandstone Cafe but had decided, in light of the work Susan was having her do, that it was inappropriate to be sitting in Matt's premises plotting against him. Not that she considered it to be plotting. As Susan had said, it was purely business, and the most likely scenario was that she would allow Matt to buy her out of each of the projects.

"Jenna," Charlie said. "I have a favor to ask you. A very big favor, so I will understand if you say no."

Jenna closed her laptop and invited Charlie to sit down. "What can I do to help?"

Charlie looked around the cafe as if checking to see if anyone was listening. He lowered his voice to a whisper. "I need to go to the city tomorrow for an appointment. An appointment I don't want anyone to know about. I know from the kindness you showed Matthew when his father died that you are the type of person I can ask to help with this."

Jenna's heart swelled. "What time would you like to leave?"

"Early. Six o'clock, if it isn't too much trouble."

"I'll pick you up from your house at six," Jenna said. She reached across the table and took the old man's hand. "Are you okay? It's not about your health, is it?"

Charlie squeezed her hand. "I will tell you more tomorrow. It's not specifically to do with my health, but the outcome could be beneficial for my long-term outlook."

Jenna smiled. "I'm intrigued, that's for sure, and yes, I'll take you. I'm flattered to be asked." And she was. She hadn't had much to do with Charlie since returning to Hope's Ridge and was surprised he'd asked her. She would need to let Susan know she wouldn't be available for their eleven o'clock video chat, but otherwise, she should be able to shift her day around.

Charlie let go of her hand and stood. "You make me happy, Jenna. I see a bright future, including a man who is going to love you and never let you down or break your heart."

Jenna felt herself blush. "I hope you're right, Charlie. I really do."

Charlie tapped his nose. "It will happen sooner than you think, and when it does, you will at first be surprised, and then you will realize that the feelings you have for this person have been with you for a lot longer than you've allowed yourself to admit."

"Now I'm intrigued. Is it someone I already know?"

"I did not say that. But now I must go. I will be waiting at six."

Jenna reopened her computer as the older man left the table, wondering if he possessed intuition or whether he was saying what he thought she might want to hear. She quickly typed a message to Susan, asking if they could postpone their meeting, and then continued on with the report. Regardless of whether Charlie's predictions came true or not, it was nice to think it was a possibility. It was also a relief to realize at least two days had passed since she'd last thought of Brad.

Jenna pulled up in front of Charlie's sandstone-fronted house a few minutes before six. Charlie was, as she'd expected, waiting by his front gate. She imagined he'd been there for at least twenty minutes and wished she'd come earlier.

She got out of the car and went to open the passenger side for him. "I could have come earlier, Charlie, you should have said."

"No, six is more than early enough, Jenna," Charlie said, climbing into the passenger seat. "In my ninety-seven years,

I am always early. Now, let's go. We have important business to attend to."

Jenna pulled away from the curb and drove toward the road that led out of Hope's Ridge toward the highway. "I thought you were only ninety-six."

"I had a birthday last week."

"I'm sorry. If I'd known, I would have thrown a party. Did anyone know?"

Charlie shook his head. "Only Ying Yue, and I'm sure she celebrated for me in heaven. She was big on birthdays."

"You must miss her," Jenna said.

"Every day there is something I think of and go to tell her and am reminded again that she is no longer with me. Every day I am crushed with that grief. Only for a second, but enough to remind me that I am human, and I am flawed."

Jenna looked across to Charlie. "You believe you are flawed because you're human?"

Charlie nodded. "Yes, all humans are flawed. We make terrible mistakes and often do not have the courage to correct them."

"I can't imagine you've made too many terrible mistakes, Charlie."

"I have had a long life, Jenna. Many mistakes have been made. I am hoping that today a mistake will be corrected. Not one that I made this time, but one made by a friend."

"Is that what we're going to do in the city?"

"Possibly. Now, I am tired and must sleep." He handed her a piece of paper. "Here is the address. Please wake me five minutes from arrival."

Jenna had to bite the inside of her cheek not to laugh. She was his taxi driver. She glanced at him as he closed his eyes and leaned his seat back. His face was wrinkled and aged, but he certainly didn't look ninety-seven. She wished she'd known it was his birthday. She'd talk to Asha when they returned and suggest a belated celebration at Irresistibles. As much as she was avoiding him, she imagined Matt would want to celebrate with Charlie too.

Her thoughts wandered from Matt to Susan as she drove up over the ridge and joined the highway. She'd been surprised to wake to a rather curt email saying the eleven o'clock meeting was important, and she would appreciate Jenna rescheduling whatever had come up. Jenna had stared at the message for five minutes before responding. The eleven o'clock meeting wasn't important, but Jenna was beginning to see a side of Susan she didn't like. The easy-going woman she'd first met now appeared self-absorbed and controlling. Jenna wasn't interested in working for anyone who talked down to her or expected her to jump through hoops because she was being paid. She'd emailed Susan back an equally curt response saying she would be unavailable until late afternoon. She'd already decided she would avoid checking her email now until she was home again.

The drive went relatively quickly, with Charlie breathing quietly as he slept. Five minutes before their arrival time, Jenna nudged him gently. "We're nearly there."

Charlie opened his eyes and looked around. "Good, very good."

"Are you going to tell me why we're here?"

"No. The only thing I ask of you is that you trust me and that you listen carefully to everything that is said."

"Did you need me to take notes?"

"No, that won't be necessary. What is important is that

you come in with me, and you do not leave until I am ready to go."

Jenna nodded. The way Charlie put it was rather strange, but she understood the underlying message. He needed her by his side, and that's where she would be.

———

Jenna pulled up outside the cute saltbox house Charlie's directions had led them to. Its long-pitched roof sloped down the back, with its central chimney providing a lovely focal point. While they were on the outskirts of the city, it wasn't the type of house Jenna had expected to see. She looked across to Charlie. "Is this the place?"

"Yes." He turned to face her. "I will be honest with you. I have done something that could make you angry, or it could make you happy. I am not completely sure which."

Jenna frowned. "This has to do with me? I thought it was to help a friend of yours."

"Yes, we are here to help a friend of mine, but I'm not sure if you will find it appropriate."

Jenna pushed open her car door. "We've driven all this way, and whether it's appropriate or not, I'm intrigued. I can't imagine anything you could do that would upset me, Charlie. If you do well, I'll deal with it."

"Very good," Charlie said and opened his car door. He stood for a minute when he got out. "My legs are a little stiff," he admitted. "It was a long time sitting."

Jenna moved toward him and took his arm. "Let me help you. You might need me to do this for you in twenty years, when you're one hundred and seventeen, so it's a good chance for some practice."

Charlie laughed. "You are sassy, Jenna Larsen, very sassy."

Jenna grinned.

They walked up the pretty flower-lined garden path and stopped outside the freshly painted blue door. Charlie drew in a deep breath.

"Ready?" Jenna asked.

Charlie nodded, lifted his hand, and rang the doorbell.

Jenna heard footsteps approaching the door. The door opened, and a tall woman in her early thirties with luscious red hair smiled nervously at Charlie.

"Hello, Charlie, come on in." She looked at Jenna, a strange expression crossing her features. "And you must be Jenna. Come into the living room. I have tea and cake ready. I know you've had a long drive."

"That is kind of you, my dear," Charlie said. "I do enjoy a slice of cake. Hopefully, we will have enough time to enjoy it."

"We're not in any hurry, Charlie," Jenna said. "We can take as long as you need."

Charlie and the woman exchanged a look. "We'll see," Charlie said.

Jenna followed them into the living room, realizing she still had no idea who this woman was. She hadn't even introduced herself. She was about to ask when Charlie pointed to a chair. "Sit, Jenna. There is a lot to discuss, and I do ask you to remember your promise. That you will stay until I am ready to go."

"Of course I will." She looked across to the other woman. "Do you know why we're here? Because I'm afraid Charlie's kept me completely in the dark. I don't even know your name."

The woman drew in a breath and wrung her visibly shaking hands together. "I do know why you're here. Charlie tracked me down yesterday and asked me to speak with you."

"With me?"

She nodded. "You and I have something in common."

"Do we? What?"

"Brad Campbell."

Jenna gripped the edge of the chair and looked at Charlie. "What is this? Brad's the last person I want to talk about."

"Me too," the woman said. "But I promised Charlie I would speak with you." The woman paused and broke eye contact with Jenna. She clasped her hands together, fidgeted in her seat. She took a deep breath before meeting Jenna's eyes. "I had a relationship with Brad."

"Okay, so we have that in common."

"I was seeing him when he was engaged to you, Jenna. My name's Nadia, and I only found out about your relationship with Brad when I arrived at your wedding, thinking I was Brad's date."

An ache pounded in Jenna's chest. *This* was Nadia. Her eyes flicked between Charlie and Nadia and back again. Why had she automatically assumed Nadia was the woman who worked with Brad? She was so stupid. Although Matt's description of the redheaded Nadia also matched the Nadia Brad worked with.

"I'm sorry to shock you," Charlie said, "but I needed to find a way to show you that Matt has not done anything to hurt you. He was standing up for you."

"How..." Jenna began and stopped. She took a deep breath and tried again. "How do I know this is for real. If I ask Brad, he'll deny having a relationship with you. How do I know this isn't Matt throwing his money around and paying you to say this?"

Charlie's face turned a deep shade of red. "Jenna, I assure you, I would never be part of a scheme like that."

"I'm sure you wouldn't, but we don't know Nadia, if that's even her name. Sorry," she added, realizing how rude she sounded. "Matt will go to any length to lie and cheat, and it wouldn't surprise me if this was one of his schemes." She turned her attention to Nadia. "My family runs the largest mill in our area, and my father is refusing to work with Matt. It's affecting his business, and I imagine he'd do anything to cheat his way back into our lives."

Nadia stood and crossed over to a bookshelf. She picked up a small box and handed it to Jenna. "Brad and I dated for two months. I printed all of the photos I had of us from my phone. They're in there."

Jenna opened the lid of the box and took out the pile of photos. She closed her eyes momentarily as Brad's smiling face looked back at her, his arm casually draped over Nadia's shoulders. She opened her eyes again and started flicking through the photos. She stopped at one taken on a beach. The sun was setting, and Brad and Nadia were lying together on a beach chair, looking like a happy couple in love. She held it up to Nadia. "When was this taken?"

"A month before your wedding," Nadia said. "We went to Cape May for the weekend."

The weekend Brad told her he was away on a team-building retreat for work.

Jenna put the photos back in the box and placed it on the coffee table. "I don't need to see anymore." She hung her head, not sure what to say or where to look. This was the final humiliation in her relationship with Brad.

"I'm sorry, Jenna," Nadia said. "I had no idea Brad was in a relationship and certainly didn't know it was your wedding when I turned up. He'd mentioned he had an ex called Jenna, but that was the only time I'd heard of you. I knew he was going to a wedding, and I wanted to surprise him and join him as his plus one."

Jenna looked up as Nadia shook her head.

"The surprise was on me, as it turned out. All I can say is thank goodness Matt saw me and stopped me before I completely humiliated myself."

Jenna gave a strangled laugh. "I guess that honor was left for me instead."

Nadia's hand flew to her mouth. "I'm so sorry. I wasn't thinking."

"I am sorry, too, Jenna," Charlie said. "I know this is hard for you to hear, but my loyalty lies with Matthew, and I did need to help clear his name."

Jenna nodded, doing her best to push an image of Matt's distraught face from her mind. She let out a low moan. "I've been so awful to him, and my family has too. His business is suffering because of us, and at a time when he needed our support."

"That can all be fixed," Charlie said. "For now, it is you that I'm worried about. Brad was not a good man."

"You can say that again," Nadia said.

Jenna locked eyes with her. "I'm sorry too that you had anything to do with him. I honestly had no idea he was seeing anyone else."

"He's an awful person," Nadia said and then blushed. "I

did something I'm not proud of, but I honestly couldn't believe he'd lied to me. I thought we had a future together."

"What did you do?" Jenna asked.

"I followed him," Nadia said. "He went out with two guys who I learned are his good friends. They went to Bradshaw's, a downtown club, and Brad was quick to pick up a woman and leave. Once he was gone, I spoke to his friends who'd had a few drinks by that time and were happy to fill me in. Apparently, he has four other women he sees on a casual basis. I asked why he was doing that if he was supposed to get married a few weeks earlier. One of the guys said Brad was securing his future with the wedding. That you were gorgeous and intelligent, so that would work in his favor when he had a work event or something he needed to look respectable at. He also suggested that a partnership was available with the realtor he works for, but only married employees would be considered since they are deemed more stable and committed. But the rest of the time, he intended to continue with his casual affairs, and in years to come, when you came into money, he'd have the finances to do whatever he wanted."

Jenna shook her head. "I can't believe the mill was part of his plan." She gave a little laugh. "No wonder he looked so shocked when I told him I wouldn't be inheriting any of it. It will go to my brother." She continued to shake her head. "I can't believe this."

Charlie passed her the plate with Nadia's cake on it. "Comfort food. It is good for this type of situation."

Jenna took a slice, not sure whether to laugh or cry. She decided on the former and let out a throaty chuckle. Charlie and Nadia looked at her as if she was crazy. "Sorry," she said. "It's so ridiculous. I thought I was good at reading men and working out those who were genuine versus those who were players."

"Definitely not," Charlie said in such a firm voice, both Jenna and Nadia stared at him.

"I'm sorry, Jenna, but your experiences with both Brad and Matthew prove my point. You are a terrible judge of character." He smiled and took a large bite of his cake.

Jenna shared a look with Nadia. Charlie was a straight shooter, that was for sure.

"What I don't understand is how you found Nadia, Charlie."

Charlie finished his mouthful and brushed crumbs from the sides of his mouth. "Delicious. It was Asha who helped me find Nadia."

"Asha? But she didn't believe Matt." Jenna was confused. Why hadn't Asha spoken to her if she believed Matt was innocent?

"No, she didn't. She spoke scathingly of him. But when I mentioned I was trying to track someone down, she gave me the idea of finding the taxi driver who drove Nadia away from the wedding and speaking to them."

"And you did that?"

Charlie nodded. "Asha was right that bribery goes a long way. The taxi driver was happy to drive me to Nadia's door for the right fee."

"He paid eight hundred dollars," Nadia said. "Matt must be pretty special."

"He is," Charlie said. "And eight hundred dollars is nothing in the scheme of everything." Charlie finished his tea and rubbed his hands together. "A most successful morning." Using the arm of his chair, he pushed himself to standing. "Thank you for your time and hospitality,

Nadia, but now Jenna and I need to start the journey home."

Jenna stood, realizing she'd hardly touched her cake or tea. It appeared they were on a schedule.

She turned to face Nadia when they reached the front door. Impulsively she leaned forward and gave her a quick hug. "Thank you for allowing Charlie to bring me here today, and I'm sorry either of us has had to go through this."

Nadia squeezed her back. "I'm sorry too, Jenna. And no need to thank me, it's Charlie who you should thank. I'm not sure too many people would go to this effort, let alone a man his nineties. Matthew is obviously important and worth the effort."

Jenna didn't respond. She wasn't sure what to think about Matt right now. The only thing she knew for certain was she owed him a huge apology.

———

A sense of calm settled over Matt, as it always did when he spent time at the wellness retreat. Even with the multitude of worries he was carrying, spending time at the retreat energized him. He hoped the incredible energy Steph had created would be felt and noticed by others as Holly's became operational.

As calm as he felt, it didn't stop a thought going around in his head. "I'm worried about Charlie," he said as he and Steph walked through the near-complete resort rooms at Holly's. Other than some minor electrical work, the rooms were almost ready to be furnished.

Steph stopped walking and turned to Matt; her eyes filled with concern. "What's wrong with him?"

"I'm not sure," Matt said. "It's not about his health. He's been acting strangely this last week. He seems jittery. If I didn't know better, I'd say he was hiding something. I hope he hasn't got himself into any trouble."

"He'd tell you, wouldn't he?"

"I'd like to think he would," Matt said, "but he's the sort of man who would probably want to save face at any cost. I'm not sure how much he would reveal."

They continued walking past the main entrance and up to the raised boardwalk that connected the buildings with the yoga studio and pool area. The steel coping had been fitted to the pool's walls the day before, and the concrete would be poured the next day. "It's coming along, Matt." The excitement in Steph's voice was impossible to miss. Matt only wished he could share her feelings.

"Everything okay?"

Matt nodded. "A few things on my mind, that's all." He didn't have the courage to discuss his finances with Steph. Of all of the projects that he might be forced to walk away from, Holly's was going to hurt the most. It was personal. The wellness retreat meant so much to him and to Buster and Steph. It was special to all of them for different reasons.

"Are you going to speak to Charlie?" Steph asked as they reached the entrance to the yoga studio and office they'd created.

Matt nodded. "I am. I called him earlier, but he said he was coming back from the city." He glanced at his watch. "He asked me to go to his house in about half an hour. He said he needs to speak to me, so perhaps he's going to tell me what's going on. I hope he's okay. As I said, I don't think it's his health, but I don't know for sure. I don't think I could handle any more loss right now."

Steph squeezed his arm. "Let me make you a cup of peppermint tea. Help you gather your thoughts before you see him. My gut says Charlie's going to live forever, so there's probably nothing to worry about."

Matt smiled. "Let's hope your gut's right."

Charlie's front curtain flapped as Matt pulled into the driveway and cut the engine on the pickup. He was tempted to laugh that the older man would be watching for him, but he didn't as Charlie prided himself on living in the moment. Peeking out of windows waiting for Matt wasn't in his style.

Matt hurried up the cobbled pathway to Charlie's front door and knocked. He heard Charlie's shuffling footsteps, and then the door opened.

"Matthew, come in."

Matt was pleased to see that the shiftiness Charlie had displayed earlier in the week was gone. His beaming smile was fixed firmly on his face, and everything seemed back to normal.

"I have peppermint tea and muffins for us to share," Charlie said. "I would take credit for baking them, but I know you'll recognize them, so I won't even consider lying. Asha was pleased to provide them."

"Then she obviously didn't know I was your guest today. She's still angry with me." He sighed, sitting down at the dining table situated off the modern kitchen. A teapot, three cups, and three muffins sat in the middle of the table. Was Charlie expecting someone else?

"I think that will change, Matthew. I spoke with Asha

this morning. She seemed open to believing that you are the good person I know you to be."

Tears filled Matt's eyes, causing Charlie to hurry to his side.

"Oh Matthew, I'm sorry. I've upset you?"

Matt shook his head and wiped his eyes. "Sorry. You're so nice to me, Charlie. I don't deserve your kindness." He gave a small laugh. "I think I'm very tired. I haven't been sleeping well, and on the one hand, I'm missing and grieving Dad, but on the other, I'm finding it hard to forgive him for the situation he left me in. Not that I can blame him completely. If the situation with Jenna and the Larsens hadn't happened, things might not be quite as bad as they currently are."

"You have had a hard time, Matthew, and I am sorry about that."

"No need to be," Matt said. "A wise woman recently told me that she hoped karma would come back and bite me one day and that I deserved every horrible thing that could possibly happen to me. I think that karma has finally come knocking on my door."

"No, it hasn't."

Matt swiveled in his seat; his face practically aflame with embarrassment as Jenna walked into the dining area. He glanced at Charlie. "Why didn't you tell me Jenna was here." Had she heard all that he'd said?

Charlie stood. "You did not ask, Matthew." He winked. "I am not a mind reader. There are three plates, three cups. Who did you think would be here? But for now, I must get on. I will return soon."

Matt stood. "I should go too." He was beyond embarrassed.

Jenna placed a hand on his arm. "No, please stay. We need to talk."

Matt sat back down. The softness in Jenna's face and eyes was unsettling. She was easier to read when she was angry with him.

Jenna sat next to him. "I'm here to apologize."

Matt raised an eyebrow. "For what?"

"For everything. For not believing you when you told me about Brad. For turning the town against you when you punched him at the wedding and for being so horrible to you."

"Okay," Matt said, waiting for the *but*. "I appreciate the apology. I'm not sure where it's coming from, but it's appreciated."

"It's coming from me having learned the truth this morning. Charlie tracked down Nadia, the one you saw Brad with."

"She works with him, doesn't she?"

"No. But the Nadia I saw today looks very similar. Tall, wavy red hair, flawless skin. There were a lot of similarities between them."

Matt's eyes widened. "How did Charlie track her down?"

"A big bribe to a taxi driver. The one who took her from the wedding. Anyway, I met her this morning and learned all about her relationship with Brad." Her cheeks colored. "I can't believe I was such a poor judge of character."

"He was a pretty experienced cheat. I wouldn't beat myself up too much. Just be more careful in the future." Matt smiled as a wave of relief settled over him. "You've got no idea how relieved I am that you know I wasn't trying to sabotage anything. You're my friend, Jenna. I was looking out for you."

Jenna nodded. "Which is why I feel so bad. I'll tell the town, and Dad. I'm sure he'll offer to do business with you again, although we'll understand if you want nothing to do with us after the way we treated you."

Matt laughed. "If Roy's willing to supply my projects, I won't argue. Sourcing material from Tall Oaks is a nightmare."

"I am sorry, Matt. I don't know how I'll ever make this up to you."

Butterflies flitted in Matt's stomach. He stood and put his hand out to Jenna, pulling her to her feet. "There's something I need to say."

Jenna stood, and they faced each other.

"I'm going to be completely honest with you. When I found out Brad was cheating, I was angry, but I was also relieved. I couldn't believe someone as wonderful as you would marry a guy like that. It made me look at my life and what must be wrong with me if a guy like that can get a girl like you when I haven't had a girlfriend that's lasted beyond a few dates."

"It doesn't say a lot for me that I'd fall for someone like that."

Matt shrugged. "As I said, he had plenty of experience cheating people. Smashing him in the face was one of the most satisfying things I've ever done. But I do still owe you an apology because there was part of me that wanted to see your relationship with him fail, even if he hadn't done anything wrong."

Jenna's eyebrows drew together in confusion. "You

would have punched him anyway? Even if he hadn't cheated?"

"Definitely not. I would have wanted to, but I wouldn't have acted on it. I've always known you were way out of my league, Jen. It's why I've never asked you out. I knew you'd laugh at me and make me feel like an idiot. So, while I've never had any false idea that we'd get together, it was satisfying to know you wouldn't be with him either."

Jenna's mouth dropped open in surprise. "I would never have laughed at you. And regardless of whether you were jealous or envious, I'm still grateful for what you did. I need you to know how sorry I am. I will make this up to you, I promise."

Matt stepped forward, closing the distance between them. "There's only one thing I want from you, and not as forgiveness or because you think you need to make something up to me. I would want it only if you want it too. I don't imagine you'd be ready right now, but if or when you ever are, I'll be here waiting." He drew her to him and kissed her lightly on the lips.

Jenna froze as Matt's lips met hers. If she'd imagined any reaction to her apology, this was not the one.

He pulled away, apprehension filling his eyes. "Sorry, I know that's out of left field. I'm not even sure that I realized until now how much I've wanted to do that."

Jenna would be lying if she said she felt nothing. The tingles that had run through her body at Matt's touch surprised her. "I..." She was lost for words.

Matt stepped back and ran a hand through his hair. "I

can't believe I did that. We've just reached a place where we can be friends and be normal again, and I go and ruin it."

Jenna stepped toward him. "You haven't ruined anything. You took me by surprise. I came here today expecting you to be angry with me for not believing you in the first place. Your reaction was far from that."

"Phew." Matt wiped his forehead, exaggerating his relief.

"But the kiss, Matt."

Matt's smile fell. "I know, I'm sorry."

Jenna reached for him. "Don't be sorry." She tilted her head up, her entire body on fire as Matt's lips met hers. This time the kiss was longer, filled with a passion Jenna hadn't expected. When they pulled apart, it was Matt whose expression was one of surprise.

"I wasn't expecting that."

"I was!"

They both turned as Charlie moved toward them, a beaming smile on his face. "And it's about time. All the pent-up aggression you two have felt for each other can finally be put to good use."

Jenna was sure her face was burning as brightly as Matt's red cheeks were.

"We have you to thank, Charlie," Matt said.

Charlie rubbed his hands together. "No, the universe is who you thank. Things have a way of working out."

Matt laughed. "You sound like Steph."

"A wise woman, that Stephanie Jones. Very wise indeed. You are surrounding yourself with good people, Matthew. Steph, myself, and now Jenna. An A-team, as some would say. Now, it is time to celebrate. Shall we have tea or champagne?"

Jenna looked to Matt. She wasn't sure what had happened or what was happening next. Charlie moved next to her and took her arm. "Live in the moment, Jenna. What comes next will unfold as it should. You do not need to worry or be concerned. You need to enjoy this moment."

A sense of calm settled over Jenna at Charlie's words. He was right. She didn't need to know right now what came next. The entire day had been completely unexpected, so she needed to go with it. She smiled at Charlie before shifting her focus to Matt. His eyes drank her in. They were so full of hope and happiness. Why had she never seen this before?

Her phone pinged with a text as Charlie made the decision to open the champagne.

She slipped the phone from her bag and glanced at the screen. Guilt instantly enveloped her. It was Susan Lewis. She wanted to hang her head in shame. She'd been working with Susan behind Matt's back, thinking he deserved everything he got, and now he was likely to lose everything he'd worked so hard for.

She stood. "Sorry, I'm going to have to go."

Concern flashed across Matt's face. "Is everything okay? Can I drive you or do anything to help?"

Jenna forced a smile. "No, something I need to take care of, and it can't wait. I'm sorry."

Matt stood, but Jenna waved him back down. "Sit and enjoy a drink with Charlie. He needs to be thanked for finding Nadia and everything he's done. Let's talk later, okay?"

Matt nodded as Jenna gave Charlie a quick hug and hurried down the hallway and out the front door.

11

*M*att whistled to himself as he pulled into the parking lot of Holly's. He couldn't believe how the day was working out. *Jenna had kissed him!* His grin was wide as he pushed open the door of the pickup.

He stopped as Steph walked from the yoga studio with two men in suits, one of them Andy Farley, the town's realtor, next to her. He frowned. What was Andy doing here?

Andy smiled as the small group reached Matt. He put out his hand. "Matthew, so great to see you."

Matt shook his hand, his eyes traveling to the other man.

"This is Dwight Langdon," Andy said, introducing them.

Matt nodded, his eyes meeting Steph's momentarily. She looked wary and upset.

"You've got a fantastic place here," Dwight said. "It's blown me away, as has Steph and the entire setup. I'd love to be part of it."

"Um, okay," Matt said. "Sorry, I'm not completely sure

under what guise you're being shown around? We're not looking for investors at this stage." Steph's sigh of relief was audible.

Andy's forehead crumpled into a frown. "I was under the impression that a percentage of the business was coming on the market soon. Dwight's a friend of mine who is looking for an opportunity like this, which is why I've shown it to him early."

Matt looked to Steph. "Buster's not thinking of selling, is he?"

"Definitely not," Steph said.

"Then some wires have been crossed somewhere," Matt said. "Sorry, Andy, the center hasn't even opened yet. It's definitely not being sold."

"Matt, Susan Lewis's assistant, contacted me last week. She said Susan has a controlling interest in the business and is planning to sell it."

"If she does, I'll buy her out," Matt said.

"I think you need to speak with her," Andy said. "She was adamant that it was being sold, and you would not be in a position to buy it."

Anger boiled inside of Matt. "She had no right to discuss this with you. My father's estate isn't even settled yet, and nothing has been worked out."

"What about the Sandstone Cafe and Sandstone Apartments?" Andy asked. "I've got prospective buyers lined up to look at both of them over the next couple of days, and I believe Ms. Lewis has her assistant dealing directly with one at five o'clock today."

Matt shook his head. "I can't believe this. My father's been dead for less than a month and she's trying to gain from it. Andy, until the will is finalized, and Susan and I have negotiated an agreement with regards to the properties, they're not available. Don't discuss them with anyone. Okay?"

Andy nodded. "I'm sorry, Matt, but Susan's assistant was convincing when she spoke to me. She said you knew about selling the properties and were supportive of your father's decision to move his investments from Hope's Ridge. She made it clear that you were not in a position to buy Susan out, and therefore she'd be selling to the highest bidder. To be fair, the market is strong, and I was assured that the prices of the business would be outside your reach."

Matt pushed a hand through his hair and did his best to take a deep breath. If Andy didn't stop, he was likely to lose it with him. It wasn't Andy's fault, he knew that, but it didn't make this moment any easier.

"Andy," Steph said. "How about Matt or Buster calls you in a day or two to confirm what's happening. You've blind-sided Matt, and I imagine he needs to speak to Susan Lewis."

Andy clapped Matt on the back. "Sorry, buddy. If I receive instructions from Ms. Lewis or her assistant regarding any of your other properties, I'll call you."

Matt released the breath he'd been holding and did his best to force a smile. "Thanks, Andy. I appreciate it." He turned to the other man. "Sorry that your time's been wasted today."

"Not a waste. I'm definitely interested if and when the time arises that you're looking to sell. If it's meant to be, it'll happen."

Matt moved next to Steph as the two men got into Andy's car, and the engine started.

Steph waited until the car had pulled out of the parking lot before turning to Matt. "You'd think Susan's priority would be developing a relationship with you rather than rushing to sell your father's investments."

"It's definitely not high on her list of priorities," Matt said. "I guess I'd better make an appointment to speak to the bank and see what my position is. I actually came to discuss the staffing issues with you for when we're up and running, but I think a visit to the bank and a chat with Susan take priority. Until the will is finalized, she needs to stop. Right now, she has no ownership of any of these properties."

"Okay," Steph said. "Let me know how it goes." She smiled. "It's never smooth sailing with you, is it, Matt? All the problems with Jenna and then the mill not supplying, and now this."

Matt took his car keys from his pocket and twirled them around his finger, unable to hide his grin.

Steph raised her eyebrows. "What?"

"Let's say that one of my problems has been resolved today. I think the mill will start supplying again."

"That's fantastic!"

"It is." He glanced at his watch. "It's three o'clock already. I might make the calls to the bank and Susan from the cafe and grab a bite to eat. Then I can intercept this assistant of Susan's and the prospective buyer and make it clear that the cafe and apartments are not for sale." He stepped toward his pickup, realizing how erratic his mood was. When he thought of Jenna, a weight lifted from him and happiness filled his chest, but the next second he had Susan Lewis and his business to worry about. He needed to fix all of this so he could concentrate on Jenna.

Jenna hurried from Charlie's house, dread filling the pit of her stomach. What was Matt going to think when he learned she'd been working for Susan? Not only working for her but privy to the information that showed the major impact Susan's plans would have on Matt's businesses, possibly even ruining him.

She climbed into the Jeep and slammed her hands down on the steering wheel. For weeks she'd been telling anyone who'd listen what an awful person Matt was, and it turned out *she* was the awful person. Matt had leaped to her defense when he learned what Brad was up to. He'd tried to tell her and her family what was happening, and then he'd taken it into his own hands on her wedding day. Yet Jenna, when being made aware of Susan's plans, had, for the most part, felt satisfaction that Matt would get what he deserved. She shook her head as she started the vehicle. She was an awful person.

Minutes later, she pulled into the driveway of her parents' house, flung open the driver's door, and hurried up the garden path. She'd make the call to Susan from her room.

Her father stepped out of the kitchen as she closed the front door behind her.

Jenna stopped. "Shouldn't you be at the mill?"

Roy nodded. "About to head back. I decided to come home for lunch today, that's all." He grinned. "I could smell your mother's leftover lasagna from the mill."

Jenna managed a small smile. "That's great. I have to make a call, but then I need to talk to you. Will you be here much longer?"

Roy glanced at his watch. "About five minutes, but I can wait if you like."

"That would be great, thanks," Jenna said before hurrying up the stairs. She sat down at the small desk she'd set up and took out her notebook computer. Susan wanted to meet with her today, so hopefully, she'd be available.

"Jenna, finally!" Susan's face appeared on the screen moments after Jenna placed the video call. "I needed you earlier this morning. I was hoping you'd be able to go to a meeting at the wellness retreat this afternoon. The realtor was showing someone around."

Jenna's heart raced. "But you don't own any of the property yet. Don't you need to run that by Matt and Buster?"

"No, I don't. The moment the will's settled, I'll be selling my shares. You've seen the figures. I'd be crazy not to."

"Possibly," Jenna said, "but don't you think telling Matt first would be courteous? I'm worried that the way you're approaching this could cause problems with him."

Susan laughed. "You're the last person I thought would care about Matt. With everything he's done to you, I thought you'd like to see him crucified."

"But what about you?" Jenna said, deciding not to correct Susan. "He hasn't done anything to hurt you, and he's your family."

Susan snorted. "Family that I learned about thirty years later. A father that didn't contribute one cent to my life. They owe me, Jenna, and they'll pay."

Jenna's gut twisted as she listened to the venom in Susan's voice. It appeared her true colors were beginning to show. She was out for revenge.

"Enough about Matt," Susan continued. "I have an

investor interested in looking around the Sandstone Cafe at five. Can you show her around?"

Jenna shook her head.

"What now?" Susan demanded. "It's bad enough you weren't there for the wellness retreat, Jenna. I employed you for a reason. I can't be on the ground in Hope's Ridge every day, so I need to know I can rely on you. If I can't, then say the word, and I'll find someone else."

Jenna bit her tongue to stop a scathing remark from whipping out. Susan's threatening tone was truly awful. It certainly reminded Jenna of the few times she'd seen Walter Law address the town when she was a teenager. He hadn't been someone she remembered being particularly nice.

"Well?" Susan demanded.

"I think," Jenna said, "that would be a good idea."

"Good. The investor's name is Sally Davido. Make sure you're there before five and—"

"No," Jenna interrupted. "I meant it would be a good idea if you found someone else to work for you. I'm not interested in destroying Matt's businesses or bringing strangers into the town to replace him."

Susan laughed. "It's not an option, Jenna. You can leave, sure, but you signed a contract that says you must give two weeks' notice, and I expect you to work those two weeks."

"I'd prefer to stop now, Susan. You don't have to pay me for the last week if that makes it easier for you."

"No, it doesn't. I need you at the cafe at five, and you need to remember the nondisclosure agreement you signed. If you mention anything to Matt about what I'm doing, I won't hesitate to contact my lawyer."

Jenna swallowed. How did she handle this? Susan was

right. There was a contract in place, but would Susan go to these lengths to enforce it?

"Don't even consider testing me, Jenna," Susan said. "You made a commitment, and you'll see it through, or you'll be sorry. Call me after the five o'clock meeting." The line went dead.

"Everything okay?"

Jenna jolted around at the sound of her father's voice. She shook her head, waves of shock crashing over her. She knew Susan was uncompromising, but that was a reaction she hadn't anticipated.

Roy stepped into the bedroom. "Anything I can help with?"

Jenna took a deep breath. "I hope so, Dad, I really do."

Roy sat down on the bed as Jenna began to talk. He didn't speak until she finished.

"We owe Matt Law a huge apology."

Jenna nodded, tears filling her eyes. "I've already spoken to him about what he tried to do to help me with Brad. I apologized and thanked him."

"That's a good start," Roy said. "I'll go find him and talk to him as soon as you and I have finished." His eyes flashed with anger. "And then I've got a good mind to go find Brad and let him know what I think of him."

"Don't," Jenna said. "He's not worth it. We're better off concentrating on fixing the situation on this end. I don't know what I'm going to do about Susan. I can't continue to work for her. But she's threatening legal action if I don't. I'd hate for Matt to hear that I'm helping her ruin his business."

"Did you know that that was what she was doing?"

"I knew she was going to try to sell the businesses for a

lot more than Matt would ever be able to afford, but it's only now that she made it pretty clear she's looking for some kind of twisted revenge. It's hardly Matt's fault that his father had another child and didn't support her."

"I thought he didn't even know about her until recently."

"That's what Matt was led to believe," Jenna said.

"I think you need to talk to Matt," Roy said. "It's likely he'll find out you've been working for Susan, even if you stop now. It's best he hears it from you. But I do think you'll have to work your two weeks. A contract is a contract, and if she chooses to seek legal action, it could cost you a fortune."

Jenna sighed. "You're right."

"Perhaps look for opportunities to help Matt and his business over these two weeks," Roy said. "There might be something that can be done to help him." He frowned.

"What?" Jenna asked.

"Matt's shown interest in investing in the mill before," Roy said. "Perhaps we reverse the idea."

"I'm confused," Jenna admitted. "I have no idea what you're talking about."

"Imagine if Susan did sell off her percentage ownership of the businesses and we bought them. The mill has a surplus that could definitely be invested."

Jenna's mouth dropped open. "You'd seriously consider doing that?"

Roy rubbed his chin. "We've questioned Matt's integrity. Not only that, but I've stopped supplying his businesses, and I've made that public knowledge around town. We had the town boycott his businesses too. When I say it out loud, I can't believe I did that." He shook his head. "And I can't believe Matt defended your honor to the extent he did. I have a lot to thank him for. We obviously misjudged him."

Jenna nodded. "We did, and you're right. I need to speak to him." She glanced at her watch. It was already four-thirty. "I'd better go and see this investor first, and then I'll track down Matt."

Roy pushed off the bed and stood. "And in the interim, I'll see if I can find Matt and right things in terms of the mill. I'll tell him that you'll come and find him later."

"Thanks." Jenna stopped. "But Dad, don't mention the investment idea yet. Matt's not aware of what Susan's up to with regards to selling off the businesses. I'll have to work out a way for him to find out without me breaching my nondisclosure agreement." Jenna leaned forward and gave her father a quick hug before pulling away and hurrying downstairs and out of the front door.

Matt set himself up at a quiet table toward the back of the cafe. It was next to one of the huge bay windows that provided sweeping views of the lake. Margie brought him a cup of coffee and placed it on the table next to him.

"Would you like anything to eat?" she asked. "I've got one of those peach cobblers you love in the oven."

Matt groaned and patted his stomach. "I'm not sure that I should. I've been eating far too many treats since you arrived in Hope's Ridge."

Margie grinned. "I'll take that as, yes, you'd love a piece."

Matt smiled. "A small piece, thanks, Margie." He took his phone from his pocket as she retreated to the counter and scrolled through his contacts until he found Susan's number. He pressed the call button, anger rising in him as he thought back to the situation at Holly's. It was one thing to explore her options. It was another to have investors already looking at his businesses. She hadn't even given him the opportunity to buy out his father's shares.

"Matt," Susan's voice was friendly and enthusiastic, throwing Matt. He wasn't sure what he'd expected, but as he was ready to rip through her, he wasn't anticipating such a welcoming reception. "How have you been?"

"I've been better if I'm honest."

"Oh? Anything I can do to help?"

Matt cleared his throat. "We need to meet and discuss Dad's shares in my businesses."

"My shares, you mean."

"No, Dad's. Probate will take months with regards to the will. Dad's only been gone for a month. You need to back off until it's settled."

"No, I don't. The investments are jointly owned, and Walter's will is quite specific in that I, as his daughter and heir, am to receive his assets. They don't need to go through probate. I spoke to Zeek Potts last week, and now that he has the death certificate, there are only a few documents to complete before the transfers are made."

"The investments are jointly owned with me," Matt said, "which means they should come directly to me."

"Not with the way the will was left," Susan said. "You could contest it, which would slow the process down. But you and I both know that it's what Walter wanted. I can't stop you from disregarding his wishes, Matt. You need to do whatever you feel is right for you."

Matt struggled to get his head around what Susan was

saying. Why hadn't Zeek contacted him if that was the case? He would call him next. He cleared his throat. "Regardless of the situation, you should be speaking with me. Don't you realize the impact it could have if you sell your ownership? These are people I'll have to deal with who will have an influence over the day-to-day running of my businesses. I'd like the first option to buy you out and thought you understood that."

"That's fine, but an evaluation needs to be done to value the businesses."

"Which I'm happy to arrange for. Andy Farley, the realtor in town, can do that for us."

"I prefer to use the market, Matt. It's the best way for me to get a real feel for what the businesses are worth because it's what someone's willing to pay."

"So the guy looking around the wellness retreat today was being used to get a feel for the market? You weren't seriously considering selling to him?"

Susan gave a little laugh. "I'm serious in selling, Matt. If he's in a position to offer a figure above anything you can afford, then I'll sell. The same with the cafe, apartments, and the properties in Drayson's Landing. Look, it's not personal. It's business." She laughed again. "From what I've heard about how you do business, I'm not doing anything you wouldn't if the situation was reversed. You're quite ruthless, from what I understand."

"But this *is* personal. We're related. Doesn't that mean anything to you? Don't you want to get to know each other, become family?"

"Sure, if that's something you want to do. But I see that as a completely separate issue."

"You're going to ruin my businesses and then expect me

to want to have a relationship with you?"

Susan sighed. "I'm not ruining anything, Matt. The situation has changed. Your father had a large ownership in your businesses. A controlling ownership in most, yet he acted like a silent partner for the most part and has let you run them. If I didn't sell and I kept them, then I wouldn't allow that. I'd want to be involved, and I'd want a say in how the businesses were run. Look, you might be lucky and have an investor buy in who wants dividends and doesn't want to be involved. We won't know until we explore further. Now, sorry, but I have a meeting and have to go. I'll have some pricing information collated within the next week to get a feel for the value of the businesses. That's the point at which we should sit down and look at whether you're in a position to buy me out."

The call ended, and Matt found himself staring out of the window, trying to process what she'd said. He needed to speak to Zeek, that much he knew, and he needed to find out whether she could do what she was doing.

"Cobbler," Margie said, breaking into his thoughts and placing a plate in front of him.

Matt's stomach churned as he looked at it. It was bad if he thought he couldn't stomach peach cobbler.

"Are you okay?"

Matt did his best to smile. "Few issues regarding my father's estate. I need to speak to his lawyer and see if I can get them resolved."

"If there's anything I can do, let me know." Margie turned to retreat to the service counter.

"There is one thing," Matt called, stopping her. "You met Susan, my dad's daughter." He cleared his throat. "My half-sister. Didn't you?"

Margie nodded. "I did. She seemed nice."

"I'm beginning to wonder about that," Matt said. "Although, that's not what I wanted to ask. She's employed an assistant in Hope's Ridge to do some work for her. Someone who's going to be coming in any minute to the cafe to show someone around. I want to speak to both of these people, but I don't know who they are." He planned to do more than speak to them. He intended to ask them to leave the premises. He wanted to find out his legal position before Susan had the opportunity to do any more damage. "Do you?"

Margie nodded as the small bell over the door rang as it was pushed open. Jenna stepped inside the cafe and seemed to be looking for someone. She hadn't noticed Matt yet, and he couldn't keep the goofy smile off his face. She was gorgeous, and hopefully, if he played it right, she might be his.

"There she is now," Margie said, causing Matt to return his attention to Margie.

"There's who?"

Margie smiled. "You seem suddenly distracted."

Heat flooded Matt's cheeks. "How could I not be. Jenna's amazing, isn't she? Stunning and amazing."

Margie's eyes widened. "She is, but I'm surprised to hear you say that."

"Let's say a few things have changed in the last few hours."

"You and Jenna?" Margie's eyes seemed to widen even further.

"Don't say anything," Matt said, "but I'm hoping maybe. She knows the truth about Brad and why I did what I did at the wedding, and I think she's realized I'm not the person she imagined."

"That's great news." Margie smiled. "Unexpected but wonderful, Matt."

"It is, but keep it to yourself for now. More importantly, back to my original question: who is this assistant? I need to keep an eye out for her."

Margie laughed and nodded toward Jenna. "If you've made up, I'm surprised she didn't tell you. Jenna's Susan's assistant, Matt."

Jenna's eyes flicked around the Sandstone Cafe. She had no idea what Sally Davido looked like, but as there didn't appear to be any single women in the cafe, she assumed she'd arrived before her.

She decided to sit at the counter but stopped. Margie was on the far side of the cafe talking to someone, her back blocking Jenna's view of who it was. When Margie moved, Jenna's heart caught in her throat. It was Matt. He was staring at Margie with an intensity that Jenna had rarely seen in him. Jenna took a step toward them. She might have enough time to tell Matt that she was working for Susan before Sally arrived. Her father was right. He needed to hear it from her before he heard it from someone else.

She stopped as Matt looked her way and locked eyes with her. She was nervous but flashed him what she hoped was her brightest smile. He didn't return it. He looked furious.

Margie turned and mouthed "sorry" before returning to the counter.

Sorry? What did she have to be sorry for?

Matt was standing by the time she reached his table.

"Hey, I was hoping to see you this afternoon. I need to talk to you."

Matt folded his arms across his chest. "Why's that, Jenna?"

All the warmth and excitement from earlier that afternoon was gone. Matt was cold and appeared angry.

"Has something happened?"

"You tell me. A couple of hours ago, I was on cloud nine. The most amazing thing happened where you not only apologized, but I thought we had a connection."

"We did," Jenna said. "We do. One I hope we can explore further."

"Before or after you help Susan destroy my businesses and everything I've worked for?"

Jenna recoiled at the venom in his voice, her stomach roiling. If only she'd arrived a few minutes earlier and had beaten Margie to telling him. She put her hands up. "Hear me out. It was what I wanted to see you about. I spoke to Susan this afternoon and told her I could no longer work for her. That was why I hurried away from Charlie's. The moment I realized that you'd done nothing wrong with regards to Brad and me, I knew I had to quit that job."

Matt shook his head, hurt flashing in his eyes. "She's planning to sell my businesses out from under me, and you knew that, didn't you?"

Jenna flushed a deep shade of red. "I did."

"And it didn't cross your mind to let me know."

Jenna hung her head. "I'm sorry. Part of me thought you deserved everything you got."

"What about the other part?"

"The other part felt uneasy at times."

"Yet you continued working for her?"

"Until today, yes."

Matt inhaled. "I'm not sure what I'm supposed to think. Can you tell me at least what she's planning? I'm not sure I believe anything she said to me on the phone just now."

Jenna stared at him, Susan's words about the nondisclosure agreement and threat of legal action playing over in her mind. "There's not a lot I can say, Matt. There are legal implications around what I can and can't reveal."

"Jenna," Margie called from the counter. "Sorry to interrupt, but there's someone here to see you."

Jenna and Matt both glanced in the direction of the bar. A woman in her mid-forties, dressed in a black pantsuit, nodded in their direction.

"Sorry," Jenna said. "I have to speak to this woman. Could we meet later and talk further? I need to explain."

"Tell me one thing," Matt said. "Are you still working for Susan?"

Jenna made the instant decision that she was going to ignore Susan's threats of a lawsuit and, following a short discussion with Sally Davido, was going to finish up. "No, I'm not."

Matt ran a hand through his blonde hair. "After weeks of calling me a liar and acting all holier than thou, you stand here and lie directly to my face." He nodded in Sally Davido's direction. "I suggest you tell your client that the cafe's not for sale."

Jenna's heart fell. He knew what the meeting was about.

He pushed past her, shaking her hand from his arm when she reached out for him. "Matt, wait. It's not what it looks like."

"It is what it looks like, Jenna, and I suggest you take your meeting somewhere else. Neither you nor your client is welcome in my cafe."

Jenna did her best to blink back tears as Matt strode toward the cafe's exit.

Matt found himself driving up the steep winding road out of Hope's Ridge. He felt sick to his stomach. Was he never going to get a break? Was this the karma Jenna had spoken about coming after him? Give him a glimpse of happiness, of possibilities for a few minutes, and then rip them from him to punish him for his past?

His eyes filled with tears, and he wiped at them angrily. Of course he didn't have a chance with a girl like Jenna. He'd always thought she was out of his league and had been kidding himself that she would be interested. But this wasn't about her being out of his league. This was about her actively working with Susan to destroy everything he'd built up. That she had had such hatred for him was devastating.

As he neared the top of the ridge, he slowed and took a left-hand turn down a narrow road that led to one of Hope's Ridge's best-kept secrets. He pulled to a stop where the road ended, climbed out of the cab, and walked in the direction of the narrow Ledge trail. He followed it for a few hundred yards through the thick forest before walking out to a clearing. Lake Hopeful spread out before him, the water rippling in the sunshine. Matt sat down on the aptly named Ledge the flat rocks created, and stared. It was beautiful, there was no denying it, but it seemed Lake Hopeful provided anything but hope when it came to him. Maybe his dad was right, that there was nothing for him in Hope's Ridge. That the people would never trust him and would never accept him as one of the town. The only three people he could call his friends were Steph, Buster, and Charlie.

A tear ran down Matt's cheek as despair washed over him. He didn't belong anywhere. His only family was his aunt and his new half-sister, who he had no interest in getting to know. He wasn't close to anyone, and he doubted anyone would miss him if he moved away.

He wiped his eyes, an image of his father entering his mind. Anger mixed with his tears. How could his dad do this to him? Suddenly announce a new sister and then leave her almost his entire estate? It didn't make any sense and certainly wasn't fair. What he hated even more was that the mess his father had left behind made it impossible to grieve for him without flares of anger taking over. Matt didn't want that. He wanted to focus on the positives of his dad's life and remember those, to put aside memories of the disagreements they'd had and focus on the love he had for his father. He wiped his eyes again. He had loved his father. For all of his flaws, he was still his dad, and he missed him.

He let the tears flow; his sleeve saturated by the time they eventually stopped. He took a deep breath, picked up a rock, and threw it toward the lake. It would never reach. He was high up but also a long way from its edge. The rock disappeared into the scrubby trees below, causing a bird to squawk and a flurry of feathers to fly from the trees as a flock of birds were disturbed.

Matt shook his head. "Sorry," he called to the birds. He couldn't even throw a rock without consequences.

His mind drifted back to Jenna's face when he'd spoken to her in the cafe. She was a good actress. He'd give her that. If he didn't know better, he'd say he saw genuine remorse in her eyes as she admitted to working with Susan. But why did she have to lie and say she'd quit when she obviously hadn't? The irony, her accusing him for so long of being a liar, yet she was the one who was knowingly going behind his back trying to ruin him. He would *never* do that.

As he had the thought, he could hear Charlie's voice in his mind. "Really, Matthew, are you sure?"

Matt felt his cheeks heat, even though he was by himself and only imagining Charlie. He'd done worse to Charlie earlier in the year, or tried to at least. It was the action he was the most ashamed of in his life, but also the one he was the most grateful for. Grateful because it had brought Charlie into his life as a friend and mentor.

He dragged himself up to standing. That was what he needed right now—Charlie's wisdom and advice.

Jenna could hardly see the path through her tear-filled eyes as she crossed the road and made her way to Irresistibles. She was devastated with how everything had played out with Matt.

"Jen, what's wrong?" Asha hurried toward Jenna as she approached the food truck.

Jenna was relieved that other than a few customers in the pavilion, there was no one waiting to be served. She did her best to muster a smile for Asha but failed miserably, her face crumpling.

"Come and sit down." Asha guided her to a private table

tucked around the side of the food truck.

Jenna allowed herself to be ushered into a seat, and Asha sat down opposite her.

"Is it Brad? Has something else happened?"

Jenna shook her head, doing her best to contain her tears. "No, it's Matt."

Asha leaped to her feet. "I'll kill him. Honestly, I will. He needs to be run out of town." Her head swung around wildly as if she was looking for him, and her eyes flashed with fury.

Jenna put her hand over her mouth, barely able to disguise the bubble of laughter that rose in her throat.

Asha stopped and looked at her. "Okay, I'm confused. Are you crying or laughing?"

Tears trickled from Jenna's eyes as she contained her laughter. "Both. Your reaction is gold. Sit down, Ash. It's not what you think. Matt hasn't done anything wrong."

"That's a first." Asha took her seat. "What happened?"

Jenna took a deep breath and started to talk. By the time she'd finished filling Asha in on all of the details, Asha's mouth had dropped open. "You kissed Matt?"

Jenna nodded. "I did, and I want to do it again. It shocked me too, but there's a connection between us. One I can't even describe. I think the fact that it is so unexpected for both of us is part of what makes it so magical."

"Magical!" Asha raised an eyebrow. "We are talking about the same man I was throwing rocks at a few months back. The same man who tried to ruin Charlie's life and the same man who flattened the groom at your wedding?"

Jenna nodded. "I know it's crazy, but I'm devastated about what happened today, which tells me that I care. A lot."

"About our Matthew, I hope," Charlie said, approaching their table. "Sorry, I am not eavesdropping, but I was waiting to be served and heard you talking. Only the last bit about caring." He grinned and turned to Asha. "Have you heard the wonderful news about Jenna and Matthew?"

Asha nodded slowly. "Jenna told me, but there's an issue, Charlie, a big one." Asha stood and motioned for Charlie to sit down. "You keep Jenna company while I make your coffee. Hopefully, you can offer some words of advice to Jenna. I'm too shocked to even think, if I'm honest."

Charlie sat down across from Jenna as her friend went to make his coffee, his smile turning to a frown. "Things are not good with you and Matthew?"

Jenna wiped her eyes as she explained to Charlie what had happened with Susan earlier, and then Matt discovering she was working with her. "He was so upset, Charlie. I don't think he'll believe me that I was planning to tell him today. I had already spoken to Susan to try to quit, but she's insisting I work the whole two weeks of my contract or she'll take legal action. She made me sign a nondisclosure contract before I started, which she says she'll enforce via the courts if I speak to anyone about what she's been doing."

Charlie nodded slowly. "So you went back to work today?"

"I did, but I was going to tell the investor that it was too early to be looking at the property. That until Susan had confirmation that she owned part of it, nothing could be done, and it was inappropriate to be looking at it. That was all I planned to do. But Matt saw me and got the wrong idea." She placed her face in her hands and shook her head. "It's such a mess, Charlie, such a mess. I have no idea how to move forward. I don't think Matt will ever believe or forgive me."

"But you haven't done anything wrong. You've been following instructions."

Jenna blushed. "I have, but there have been times when it didn't feel right. I've seen some messages and read documents that have made me feel uneasy."

"What kind of documents?"

"To do with Matt's businesses. Susan's done a lot of research into the market here and in Drayson's Landing to find out what her options are."

"That's smart business."

Jenna nodded. "Yes, but some of this research was done before Walter died. Before she even knew she would be inheriting. That seems a little premature, considering he was in reasonable health. Sure, he'd had the heart attack earlier in the year, but he'd recovered well from that, and Matt said he was quite fit and healthy. There was no suggestion he'd die suddenly."

"Mm." Charlie was deep in thought as Jenna continued.

"That's the type of thing that if I was a good friend, I would have spoken to Matt about. At the time, I wondered if Susan had manipulated the situation somehow with Walter, but then I decided Matt deserved everything coming his way, so if she had done that, then good for her."

Charlie tutted as he remained deep in thought. "She is not operating as you would hope family would. Although, family does not necessarily mean trust and friendship. Look at my nephew Albert and what he did to me."

"I find it hard to comprehend," Jenna said. "Even though both Zane and I moved to the city when we were old enough to, coming home has always been about family. Mom and Dad, our friends, the town. There was always somewhere to fall in times of trouble. Like the last couple of months. Matt doesn't have anyone."

"He has me," Charlie said. "And hopefully, he will have you. We need to fix this problem. The first step is to ignore the nondisclosure document. I can afford the best lawyer money can buy if and when you need it. For now, it is important that Matthew learn the truth." He reached across the table and took her hand. "I am counting on you and Matthew becoming partners and eventually becoming husband and wife." He tapped his chest. "It's a feeling in here that you are right for each other."

Jenna closed her eyes briefly. Less than twelve hours ago, if someone had said to her that she and Matt Law would make a good couple, she would have laughed at them. But listening to Charlie was the strangest sensation because she knew she agreed. When Matt had kissed her and looked deeply into her eyes, he'd touched something inside her. She wanted him to look at her that way again. The adoration in his eyes, love even, had blown her away. She was blown even further away realizing she had feelings for him too.

She opened her eyes. "Thank you, Charlie. Asha and Steph are right about you. You are very wise."

Charlie blushed as Asha returned to the table with a tray, depositing steaming mugs of coffee in front of Charlie and Jenna and a selection of muffins for them to choose from. "I'd like to hope that by ninety-seven, we are all wise. That my suggestions are old age common sense."

"What's the plan," Asha said.

Jenna pushed back her chair and stood. "To ignore the

nondisclosure agreement and talk to Matt."

Matt was disappointed when Charlie didn't answer his door. He desperately needed to speak to him. He pulled out his phone and found Charlie's number. He pressed the call button and almost laughed when he heard the phone ringing inside Charlie's house. It had been the one area where Charlie had fallen short when working for Matt— remembering to carry his phone with him. Matt had insisted that he needed to be contactable during the working day by Matt and suppliers, but Charlie had shrugged. "Never had cell phones in my day, Matthew, and many buildings were built. It is not an essential tool. Hammer, yes, phone, no."

Matt had given up in the end. If he needed to find Charlie, he was usually in one of three places: on-site at the apartments, in the Sandstone Cafe, or across the road at Irresistibles. He wasn't required on-site today, so it was quite likely he was across the road enjoying Asha's muffins or in the cafe devouring one of Margie's cakes. He was beginning to wonder if the older man's entire diet consisted of baked goods.

He squinted against the sun as he looked across to Irresistibles and frowned. It could possibly be Charlie sitting in the pavilion waving his hands animatedly as he spoke to the person with him. It was certainly one of his trademarks. Matt hurried across the road, ignoring Asha as she waved to him and called him over to the food truck. He didn't want to speak to any of Jenna's friends, especially Asha, who could blow up at any minute.

He strode up the ramp of the pavilion, relief settling over him as he met Charlie's gaze. The old man smiled and waved him over. The man he was with turned in Matt's direction as Charlie waved, causing Matt to stop. Roy Larsen. Could the day get any worse? He was tempted to retreat, but Charlie was calling him over, so he continued toward the two men.

"Matthew," Charlie said, standing as Matt reached their table. "I have an errand to run, and Roy would like to speak to you. It's important." He shuffled away from them at an impressive speed.

Matt folded his arms and waited for Roy to speak.

"Sit down, please," Roy said. "I have something to say and would be more comfortable if you'd sit."

Matt unfolded his arms and sat down in the chair Charlie had vacated.

"I'm sorry, Matt. Truly sorry."

Matt let out a long breath. At least one thing might go his way today. "Thank you. I spoke with Jenna this morning and had hoped you'd come around."

"Come around? More than that. I'm mortified at the way I behaved toward you. I hope you will have it in your heart to forgive me."

Matt smiled. "Consider it forgotten, Roy. We've always had a good working relationship until now. I don't see any reason we can't move forward with that."

Roy nodded. "I think perhaps we could expand on that."

Matt leaned back in his chair. "Expand?"

Roy cleared his throat. "Jenna explained the position you've been put in as a result of your father's will. That this Susan Lewis could make it difficult for your businesses."

"Could and I think will," Matt said. "I haven't quite worked out what her real agenda is, but I'm beginning to wonder if I'm being punished for Dad not being there for her during her childhood."

"Quite possibly. Jenna said that she was looking for top dollar for her share in your businesses. Money that you might not be able to come by."

Matt sighed. "That appears to be the case. But Roy, I'm beginning to think it might be for a reason. My father wasn't welcome in Hope's Ridge, and there's been enough evidence to suggest I'm not either. Before he died, Dad was planning to move all of his investments and assets out of Hope's Ridge and Drayson's and invest in opportunities in the city. He told me that he was sick of the town enjoying the facilities he'd had to fight so hard to establish, and I'm beginning to feel the same way."

"You're thinking of leaving?"

Matt nodded. "I am. Since Charlie's taken me under his wing, I've changed. I've grown within myself and looked at what's important to me. It's not all about making money and putting my stamp on the town."

"What is important to you, Matt?"

Heat rose up the back of Matt's neck. "I want a family, Roy. A woman who loves me for me and hopefully one who wants kids. I want to settle down. To feel like I belong somewhere. Be surrounded by people who like and respect me for who I am. I don't think that will ever happen here because people know my past, and that's the person they're interested in believing I am. If I move to the city, or even somewhere completely different, I can start again."

"If you had someone willing to buy Susan's share of

your businesses and remain a silent partner, would you reconsider?"

Matt stared at him. "Are you offering?"

Roy nodded.

Matt wasn't sure what to say.

"We owe you, Matt. Big time. The mill's doing well, and it would be a good opportunity to diversify some of our investments. While you might find this hard to believe, I respect the way you've been doing business recently, and I would be happy to be involved. I can be a silent partner or possibly have some involvement if that's what you'd like." He laughed. "And the many discussions you've had with me about reducing costs on our products could be raised again. If I have a vested interest, I think you'd find much better pricing. Also, on a personal note, regardless of what you decide to do, I'm holding a town meeting on Friday. I'll be using it as an opportunity to tell the town what happened at the wedding and how I will be eternally grateful to you for what you did and to express how ashamed I am of the way I've acted toward you." He shuddered. "It makes me sick to my stomach knowing Jenna was involved with a disgrace like Brad."

"Me too," Matt said, unable to keep the anger from his voice.

Roy searched his eyes. "You care about her, don't you, son?"

Matt clenched his teeth. "I thought I did, but then I discovered what she's been doing with Susan."

"Let me ask you something. If the roles were reversed, and you were Jenna, what would you do to the man you thought had ruined your life?"

"Fair point, but Roy, she's *still* working for Susan. She

was at the Sandstone Cafe this afternoon meeting a prospective buyer. Right in front of me."

Roy groaned. "She came to find you to tell you what was going on and to get rid of the client. Susan's threatening her with legal action if she doesn't work through her two weeks' notice period and if she discloses private information to you."

Matt's eyes widened. "Really?"

"Really. She was devastated when she told me today what's been going on. I told her I'd pay for any lawyer's fees if she wants to ignore Susan, but she's worried about what a lawsuit could do to her career moving forward. She's stuck in a hard place, Matt. I know that's difficult for you to believe when she's been working for the enemy, but she is." Roy glanced at his watch. "I've got to go. I promised Janet we'd picnic by the lake later and watch the sunset and I need to buy a bottle of wine. Think about what I said, won't you? If you decide you want to stay around and you'd like to consider partnering with me, I think we could make it work."

"I appreciate it, Roy, but I couldn't take your money knowing it was because you thought you owed me."

Roy stood and clapped him on the back. "And that's a true sign of how much you've changed. I'm proud of you, Matt. Not long ago, I imagine you'd take the money regardless of where it came from. You've grown in a lot of ways, and I admire your integrity."

Matt watched as Roy walked down the ramp of the pavilion to the pebbled path that led to the small parking lot. He couldn't help but smile. *He admires my integrity.* That was not something he expected to hear from Roy Larsen, or if he was honest, anybody.

12

*T*he next morning Charlie sat in the pavilion by the lakeside, people watching. He'd hardly slept with the drama of Matt's situation worrying him. He'd bumped into Roy Larsen after Roy had spoken to Matthew and had been distressed to learn that Matthew felt he needed to leave Hope's Ridge and start again. He'd invited him to his house for dinner that evening, hoping he'd be able to change his mind.

A white Mazda Miata convertible pulled up in front of the Sandstone Cafe at the same moment Asha placed a cup of peppermint tea in front of Charlie.

"Your rent payment, sir," Asha said, joking as she usually did that Charlie only accepted food and drink in lieu of rent.

"Who is that woman?" Charlie asked, pointing a shaky finger at the convertible.

"I believe that's Susan Lewis," Asha said. "Matt's half-sister. It looks like she's coming this way, so you can ask her yourself."

Charlie pushed back his chair. "Sister, schmister. I'll be the judge of that." He hurried, on shaky legs, down the ramp and onto the pebbled pathway leading to the parking lot.

"Charlie, be careful," Asha called after him. "You'll fall if you don't slow down."

Charlie slowed for a second before hiding a secret smile. Asha was always full of good advice. He walked toward Susan Lewis, wondering if there was any chance his plan would work. She smiled as she approached him, and he did his best to plaster on a fake smile. As she got closer, he slowed and clutched his side.

Susan sped up her pace. "Are you okay, sir?"

Charlie groaned and staggered to his left.

Susan was by his side in an instant and did her best to hold him up.

"I'm sorry," Charlie said. "Don't feel good. Probably Asha's food."

"Asha!" Susan called. "Can you bring a chair?"

Charlie didn't look back to the food truck to see whether Asha had sprung into action or not. He knew her well enough to know she'd be worried, and would no doubt arrive with the chair any second, which meant he had to be quick. He groaned again, his arms flinging out, pushing Susan away. "Sorry," he managed. "I can't control..." He swung his arms wildly again and stumbled. This time Susan stepped forward to meet him and placed her arms around him to steady him.

He straightened for a split second before falling. He half prayed he wouldn't injure himself but knew that if he could get what he was after, even a broken hip would be worth it.

Susan cried out as his hands flung out, grabbing on to

her hair in one hand and arm in the other as he went down. He heard footsteps running toward them and someone calling out.

Holding on tight to Susan had the added advantage of her breaking his fall. The next thing he knew, he was lying on his back, his fists still clinging to Susan's hair.

"So sorry," he gasped as he released his grip on her, a handful of her hair stuck to his palm.

"It's okay," Susan said, rubbing her head. "But we need to get you help. Don't move."

"Yes, Charlie," Asha said. "Susan's right. Stay still, and I'll call an ambulance."

He could hear the fear in her voice and wanted to reassure her that not only was he fine, but he had a plan. But instead, he lay moaning on the ground until the ambulance arrived.

Matt lay on his back with his eyes closed, enjoying the sounds of Steph's calming voice as she led the class through the final relaxation and vinyasa. He would certainly miss yoga if he did leave Hope's Ridge. He'd decided to start avoiding the town as much as possible and immerse himself in yoga, hiking, and some rock climbing instead. He needed a break to regroup and think about what he was going to do.

Fifteen minutes later, he left the yoga studio and climbed back into his truck. His phone pinged with a text as he pulled his seat belt on. He glanced at his phone, his heart rate increasing as he saw Jenna's name. She was the last person he expected to hear from.

. . .

Hi Matt. I know you don't want to hear from me, but Susan's in town. Didn't want you being blindsided (again) if you bump into her. Take care. J x

Blindsided? Matt started his car, his yoga calm replaced with anger. It was not him that was going to be blindsided today. Within minutes he was driving along Lake Drive, the Sandstone Cafe in view. He jumped out of his pickup and walked to the front door of the cafe. He hadn't planned to talk to her yet, but her being here annoyed him. Why couldn't she stay away until she had her hands on his father's money?

Matt stopped as he entered the cafe and saw Susan sitting at a table with a small group, including Margie and Ryan, surrounding her. Margie leaped to her feet as soon as she saw him and hurried over, concern etched on her face.

"I was about to call you."

"Everything okay?"

Margie shook her head. "It's Charlie. He suffered an attack of some sort about an hour ago. We had to call an ambulance. He didn't look good."

Chills ran through Matt. He could not lose Charlie too. "Where did they take him?"

"The medical center in Drayson's Landing. They were hoping he could be treated there and not have to go to Tall Oaks or the city."

"Okay, thanks." He turned, all thoughts of Susan and what he wanted to confront her about forgotten.

"I'll come with you." He stopped at the sound of Jenna's

voice. "I just heard too," Jenna assured him. "Let me drive you."

Matt shook his head. "No, this has a sense of deja vu. The last time you drove me, my dad died."

The color drained for Jenna's cheeks. "That wasn't my fault, Matt."

"I know, but I don't want to jinx anything."

"Then you drive," Jenna said. "I'm coming whether you like it or not."

"Fine." Matt wasn't going to argue anymore. He needed to get to Charlie.

Thirty minutes later, after a torturous car ride where neither of them spoke, Matt and Jenna were shown by a nurse to Charlie's room. They could hear his voice as they neared the room, clearly objecting to whatever treatment was about to be administered. "There's nothing wrong with me. I'll be discharging myself shortly. I am waiting to speak to the doctor about some tests."

"But Mr. Li, we haven't done any tests."

"But I would like you to," Charlie said. "Please tell the doctor to hurry."

Matt and Jenna reached the door to Charlie's room and waited while the nurse finished her conversation. She rolled her eyes at Matt and Jenna as she said her farewell to Charlie and left the room.

"Charlie," Matt said, stepping into the room. "You've had me worried sick. How are you feeling?"

"Fit as a fiddle," Charlie said. "You can take me home soon. I need to speak to the doctor." He looked from Matt to Jenna. "You have made up?"

Matt looked across at Jenna. "No. We both happened to

be in the cafe at the same time that Susan shared the news that you'd fallen."

"You will make up," Charlie predicted, "sooner rather than later, I hope."

Neither Matt nor Jenna responded.

"And Susan," Charlie continued. "What an interesting character."

"Not how I'd describe her," Jenna said.

"Or me," agreed Matt.

"Mr. Li, I believe you wish to speak to me?"

Charlie looked from Matt to Jenna as a doctor entered the room. "Matthew, could you please go and find a decent coffee for me? This hospital doesn't sell anything drinkable. Perhaps from the cafe across the road?"

"I can go," Jenna volunteered.

"No," Charlie said. "I'd like Matthew to get it. Jenna, I'd like you to stay with me."

Matt didn't miss the wink Charlie gave Jenna.

"This doctor is good-looking and possibly single. You may wish to speak with him after I do."

Jenna's cheeks flushed red, and Matt was annoyed to feel a spark of jealousy at Charlie's suggestion.

"Matthew? Coffee."

Matt stood and made his way out of Charlie's room, wondering what Charlie was up to. One minute he was saying he and Jenna would make up, and the next, he was setting her up with a doctor. Knowing Charlie, nothing was what it appeared. In the time he'd spent getting to know him, he'd quickly learned that the older man was quite devious. He hoped whatever Charlie was scheming didn't involve him.

The doctor waited until Matt left the room before turning back to Charlie. "Now, Mr. Li, how can I help you? The nurse mentioned some tests?"

Charlie nodded then turned to Jenna. "Check that Matthew has gone. I do not want him hearing this."

Concern filled Jenna. Charlie must be really sick if he wanted to protect Matt.

She walked to the door and poked her head out. Other than a nurse walking into another room, the corridor was clear.

"He's gone," she said, moving back into the room. She sat down in the chair next to Charlie, bracing herself for the bad news.

Charlie took a handkerchief from the cabinet next to him and placed it carefully on the bed. "I need you to test this," he said to the doctor.

"Your handkerchief?"

Jenna wondered if Charlie had hit his head when he fell. She was about to ask the doctor if he'd been tested for concussion when Charlie spoke up, the annoyance in his voice obvious.

"No, the hairs inside it."

Hairs?

"I need a DNA test."

"I'm going to need more information, Mr. Li," the doctor said. "Is this your hair?"

"No. I do not need a DNA test. I know who I am."

Jenna did her best to hide her smile at the incredulous look on Charlie's face. "Charlie, neither the doctor nor I understand. You need to provide more information."

Charlie sighed. "Fine. This hair is from Susan Lewis."

"What? Why do you have that?" Jenna asked.

"I may have grabbed her hair when I fell. Purely self-protection, but now it comes in handy."

"Okay," the doctor said, "if I was to set up a DNA test, we would need a second sample to cross-match it with. Do you have that?"

Charlie's face fell. "I did not think of that."

"And," the doctor added, "it isn't something we do here. You'll need to find a lab that specializes in DNA testing. Usually, you require the consent of the person whose hair you are testing. Now, Mr. Li, I can organize your discharge papers if there's nothing else."

Charlie nodded, disappointment clouding his features.

"A nurse will come and see you in about ten minutes," the doctor said. "You'll then be free to leave."

Jenna waited until the doctor had left the room before turning to Charlie. "What's going on?"

"Susan Lewis is not behaving like someone who has discovered who her father is and that she has a brother. It concerns me," Charlie said.

"She's behaving as Walter Law did," Jenna said. "That's probably enough to prove she's related to him."

Charlie shook his head. "Perhaps. But I would like concrete evidence that she is his daughter. I'm surprised Matthew hasn't done this himself."

"What don't you speak to him about it? You'll need his or Walter's DNA to do the test."

"I don't want to get his hopes up," Charlie said. "If she's not related, then he has a real reason to contest his father's will."

"If who's not related?"

Jenna jumped as Matt entered the room, a tray with three cups of takeout coffee in hand.

"No one," Charlie was quick to say.

Matt shook his head and looked to Jenna. "I heard enough of that to know something's up. You're questioning whether Susan's my father's daughter?"

Charlie nodded. "I don't trust her behavior, Matthew. If she is your sister, then that is bad luck. But if she's not, then she should not be allowed to impact your life as she is."

"Dad insisted on a DNA test when he first learned of her," Matt said. "She mentioned it when we first met."

"That means nothing," Charlie said. "She might be a professional hustler for all we know, and that was part of her act."

Matt laughed. "I doubt it."

"It's possible, Matt," Jenna said. "And once you hear the trouble Charlie went to to get a DNA sample from Susan, I think you'll take this seriously."

Matt's laughter stopped. "What trouble?"

Jenna turned to Charlie. "Did you land yourself in the hospital on purpose so you could get a DNA test done?"

Charlie averted his gaze to the window overlooking the main street below.

Jenna looked at Matt. "He grabbed Susan by the hair when he fell and conveniently took a handful with him."

Matt's eyes widened, and Jenna had to hide her mouth behind her hand as she tried not to smile. She couldn't believe the old man would do something so extreme.

"You did that for me?" Matt asked, his voice breaking a little.

Charlie moved his gaze back to Matt. "You are family to

me, Matthew. The son I never had. If Susan is your sister and you choose to get to know her, then I am happy to welcome her too. But if my gut is right, and she is not, I do not want her hurting you and everything you have worked toward."

Jenna moved toward Matt as she saw his eyes fill with tears. She squeezed his arm. "We both care about you, Matt. A lot."

Matt wiped his eyes. "Sorry. I don't know what's come over me. Thank you, Charlie. It means a lot to me, what you've done and what you said. I'd be honored to be your family, absolutely honored."

Jenna had to clear her throat, her eyes also welling up with the emotion in the room.

"Now, back to the DNA test," Charlie said. "We need to figure out a way to get one done. We'll need your DNA, Matthew, or your father's, if that is possible."

"I'm not sure about Dad's, but we can use mine."

"I know someone who might be able to help us," Jenna said. "The wife of one of the guys I used to work with deals with DNA. I met her at the company's Christmas party one year and had a fascinating conversation about how she uses different samples for discreet tests. They can use all sorts of items, and hair is definitely one of them."

"Could you contact her?" Charlie asked. "This is very important, and I think urgent."

Jenna slipped the phone from her pocket and scrolled through her contacts. "I'll call Kurt, her husband, and see if he'll give me her number."

Jenna turned away from Charlie and Matt and walked toward the window as she found Kurt's details. Matt was looking at her strangely, and after everything that had happened in the last few days, she wasn't sure she wanted to know why.

13

*M*att paced up and down in Charlie's living room, his thoughts running a million miles an hour.

"You'll wear a hole in my carpet," Charlie said from the armchair where he sat watching Matt. He glanced at his watch. "She'll be here any minute."

Matt stopped pacing and forced himself to sit opposite Charlie. "I've hardly been able to sleep since we brought you home from the hospital."

Charlie nodded. "Me too. It has been a long two days. I told Jenna to offer her friend as much money as possible to get a quick result, but it seems this was the quickest that could be managed."

The wife of Jenna's colleague had agreed to test the samples, but as the turnaround was usually five days, getting results in two was the best she could offer.

A knock on the front door had Matt leap to his feet. "I'll get it." He hurried down the hallway and pulled open the door.

Jenna stood in front of him, her blonde hair hanging loose around her shoulders. Her green eyes connected with his.

"Hey," Matt said. All of the anger he'd felt for Jenna seemed to have disappeared. The extent she'd gone to in order to help him had made him rethink his feelings toward her. Roy Larsen's words that Jenna had been *devastated* by what she'd done had affected him. He knew that feeling of wishing with everything he had that he could turn back time and change his behavior. And the difference between him and Jenna was his awful behavior had been fueled by his own greed, whereas Jenna's had been fueled from hurt and betrayal that she'd thought, with good reason, he'd caused her.

She held up a white envelope. "I've got it."

"Did you open it?"

Jenna lowered the envelope, her eyes wide. "It's your private information."

Matt managed a nervous smile. "Sorry, part of me hoped you had and could tell me the results."

"Can I ask you something?" Jenna said.

Matt nodded.

"Are you hoping you have a sister, or you don't?"

"Honestly, I've given that so much thought," Matt said. "In an ideal world, I'd want a sister. I've felt very alone recently, and it would mean a lot to have family I could become close with. But it's not an ideal world, and the way Susan's behaved so early on in our relationship tells me that we'll never be close." He gave a little laugh. "She's another level of ruthless than I'd ever want to be. It's been a real eye-opener. She's a great inspiration for how *not* to do business. So, in answer to your question, I'm hoping we aren't a match. I contacted Dad's lawyer, and he confirmed that Dad's will is specific in identifying Susan as his biological daughter, and that is why he made provisions for her. His will also said that if she was to predecease him that his estate would go to his biological son, being me. It's clear that biological children would benefit and no one else."

"What's happening out there?" Charlie called from the living room. "Unless you're proposing, Matthew, get in here at once."

Matt smiled. "He's insistent that we get together."

Jenna laughed. "From what I've seen about Charlie, and heard from Asha too, Charlie usually gets what he wants."

Matt took a step closer to her and lowered his voice. "Do you think it might be what you want?"

"Definitely." She said it without hesitation, her eyes sparkling, filled with love.

Matt drew in a breath, hardly able to believe she was so sure.

She squeezed his arm. "Come on. We shouldn't keep Charlie waiting. We can chat about us, if there's going to be an us, once this is done." He followed her down the hallway, a flurry of emotions whirling inside him. He'd been anxious all morning worrying about the DNA test results, but now he was filled with hope. Could he and Jenna move past all that had happened?

"Results?" Charlie demanded as they entered the living room.

Jenna handed Matt the envelope and sat on the edge of the couch.

Matt gave a shaky smile then turned his attention to the envelope. He tore along the top and took out the document.

"Dear Mr. Law..." he read and started to scan the letter.

He turned the page to the official results document. A wide smile formed as he read aloud. "The DNA data does not support the biological relationship."

Charlie pumped the air with his fist. "I knew it."

"Thank goodness you did," Jenna said. "What happens now?"

Jenna and Charlie looked to Matt.

"First, I'll confront Susan, and then I will contact Dad's lawyer and ask him to order a legal DNA test. Because Susan didn't agree to this one, it won't stand up in court, which we'll need in order to contest the will." He frowned.

"What's wrong?" Jenna asked.

"I was thinking of Dad, that's all. He was led to believe Susan was his daughter and was manipulated into leaving her most of his estate. It's sad that he died before the truth came out."

Charlie shook his head. "No, Matthew. Your father died happy thinking he had two children. While this is not true, hopefully, it gave him peace in his last moments. If he'd learned of the deceit and then died, he would have been very unhappy."

"Maybe." Matt sighed. "I guess we'll never know. I wouldn't want to be cheated like Dad was. I wonder what hold Susan and her mother had over him? Dad's not stupid. It's surprising he fell for their scam, assuming it was a scam." His phone rang. "Sorry, I'll turn it off." He slipped it from his pocket and glanced at the screen before looking up at Charlie and Jenna. "It's her."

"Take it," Charlie said. "Arrange a meeting."

Matt nodded. "Susan, hi."

"Hi, Matt, I'm in town this morning and hoped you'd have time to meet. I've had some figures presented to me regarding the Sandstone Cafe and wanted to run them by you like I promised I would. Hopefully you'll feel the figure is reasonable and will be in a position to counteroffer."

"Okay," Matt said. "Can we meet at the cafe in ten minutes? I'm not far away."

"See you there."

Matt ended the call. "Susan's going to present me with a figure she wants me to buy her out of the Sandstone Cafe for."

"Do you think any of these investors are real?" Jenna asked.

"I met one of them, and so did you," Matt said. "They looked real enough to me."

"I mean, do you think they're in a position to buy the businesses? I'm beginning to wonder if this is a complete setup. First she managed to become Walter's heir, and now she's giving you the option to pay her—I assume more than his ownership is worth—to retain what should be yours."

"Revenge," Charlie said, tapping his nose. "I smell revenge."

Matt frowned. "But I've never met her before all of this and certainly haven't given her a reason to want revenge on me."

"Not on you," Jenna said. "On your dad. I'm guessing Walter's done something to her that you're paying for."

Matt rubbed his hands together and stood. "I guess I'm about to find out." He looked from Jenna to Charlie. "And thank you, both of you. You've both done so much to help me."

Charlie waved away his thanks. "You would do the same for us. Now go on, go and meet Susan and deal with her once and for all."

Matt glanced at Jenna. "Can we meet later?"

Her face lit up. "Definitely."

Susan was already sitting at a table when Matt entered the cafe. He waved at Margie, who was serving behind the counter, and made his way over to the table by the window.

Susan smiled. "Lovely to see you, Matt. How have you been?"

"Fantastic," Matt said, sitting down opposite her.

Curiosity flashed in Susan's eyes. "Has something happened?"

Matt nodded. "A lot. But nothing I want to discuss. Now, what did you want to see me about?"

Susan pulled out a document. "As I told you, I wanted to have the market value of the property. While I know I'm not in a position to sell it yet, I'm getting everything in order so I can sell immediately when Walter's shares become mine. I don't want to spend any more time than I have to in Hope's Ridge or Drayson's Landing. I can see why Walter was quite scathing about both places."

Matt raised an eyebrow. "You've only been here a few times."

"Yes, but I've spoken to enough people to realize how backward the town and people are when it comes to development and investment. Anyway, it doesn't matter what my reasons are for selling. That's what's happening, and it's whether you're interested in buying that we need to confirm." She pushed the document across to Matt. "That's the offer. You'll see there are two offers. One to buy the entire building and business, the other to buy my share."

"I never said I was selling."

"I know. But the figure is good, so you might want to consider it."

Matt passed the document back to Susan. "Not interested."

"In selling your share or in buying mine?"

"Either."

Susan's brow furrowed. "I don't understand. I thought you wanted the first option on my part of the properties."

"What I want right now is some answers." Matt took the paper with the DNA test from his pocket and slid it across the table to Susan.

"What's this?"

"A DNA test. You're not my sister, and you're not Walter's daughter."

Susan's face paled. "What? Yes, I am. And how did you have this done without my consent?"

"That's not something you need to worry about. I will be advising Dad's lawyer to request a legal DNA test as part of my case to contest Dad's will."

"What? That's ridiculous. Walter and I had a test done when I first met him. It was a match. I imagine he sent it to his lawyer, so it should be on file."

"Then you won't have a problem having another one done, will you?"

Susan stood, the color returning to her face as anger flashed in her eyes. "Our father would be turning in his grave right now if he knew what you were doing."

"I'm not doing anything he wouldn't do himself if he had suspicions, Susan. You'll hear from Zeek Potts later today regarding the DNA test."

Susan didn't reply. Instead, she stormed out of the cafe,

and moments later her white convertible sped away from Hope's Ridge.

———

A week had passed since Susan stormed out of the Sandstone Cafe, and Matt had spent most of that time free climbing up at the Bluff and avoiding everyone and everything to do with Hope's Ridge. He wasn't sure why he'd reacted that way. After all, things were back on track with the mill supplying his businesses, and a future with Jenna was possible. But until the Susan Lewis situation was resolved, he felt a need to put everything on hold. Waiting for the DNA test results gave him an unexpected breather —a chance to grieve properly for his father and to think about his future.

He'd arrived home mid-morning on Friday, his body tired but his mind exhilarated from his sunrise climb. He opened the fridge when his phone rang. It was Zeek Potts.

Ten minutes later, Matt ended the call with Zeek and fist-pumped the air. The DNA results had returned confirming Susan was not his sister and no biological relation of his father's. Zeek confirmed that contesting the will would take time, but he was confident that Susan would have no claim on anything, and the estate would revert to Matt. The relief Matt felt was palpable. He needed to celebrate. His thoughts went to Jenna. He hadn't seen her since they'd read the first DNA results at Charlie's house. She'd messaged him, but he'd asked her for some space, explaining he had the Susan situation to deal with, and then he'd be in touch. He also realized he could tell Steph with confidence that he'd be retaining his ownership in the retreat and also lay any concerns Margie and Ryan had about his ownership of the cafe to rest. It was more than a relief. It was amazing.

He wondered if he should call Jenna. He'd like to share the news with her and Charlie together if they were free. Maybe he could take them out for a special lunch or at least somewhere where they could order champagne. He picked up his phone and called her number.

"Hey, stranger." Jenna's voice was tinged with apprehension. He didn't miss the meaning of the word *stranger* in her greeting either. When he'd last seen her, he'd asked her if they could catch up later and then had never called her. She was owed an explanation.

"I deserve that," he said. "I've been hiding from everyone. I wanted to be alone until we had the DNA results."

"You weren't avoiding me?"

"A bit, but not for the reasons you're probably thinking."

"I'm thinking you're still mad and upset with me over working for Susan."

Matt shook his head. "No, I realized that if our roles were reversed, I would have done the same and wished all sorts of disasters on you. I wanted an answer on this DNA stuff and where I stand with my businesses before I could think about anything else."

"And you have the results?"

"I do. And I was hoping to take you and Charlie out for lunch to celebrate."

Silence greeted him. "Jenna?"

"Sorry. We're celebrating, so that means you're not related?"

"We're not. Now can I pick you up?"

"No, I can't come. I'm in Tall Oaks about to go into a job interview."

Matt's smile vanished and a pain developed in his chest. He'd hoped to share his news with Jenna and Charlie and then ask her if they could start again. Go on a date and see where it led. But Tall Oaks? "A job interview? You're moving?"

"Nothing's definite. It's a good opportunity to move into a creative director role. Look, I'd better go. The interview's in five minutes, and I need to get my head in the right place. Can we catch up for a drink tonight, perhaps? I'll be back in Hope's Ridge by five. I'm happy if you want to ask Charlie too."

"Sure," Matt said. He was doing his best to hide his disappointment. "And Jenna, good luck. They'd be silly not to offer it to you."

"Thanks, Matt."

The call ended, and Matt stared at his phone. Steph would be the first to say that life would turn out how it was meant to, and right now, the universe was sending him a clear message—that he and Jenna were not meant to be together.

———

Jenna ended the call with Matt and sat for a few moments staring into space. The interview wasn't for another hour, but she'd wanted to end the call. She shook her head as a waitress walked past her table and held up a coffeepot. She'd drunk enough coffee that morning already. Not hearing from Matt for a week had thrown her. She'd thought there was something happening between them, but then when he hadn't called her to meet up after he'd seen Susan, she'd begun to second guess everything. Then she'd received the phone call from Bridget, a colleague she'd worked with two years earlier, who was now running a graphic design studio in Tall Oaks and who was looking for a creative director. If she wanted a fresh start, then she couldn't think of a better place to get one. Tall Oaks was larger than Hope's Ridge but nothing like the size of the city, and better still, other than Bridget, she didn't know anyone. It would also give her the chance to get out of her parents' house. She was almost thirty, and living back at home wasn't something she ever thought she'd be doing.

"Jenna?"

Jenna looked up to find Susan Lewis standing next to her table.

Susan pointed to the window. "I was walking past and thought it was you. What are you doing in Tall Oaks?"

"I could ask you the same."

"Visiting my mom, she's in the hospital here."

"Oh, I'm sorry," Jenna said. "I didn't realize she lived here. I assumed she was in the city."

"No, she's lived here all her life," Susan said. "Can I join you?"

Jenna nodded, and Susan placed her bag on an empty chair and sat down.

"I owe you an apology," Susan said. "For the way I spoke to you when you wanted to stop working for me." She gave a wry smile. "I think I was going a bit crazy and wanted tasks done quickly, without questions, and without any hassle. It's not how I usually operate, but the Law family sparked a weird drive in me. It's hard to explain."

"Okay," Jenna said, "thank you, I guess. I'm assuming

that your plans for the cafe and the rest of Matt's businesses have fallen through?"

Susan laughed. "A shame for both of us."

"As in you and me?"

Susan nodded. "I thought you'd be the first person to wish bad things on Matt Law. After everything he did to you. You were the perfect assistant up until you decided to leave. What was that about anyway? Did you feel guilty?"

Jenna nodded. "I realized that I was no better than Matt with what was being done to his businesses."

"But you didn't initiate any of that. You were following instructions."

"Instructions that didn't sit well with me. I might not like the way Matt conducted himself in the past, but I didn't want to be involved with bringing him down either."

"Really? Well, that is a surprise. I thought you'd be lining up to watch him fail."

Jenna made the snap decision not to tell Susan that she'd made a mistake about Matt. Her gut told her she was going to learn more about Susan if she didn't. She shook her head. "No point sinking to his level. But what about you? Was this all some kind of scam? What did Matt do to you to cause such an extreme reaction?"

"Nothing," Susan said. "I almost felt a little bad for him. Almost, but not enough to stop what I had planned. And no, it wasn't a scam. It was a case of a debt needing to be repaid. It wasn't Matt. It was his father, Walter. He was a despicable man, and after learning certain facts I decided to go after him."

"Go after him? That sounds pretty extreme. He obviously knew your mother. Knew her well if she was able to convince him you were his daughter."

"Mom didn't convince him, I did. He met her thirty-three years ago. My father worked for him and was in charge of finances for his company. It was a well-paid job, and Dad felt lucky to be part of the business."

"But?"

"But," Susan's mouth contorted with anger, "Walter used his position of power in the most horrendous of ways. He met my mother at a function and took a liking to her. It's only recently that I learned what he did."

Jenna's gut clenched. She had the feeling she didn't want to hear this.

"He charmed her initially, built up her trust, and then made a pass at her. Mom was flattered but quick to reject him. She loved my dad and would never have considered cheating. Walter Law, however, gets what he wants. So he threatened her. Said if she didn't sleep with him, he'd fire my dad and make sure he never worked in finance again."

"Oh no," Jenna said. "I'm so sorry, Susan. So sorry." Her legs began to tremble. She hated to imagine how Matt would feel learning this about his father.

"So, she did," Susan continued. "She thought if she got it over with and only did it once, he'd leave her alone, but he didn't. It went on for about two months until Mom could no longer handle it. She felt guilty and depressed and realized what a huge mistake she'd made. She'd done it to put Dad's happiness first, thinking he'd be devastated to lose his job, but Mom being so unhappy caused Dad to be unhappy too."

"She told him?"

Susan shook her head, her eyes filling with tears. "No, she felt she couldn't. She told Walter instead that it was over. He fired Dad that afternoon."

Jenna's mouth dropped open. "No."

Susan nodded. "He did."

"Did your mom finally tell your dad what had happened?"

"She never got the chance," Susan said. "She was right that Dad was a proud man, and losing his job was devastating. He couldn't look my mom in the eye and tell her he'd been fired, so instead, he threw himself off the cliffs at Morningside."

Jenna froze. This story was more horrific than anything she could ever have imagined.

"Mom never knew if Walter told Dad that he'd been sleeping with her too. So she's spent every day since it happened beating herself up."

"That's awful, Susan. I'm so sorry. I honestly don't know what to say."

"You don't need to say anything. I guess I wanted you to know that I wasn't going after Matt's businesses and Walter's money without good reason. I found out about Walter earlier this year. Mom had told me that my dad died in a car accident when she was pregnant with me, but I found out the truth from some old letters that he'd taken his life. She then told me the whole story, and I decided Walter Law wasn't getting away with it. He was responsible for my father's death and for ruining my mother's life."

"Did you blackmail him?"

"No, I took the subtle approach. I contacted him and said I believed I was his daughter. We met, and I produced a DNA kit, which he was happy to let me deal with. I had some very official and very fake documents prepared that showed I was his daughter. I then made it clear that I wanted compensation for what he did to my parents. He didn't want anyone knowing about his background with my mother, particularly Matt, so he was happy to pay."

"You were given money?"

Susan nodded. "Yes, but so much of his money was tied up that accessing it was difficult. That's why I had him change his will to ensure that I'd at least get something when he died. It's unfortunate for me that Matt decided to get a DNA test done, or it would have worked out well."

"If you could have lived with yourself after ruining Matt and stealing his inheritance."

Susan's cheeks burned red.

"At least you don't share Walter's genetics. You must have wondered if your mom and Walter were together around the time you were conceived."

"I did, and yes, it is a relief, but also upsetting in that he gets away with what he did."

"Are you going to tell Matt?"

"Part of me thinks I should, and another part thinks I should walk away. We got enough money from Walter that I can pay for any medical costs for Mom and for good quality care as she gets older. That's one thing, at least. Walter's own life was shortened by his heart attack." She gave a wry smile. "Quite a fitting way to go for a heartless man."

"To walk away shows you to be the strong and much better person. Matt's had a pretty rough time the last few months. With his father dying and then concerns for his businesses from both your involvement and my family cutting off supply to him from the mill."

Susan raised an eyebrow. "I thought you hated Matt."

Jenna blushed. "I did, but I found out that he didn't do anything to hurt me."

"But the wedding?"

"Every word he spoke about Brad turned out to be true. I spoke with the woman Brad had been cheating with."

Susan's mouth dropped open. "So Matt flattening him at your wedding was a good thing?"

"It was, and it showed me how much Matt cares about me and what a good friend he is."

"Friend?"

Jenna's blush deepened. "I'm open to something beyond friends."

Susan leaned back in her chair. "This is a most unexpected conversation." She cleared her throat. "What about the rest of the town? I had the impression that everyone thinks Matt's a bad person, like his father was. The other terrible things he's done had me believing he was just as awful."

Jenna shook her head. "No, the other things were done some time ago and he's really changed and redeemed himself. The whole wedding situation caused a lot of animosity to resurface, which was very unfair on him."

Susan's face paled. "I'm beginning to think I owe Matt an apology. It was easy to go after his businesses thinking he was as bad as his father and deserved it. But this changes things if he isn't as horrible as I was led to believe."

"He's not," Jenna said. "He's been lucky to have been taken under the wing of a ninety-seven-year-old gentleman who's been teaching him about integrity and being the best person he can be. I don't think anyone in the town can believe the transformation, but I know it's genuine. The way he's reacted lately proves that." She glanced at the antique clock on the far wall. It was ten minutes until her job interview.

"Do you need to go?" Susan asked.

"I have a job interview in ten minutes."

"But then you'd be moving to Tall Oaks. That's hardly going to allow you to *be open to something beyond friends.*" Her eyes twinkled as she teased Jenna.

"You're right." Jenna slipped her phone from her bag and scrolled through her messages, finding the number for Bridget. She called it, relieved when her former colleague picked up. She canceled her appointment, apologizing for the late notice, and confirmed she wouldn't be in a position to apply for the role. Once she finished, she slipped her phone back into her bag and grinned at Susan. "Thank you. I think I needed to say out loud that I was interested in Matt to believe it myself."

"Good for you," Susan said and picked up a menu from the table. "How about some lunch before you drive back? I don't know about you, but telling so many truths makes me hungry."

Jenna picked up a menu, surprised by the way the day was turning out. She opened it then placed it down on the table again. "You never said whether you were going to tell Matt."

Susan looked at her quizzically. "Are you? You know the whole story too."

Jenna shook her head. "He'd be devastated, and I don't want to be the one to do that to him. If you plan to tell him, then I'll tell him I saw you today and that we discussed something you need to talk to him about, but otherwise, I don't think it will achieve anything. Matt didn't have a great relationship with his father, but he was still his dad. He's had a hard enough time coming to terms with how his dad's will was left, but this is a whole other level."

"It would explain to him why the will was left that way," Susan said. "Maybe that's more important to Matt than learning about my mom and what Walter did."

"Maybe," Jenna said and opened the menu again, deep in thought.

———

Jenna arrived back in Hope's Ridge after five and was knocking on Charlie's door within minutes of her arrival. She'd sent Matt a message on her way home saying she was running late and could she meet him by the lake at six. It was a beautiful day, and the sun wouldn't set until closer to eight, so they had plenty of daylight hours.

He'd sent her a message straight back saying he'd bring a blanket and some drinks.

After speaking to Susan, Jenna knew she needed advice.

"Oh gosh," Charlie said. "This is not good. Not good at all."

Jenna had launched into the story of meeting Susan and what she'd learned the moment Charlie opened his door. "I don't know what to do," Jenna admitted. "I think it's best that Matt doesn't know about his father, as it will upset him so much, but I don't want to have secrets from him either."

"Sometimes secrets are necessary," Charlie said.

"But what if Susan changes her mind and decides next week, next year, or years down the road to tell Matt, and then he finds out that I knew all along."

Charlie smiled. "You see a future with Matt. That is very good."

"It's not the point," Jenna said. "The point is, what do

I do?"

Charlie sat in silence for a moment before standing and crossing the room to a shelf that contained a pretty metal urn. He picked it up. "We'll ask Ying Yue for help."

Jenna swallowed. She'd noticed what she'd thought was a pretty ornament before but hadn't realized it was an urn containing Ying Yue's ashes.

Charlie held the urn and closed his eyes.

Five minutes passed before he opened them and set the urn back down.

"Ying Yue is the wisest person I know," Charlie said. "Now, this is what you must do."

Nerves flitted in Matt's stomach as he placed a bottle of Bollinger on top of the picnic blanket he'd already placed in a basket he'd taken from the Sandstone Cafe. He'd taken glasses, and Margie had insisted he take a container full of soft cheeses and antipasto. "It's Jenna's favorite," she'd said.

Now, as he crossed the road and waved to Asha as he passed Irresistibles, his stomach churned. He and Jenna still hadn't had a chance to talk properly, and he hadn't had a chance to tell her how he felt. But it was quite likely they'd be celebrating her new job in Tall Oaks and not discussing anything to do with them.

He found a spot by the lake that he knew Jenna would see from the path and spread the picnic blanket. He placed the basket of goodies on it and, with hands in pockets, found himself pacing. It was a nervous habit he seemed to have developed. He took a deep breath and forced himself to stop. Instead, he turned and faced the lake, hoping some of its calm would rub off on him. His eyes wandered along the shore, settling in the distance on the Lake House. He'd tried many times to find out who owned the house, hoping to buy the prime real estate, but had hit a wall each time he'd tried. He'd made it as far as learning that the owner was a recluse who was waiting for the right time to return to Hope's Ridge. *Return.* That had intrigued him as it suggested they were from the area. He shook his head, trying to imagine who would have the money to own a waterfront lake house and allow it to sit empty for years.

He jumped a few moments later as an arm slid around his waist. He turned to find Jenna smiling at him, both her arms encircling him.

"This is nice," he said, "a little confusing, but nice."

Jenna leaned toward him and kissed him softly on the lips. She pulled away, a shyness on her face he wasn't used to.

"I wanted to start our catch-up the way I'm hoping it's going to end," she said. "There seems to be constant confusion when it comes to you and me, and I want to stop that right now and straighten out a few things."

Matt nodded. She came across so strong and so assertive, but he couldn't help but notice the tremor in her hands and the vulnerability in her eyes. It was so attractive.

"After I spoke to you today, I decided not to interview for the job."

Matt's eyes widened. "You canceled?"

Jenna nodded. "What's the point of being three hours away and trying to start a relationship? It would never work."

"A relationship?"

"Yes," Jenna said, "that's what we're looking at here. Not

a fling or another case of going our separate ways. A relationship. Charlie's gut says it's meant to be, and that's good enough for me."

Matt laughed. "It's good enough for me regardless of what Charlie has to say." He leaned forward and took Jenna in his arms. "This is turning out to be the best day ever." He kissed her with more force and passion than any of their previous kisses. They parted, and he pulled her down onto the blanket.

"I brought champagne," Matt said. "I was going to pretend to be happy if you got the job and celebrate it with you while I was secretly dying on the inside."

"Really?" Jenna said.

Matt took her hand. "Jen, when we first kissed, I thought I was the luckiest man alive, and then everything fell to pieces so quickly that I assumed it wasn't meant to be. But there hasn't been a day since then that I haven't wished things had turned out differently. And now it has, and we can celebrate us and a new beginning." He leaned forward and kissed her lightly on the lips. "And I can't believe I get to do that again."

Jenna laughed as he grinned and took the champagne from the basket. He handed her a glass, but she hesitated.

"Can we hold off on the champagne for a minute?"

Matt put the glasses down. "Please tell me you aren't about to end this before it begins."

Jenna took his hands in hers. "No, but there's something I need to tell you. I've debated over telling you, and I'm still not sure it's the right thing, but Charlie's wife says we must start with a clean slate and that if I keep this from you, it will be like a toxin slowly poisoning our relationship and our future."

Matt frowned. "Charlie's wife has been dead for many years."

"He still talks to her and takes her advice," Jenna said.

Matt's throat constricted as he saw the fear in Jenna's eyes. If he was a praying man, he'd be down on his knees right now praying that whatever she was about to tell him wasn't something that he'd be unable to forgive her for.

What she did tell him left him shocked and not needing to pray.

"You're sure," he said for the third time after Jenna finished talking.

She nodded. "I'm so sorry, Matt. I wasn't sure whether to tell you or not. I didn't want you to have this as your lasting memory of your father, but I also didn't want to hold on to this information and spend years lying by omission to you. I know it would have poisoned us eventually. Ying Yue was definitely right about that."

Matt took her hand and squeezed it. "I'm not sure if I want to know this either, but Ying Yue," he gave a small smile, "or Charlie, is right. We can't have secrets from each other if we want this to work. No lies, no secrets."

"Two open books," Jenna said.

Matt leaned across and kissed her. "Exactly."

He pulled back and took a deep breath. "Sorry, this is all a bit much." He shook his head. "Poor Susan. And her mother. It's hard to believe Dad would do something so awful. I knew he was unscrupulous when it came to business, but he should have gone to jail for this."

"I agree, but I also question the way Susan acted, Matt. It's pretty awful, what she tried to do. She gave me the impression that she saw red when she learned from her mother what had happened and has behaved irrationally ever since that point. She was very calm and relaxed when I saw her today. Seemed to accept that it was time to move on."

"That's good, at least. But I think I should do something, don't you?"

"Like what?" Jenna asked.

"I don't know. But I need to acknowledge that what Dad did wasn't okay and that he should have paid for it." He frowned. "I'll think about it. I don't want to rush and do anything I might regret. Susan's unlikely to show her face around here unless she decides to blackmail me with this information too. Do you think she'd do that?"

Jenna shook her head. "No, I doubt you'll ever see her again unless you track her down. She knows you weren't to blame for any of this. And I told her that I had it all wrong about you and the wedding and that you were a great guy." She blushed. "It was something she said that made me realize I wanted to cancel the job interview."

"Really?"

Jenna nodded.

"Then I should be thanking her." Matt grinned and poured two glasses of champagne. He passed one to Jenna. "Let's forget about all of that for now and concentrate on us. This is officially our first date, and I want to remember it for the great company, beautiful sunset, and the most gorgeous woman I've ever met. I honestly can't believe you're sitting here with me, suggesting there could be a future for us."

Jenna blushed. "Not *could*. There *will* be a future, Matt." She leaned forward, sealing her words with a kiss that took his breath away.

CHAPTER 14

ONE MONTH LATER

$\mathcal{M}$att hurried toward Steph, picked her up in his arms, and twirled her around. She was laughing as he placed her back down.

"We did it, Steph, we actually did it!"

Steph beamed back at him. "We did, and it's incredible. Come and have a look around."

Matt laughed as he linked arms with her. "Like we've done every day the past month."

"I know, but I guess as today is the official opening of Holly's, this look around is special. It's the final time Holly's is ours before guests start to arrive and staff begin working here. Life's going to be different around here from next week, Matt."

Matt nodded, his smile wide as his eyes drank in the completed buildings and landscaping that made up Holly's Wellness Retreat. "I wish Mom could see this," Matt said. "She'd be so happy."

"And proud," Steph said. "You've done something amazing here, and so many people will benefit from it."

"We have," Matt corrected her, drawing another smile from Steph.

"I hardly recognize you sometimes," Steph said. "That other Matt is so far in the distance these days; it's hard to believe he ever existed."

"I wish he never had," Matt admitted.

"You shouldn't feel like that," Steph said. "If old Matt hadn't existed, then you probably wouldn't have the relationship you have with Charlie and possibly not Jenna either. You might not have had it in you to break up her wedding and fall in love."

He laughed, knowing she was teasing. "New Matt did that, not old Matt, but you're right about Charlie. Other than Jen, he's the most important person in my life. I've learned so much from him. I can't imagine how I'll be when he's no longer here."

"Oh, is he moving?"

Matt stole a glance at Steph, who smiled at him.

"Look, I know what you mean, but he's likely to have another ten years in him. He's so fit, and he'll have Holly's to come to if he needs any help moving forward. He's coming for a weekly massage, by the way. He reminded me during the week that that was his payment for being your foreman on the apartments."

Matt laughed. "And he'll turn up like clockwork for it too, as he does for his coffee and muffins with Asha and his lunches at the cafe. He's a great example of the barter system done well."

"Come and have a look at this," Steph said, leading Matt into the first room of the Hope wing. She opened the door, and Matt drew in a breath. The room was stunning. Steph's designs had brought the browns and greens from the carved walkways and forest outside the room into the interior decor. The bed was covered in plush cushions, and a sitting area was positioned in front of a large window that looked out to the hills behind the retreat. But the real feature was the artwork. The splashes of color from Ryan's abstract pieces complimented the room perfectly.

"It's beautiful, Steph." He'd seen the room yesterday, but Steph had added the soft furnishings and artwork later in the afternoon, so he hadn't seen the finished product.

"Your idea to lease the pieces from Ryan was a great one," Steph said. "He thinks he'll end up selling most of them this way, and then it won't cost us anything." The arrangement with Ryan was that they would lease his pictures long-term, but if they sold, the lease costs would be reimbursed.

They walked into the rest of the rooms that were decorated as beautifully but with different colors and different artwork.

"We're nearly fully booked for the next three months," Steph said. "The marketing manager you employed has excelled." She nudged him as she said this. "In more ways than one by the looks of the smile on your face every day."

"Jen's done a great job," Matt agreed. "As long as you're fine working with her?" Matt had suggested the job to Jenna when he and Steph realized they needed someone to work on the graphic design side of ads for the business but also liaise with websites and magazines to place ads and book editorial pieces. Jenna's skill base was suited to the design side of their needs, but she'd picked up the rest of the job easily.

"I love working with her," Steph said. "She was always Asha's friend when we were growing up, and it's been lovely to get to know her better and become friends with her. We're a good team."

"I love that we've ended up doing this as couples," Matt admitted. "It was never the plan, but having Buster own the majority share and you running the studio, and now coordinating the staff for the wellness retreat keeps it all close to us."

"I love it too," Steph said. "Now, we'd better get ready. The guests will be here in half an hour, and there's still some setting up to do."

Matt followed Steph to the large grassy area that overlooked one of the retreat's features—the manmade lake. Tables had been set up along with streamers and balloons, creating a lovely party atmosphere.

Buster and Jenna were placing glasses on the tables as Steph and Matt approached.

Jenna looked up and rewarded him with a delighted smile. He smiled back, still wanting to pinch himself that Jenna had chosen him.

"This looks amazing," he said. "How many people do you think will come?"

"We invited two hundred, and I'm expecting closer to three," Buster said with a laugh. "You know what people in Hope's Ridge are like, free food and free drinks. They'll all be trying to get in."

"Which is fine," Jenna said, "because I arranged for catering for four hundred." She shrugged. "I think Buster's numbers are a bit conservative."

Matt laughed. "As long as everyone has a good time. I want the opening of Holly's to be special."

"And I want to know what's under that," Buster said,

pointing to a large object that currently had a black sheet draped over it by the lake.

"You'll find out soon," Matt promised, exchanging a look with Jenna. He was a little nervous about this surprise but planned to unveil it during the speech he was going to give to welcome everyone to Holly's.

"The caterers are all prepared," Steph said. "They'll bring out the food on trays and offer it around." She looked at the parking lot. "All we have to do now is wait for people to arrive."

On the dot of three, the first car arrived, and Matt grinned as Margie helped Charlie from the back seat of Ryan's Range Rover. He hurried over to them.

"Thank you so much for coming."

"We wouldn't have missed it, Matthew. The party of the decade, I believe it is being referred to."

Matt laughed. "I hope it lives up to that expectation. You're looking mighty dapper, Charlie." And he was. Charlie was wearing a smart black tailored suit with an aquamarine shirt. "Come with me, and we'll organize a drink for you."

"Drink?" Charlie said. "I assume Steph is only serving kombucha and healthy juices?"

Matt laughed again. "No, we twisted her arm. For this afternoon, there will be healthy options and party options. As in wine, beer, and champagne."

"Excellent," Charlie said. "That's what I was hoping."

Matt led them across to the area by the lake as people began to arrive. By three-thirty, the lawn was crowded, and the chatter and laughter volume was rising.

Matt was talking to Zane and Asha when Jenna took his hand. "Got a minute?"

Matt excused himself and allowed Jenna to lead him away. "I think your brother might upstage our opening with a proposal."

Jenna stopped and stared at Matt. "What makes you think that?"

"He seemed nervous and kept checking his jacket pocket. Hopefully there's a ring in it. It's about time."

"It is," Jenna said, "although I think Asha wanted to wait until they'd been together for twelve months before anything like that happened." She let out a long breath. "Let's forget about them for a minute. I interrupted because I wanted to warn you."

"Warn me?"

Jenna nodded. "Susan Lewis turned up."

Matt looked back at the crowd gathered on the lawn. "Where is she?"

Jenna pointed over to the left-hand side of the lake. "Over there talking with Margie. I think that might be her mother with her."

Matt let out an audible breath. "Come with me, would you?"

Jenna gripped his hand tightly. "Of course."

They wove their way through the guests to where Susan was laughing at something Margie said. She stopped laughing as she saw Matt and Jenna approach.

"Hi, Matt. Jenna," Susan said. "I hope you don't mind that Mom and I decided to come and have a look."

Matt smiled. "I wouldn't have invited you if I didn't want you here."

Jenna looked at Matt, surprised. Had he invited them? He squeezed her hand.

"How are you both?"

"Good, Matt, thank you. We're grateful to you too. You didn't have to react the way you have."

Jenna stared at Matt again. She had no idea what was going on here.

Susan smiled at her. "I'm guessing Matt hasn't filled you in?"

Jenna shook her head. "Not yet."

Matt turned to her, worry flooding his eyes. "I was going to. I wanted to see how Susan would react first. I wasn't keeping this from you."

"Relax," Jenna said. "I'm intrigued. I didn't think we'd see you again, Susan."

"Thanks to you, Matt and I have had a chance to talk."

"Susan contacted me after the two of you met in Tall Oaks," Matt explained. "She apologized and I decided to accept her apology and move on. I felt the real apology was owed from my family. I needed to apologize for my father."

"Which was kind of you, Matt," Susan's mother said, "but certainly not your responsibility. None of this is your fault. I am the only one here who could have changed the course of our history, and I'm sorry that you were impacted by it."

"Oh Mom," Susan said, "you did what you thought was best. Saying no from the start to Walter may have ended in the same scenario when it came to what Dad did."

"Possibly," Veronica said, "we will never know."

Jenna's heart contracted as she saw the pain in Veronica's eyes. She couldn't imagine having to live with the guilt that she must have.

"Matt's been kind to us, which considering Susan's actions is quite unbelievable," Veronica said. "Did you know I'm going to be the first guest in the Hope wing of Holly's next week?"

Jenna looked to Matt. "Really?"

He blushed. "Yes. I invited Veronica as our guest to stay for two weeks. She has some underlying health concerns that working with the wellness staff could help." He turned to Veronica. "You can stay as long as you need and come back at any time. Your visits will always be a gift from me to you."

"Oh Matthew, you are so kind." Veronica's eyes filled with tears. "I'm not sure we deserve your kindness after—"

Matt cut her off. "That's all in the past, so let's leave it there. The past links us, and my father's actions have caused you pain and grief beyond anything that's been done to me. I'll never be able to make that up to you but would like to be able to provide you with help where I can."

Veronica wiped her cheeks as tears spilled down them.

Matt smiled kindly at her. "It's time to put the past behind us and get on with the present, which means I need to make a speech." He squeezed Jenna's hand and excused himself.

"He's a good man, Jenna," Susan said. "He's offered to do a lot to help Mom since accepting my apology. I definitely underestimated him."

"A lot of the town has," Jenna said. "But that seems to be slowly changing."

"Attention everyone." Jenna turned from Susan as Matt began to speak. He'd set up a microphone and was standing with Buster by the lake.

The crowd on the lawn quieted and turned to face Matt.

"Firstly, thank you all for coming this afternoon. We're delighted that you are here to celebrate the opening of Holly's with us. As many of you know, Holly's has been a labor of love for Buster and me, but mostly for Steph, who is the face of Holly's and the person responsible for the massive transformation you see before you today."

Jenna looked across to Steph, who was standing with Asha, pink coloring her cheeks.

The crowd clapped with appreciation.

"We hope you'll all enjoy the facilities at Holly's, from the yoga studio many of you already frequent to the massage and day spa, and the accommodation and knowledge and experience of our staff, who are experts in the field of natural healing. Now," he turned to the object he had covered with the sheets. "I wanted to mark today and the opening of Holly's with something extra special." He gave a nervous laugh. "I hope I got this right. You all know that I'm good at getting things spectacularly wrong."

Quiet laughter rippled through the crowd.

Matt looked across to Jenna, who smiled with encouragement. She hoped for his sake that he had gotten this right, as although he wouldn't tell her what he was doing, she knew from the snippets he'd shared that he'd begun preparations for this months ago.

Matt took hold of the corner of the sheet. "Holly's, as many of you are aware, is named in honor of Buster's sweet daughter, Holly. She happened to share the same name as my mom, which is lovely as it reminds me of Mom too, but ultimately the wellness retreat is to honor young Holly's life. I'm hoping you'll all remember that when you visit, and I'm hoping this will be a beautiful tribute and reminder of who Holly was."

Matt pulled away the sheet, revealing a bronze statue of a little girl. A gasp went up around the group, and tears instantly filled Jenna's eyes. She wasn't the only one; she saw many people reaching into their pockets for hankies and tissues.

She looked to Buster, who'd walked over to the statue and was running his fingers over the little girl's face. He turned to Matt, his voice breaking. "It's beautiful, Matt. I don't know how to thank you."

Conversation started up among the guests, and Jenna heard many comments that made her heart swell with pride. "He's like a different man these days." "What a wonderful tribute to Holly." "How lucky we are to have Matt involved in the town." "He's certainly nothing like his old man."

That was the one Jenna knew Matt would be the happiest to hear.

Clapping began as Buster hugged Matt, wiping a tear from his eye.

"To a wonderful new business venture," Charlie called out, raising the glass of champagne he was holding. "To Holly's."

"To Holly's," the guests all cheered, raising their glasses.

"To us," Jenna mouthed as Matt met her gaze.

He held up his glass and mouthed back, "To love."

The End

FREE BONUS SCENES

Would you like to read more about our friends in Hope's Ridge? Sign up to my mailing list at www.silvermckenzie.com.au for exclusive access to bonus scenes featuring our Hope's Ridge family.

These aren't deleted scenes, they are bonus scenes written exclusively for my mailing list subscribers and new scenes are added each month. You'll also have opportunities to win free books and Amazon gift cards.

FINDING HOPE'S RIDGE
Book 1 in the Hope's Ridge Series

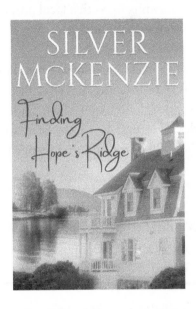

He broke your heart and destroyed your business.
Would you give him a second chance?

Asha Jones has lived and breathed the small town of Hope's Ridge her entire life. She's built a successful business on the shores of Lake Hopeful, and now, with the iconic Sandstone Cafe up for lease, she has an opportunity to expand her business and fulfill a dream.

But one mistake is all it takes for Asha's dream to crumble overnight. She's made an enemy of an influential property developer, and just when she thinks things can't get any worse, the man who crushed her heart ten years earlier returns to town.

Suffering from PTSD and dealing with the trauma of recurring nightmares, Zane Larsen returns to Hope's Ridge, resolved to recover his self-confidence and find a new direction for his life. Teaming up with a local property developer provides a new career path and gives him a much-needed reason to get up each day.

As Zane slips back into small-town life, he doesn't anticipate feelings resurfacing for Asha, the one woman in Hope's Ridge who's hated him since high school. And, while Asha does her best to ignore Zane's existence, she can't ignore the feelings for him that reappear. She can't go there again—can she?

Zane needs to redeem himself and fight for a second chance at love. But is working with the man who wants to destroy Asha's business a guaranteed way to reignite her hatred - or could it be an opportunity to change her opinion of him?

BEYOND HOPE'S RIDGE

Book 2 in the Hope's Ridge Series

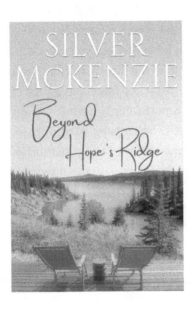

Their heartbreak was absolute. Can they help each other move forward?

Twelve months ago, Steph Jones's easy-going outlook was destroyed when she was involved in a motor vehicle accident that claimed the life of a five-year-old. Plagued with the horror and memories of that day, Steph cannot forgive herself and is unable to move on.

In the nearby town of Drayson's Landing, Henry Busterling is mourning the first anniversary of his daughter's death. How can Buster move forward when he blames himself for the accident? With his ex-wife serving a prison sentence, Buster's empty home is a constant reminder of all that he's lost.

For Steph, confronting the past is the only way to move forward. But that's easier said than done when she can't look Buster in the eye, let alone be in the same room as him. Immersing herself in her yoga is much more attractive than facing the man she's been avoiding for the past year.

When circumstances force Buster and Steph together, Steph has an opportunity to admit her guilt and ask for forgiveness. But with Buster planning to move beyond Hope's Ridge and its devastating memories, has Steph left her chance to make peace with the tragedy too late?

Available now from Amazon or
www.silvermckenzie.com.au

ABOUT THE AUTHOR

SILVER MCKENZIE is a pen name of women's fiction and domestic thriller author, Louise Guy.

Louise decided to write the Hope's Ridge series under a pen name as while the series sits nicely in the women's fiction category, the books have a stronger romantic story line than her other women's fiction titles which tend to have more intrigue and suspense. The Hope's Ridge series is also set in a fictional US town so the books are written in US English compared to Louise's other books that are set in Australia and use Australian English. She also decided Silver was a pretty cool name and it might be the only chance she has to name herself!

Silver has lived in the UK, New Zealand and Australia as well as having traveled to over thirty countries. Today, Silver and her husband are permitted to share a home in Queensland, Australia, with their two sons and a rather bossy, but beautiful cat named Pud.

If you are interested in checking out books written by Louise Guy, go to: www.louiseguy.com

And, both Silver and Louise are easy to find on Facebook.